The

Deadly

Canyon

The

Deadly

Canyon

Jake Page

Ballantine Books / New York

All rights reserved under International and Pan-American Copyright Conventions. Published in the United States by Ballantine Books, a division of Random House, Inc., New York, and simultaneously in Canada by Random House of Canada Limited, Toronto.

Grateful acknowledgment is made to CPP/Belwin, Inc. for permission to reprint an excerpt from the lyrics of "HOLD TIGHT (WANT SOME SEAFOOD MAMA)" by Leonard Kent, Dick Brandow, George Robinson, Willie Spottswood, and Leonard Ware. Copyright © 1967 by Mills Music, Inc. c/o EMI Music Publishing. Reprinted by permission of CPP/Belwin, Inc., Miami, FL. All rights reserved.

LIBRARY OF CONGRESS CATALOGING-IN-PUBLICATION DATA

Page, Jake.
The deadly canyon / Jake Page. — 1st ed.
p. cm.
ISBN 0-345-37930-6
1. Hopi Indians—Fiction. I. Title.
PS3566.A333D39 1994
813'.54--dc20   93-22130 CIP

Manufactured in the United States of America

Designed by Fritz Metsch

First Edition: March 1994

10 9 8 7 6 5 4 3 2 1

Thanks again, Lew
and, invariably, Susanne

Author's Note

Locals dwelling in the bootheel of New Mexico may be surprised to find that the Peloncillo Mountains have been slightly rearranged geologically to suit the author's felt needs.

Never mind.

This is just a harmless story. The landscape, as well as the characters and events herein, is imaginary.

For the most part.

The

Deadly

Canyon

Prelude

T. Moore Bowdre sat lumpishly in an outlandish wing chair, idly changing stations on the FM radio. The wing chair was half again as big as any normal chair, but T. Moore Bowdre was a large man and hated to perch with his knees together on furniture designed by some European colonist's version of what was polite during the time the Spanish invented the Inquisition. Spanish mission style, it was called, still a cherished part of the greater Santa Fe style.

It was amazing, Bowdre thought, how much staying power those Spaniards had. A lot of people in Santa Fe still thought they had to sit on those uncomfortable Spanish colonial chairs, all wood, angular as a nun, with their hands clasped in some kind of obeisance to the past, while their fannies turned to plastic, and probably got splinters as well. T. Moore Bowdre wasn't about to have some kind of pew in his own house. He wasn't about to offer up comfort to any greater glory, be it God or even Santa Fe style.

Mo had commissioned his chair from a young furniture

maker who inhabited an adobe shed in Algodones, New Mexico. A small town along a little-used road, Algodones is not far north of the bland and reckless sprawl of Albuquerque, which plays Grand Rapids, Michigan, to Santa Fe's Barcelona, fifty miles north.

"See, Ben, I'm not into a whole lot of right angles," Bowdre had said to the young furniture maker. "They just don't suit me. I want soft, Ben. *Soft. Round. Smooth.* No more hard places for me. I want this chair like a woman, a great big woman with the world's most welcoming lap. You make it for me like that. Place where I can sit and dream." He emitted a staccato series of noises that lay somewhere between human laughter and the bark of a large dog.

Ben giggled and said, "For you, I'll learn to upholster, to sew." Two dogs began leaping up and down at the fence in the next yard, barking hysterically. "Afghans," Ben said. "The woman drove all the way to Baltimore to get five of 'em. Broke down on her way back, somewhere in Kansas. I guess it's a bit of a problem, finding a motel where you can stay with five Afghans."

The dogs continued barking. "They're not too smart," Ben said. "Their heads aren't much more than a slight widening of the spinal column." He looked around his yard, littered with weathered, gnarled pieces of wood—all carefully scavenged from arroyos throughout the northern part of the state. "I'll make the legs from Apache plume roots, and I've got some wonderful cedar pieces for the arms."

"Sounds good. See you in a week. Check on progress."

"Make it two."

"Okay. See you in two weeks." T. Moore Bowdre pulled himself up into the passenger seat of his aging pickup truck, closed the door, and said to the woman behind the wheel, "He's a nice boy. Make me a nice chair. Needs the money."

"How much will he charge for it?" the woman asked.

"Around three hundred."

The woman looked around the yard, the most notable feature of which was an aged, pink freight car that loomed up near Ben's house like an abandoned dream. There were several old railroad cars in Algodones, she had noticed, one of them some sort of store. She looked past the low and ramshackle adobe buildings of the town, the yards filled with the pale green grays of desert scrub, wondering why a college kid from Virginia named Ben would wind up here making furniture out of old branches and roots. He had started what might be called a mini-mini-fad, and it didn't really make sense, especially not to a Hopi woman who had grown up on the Rez and had sat in the same Sears folding chairs for her whole youth around the table in the kitchen in her mother's two-room house. Chairs, she thought, were just chairs. And the Hopi had even done perfectly well without chairs for a thousand years, more than a thousand years. Now, if you had a chair, and it worked, why change it? But she understood too why T. Moore Bowdre wanted his own custom-built chair.

Two weeks later Bowdre sat in his new chair in the living room of his house on Canyon Road in Santa Fe, trying it out. Somehow Ben had managed to weave about twenty twisted and tortured roots and limbs into a graceful replica of a wing chair, the seat and back upholstered in velvet the color of Chardonnay. The big man leaned back, stretched his legs out, and let his wrists lie on the chair's arms while his big hands dangled over the edge. Then he rubbed his fingers over a smooth, gnarled piece of cedar on the chair arm. "Ben did good," he said. "You want to try this chair?"

The woman laughed in her alto voice. "You just sit there if you're happy."

Bowdre reached over and fiddled with a dial on the radio. A voice began in midsentence.

"God spare me the flood," Bowdre said. "Could that be

Billy Graham?" He listened. "By God, that *is* Billy Graham. Must be a hundred and fifty years old. Connie, listen to that voice. Listen to those words. When I was a boy, the road to redemption was like a mountain. Billy Graham, he'd stare at you from his fierce blue eyes and say, 'You, sinner, you got in front of you the *Rocky Mountains*!' Why, he sounds downright reasonable now. Listen. God*damn*, Connie, you listen to that fella now, you might even think that someone like me, maybe even you, Indian people, could be redeemed. Blessed be the Lord. How 'bout you sit in this chair with me? I was always hoping what we do would be sanctified in the eyes of God Almighty. Here's our chance."

The phone rang, and Bowdre reached out a meaty hand to pick it up. After a moment he grinned. "Of course I remember you. How the hell could I forget?"

The Hopi woman named Connie slipped out of the room.

O n e

The process—invariable and far more ancient than the human race—had begun within an hour.

They would have found it in ten or fifteen minutes if it hadn't been in a dry cave with a relatively small entrance on a ledge high up the canyon wall in so arid a land. But they came, as they always do, laden with eggs, homing in on transparent wings. With frantic determination they crawled over the surface looking for places to deposit the next generation—places that were still moist. Soon the interior temperature began to rise as countless bacteria proceeded with their version of ingestion, and the dark caverns began to swell with gas. And the blowflies' eggs gave rise on schedule to larval forms, and these swarmed blindly into the swelling caverns, eventually breaking through the integument around the gaseous caverns, and the swelling subsided. Masses of them writhed inside and out in an orgy of feeding until, each in its own time, there was yet another metamorphosis, time to leave the premises and burrow into the sandy soil nearby.

The process continued. Unerringly, beetles, large and small, had followed the chemical traces that wafted from the cave and down the canyon in the thin currents of air, arriving to feed on the tougher elements, the outer integument, the cartilage. Yet other beetles came to feed on the carrion beetles, crawling with six-legged adroitness over the remains, fierce and implacable.

It was then, well before the beetles had completed their work, which would in due and proper course have left only bones and hair behind after their departure, that a face appeared in the entrance to the cave, a long, thin face with eyes so light a blue as to be almost colorless, sunstruck eyes that squinted almost shut as they peered into the gloom of this familiar place.

"Jesus," said Daniel Ascension. "Don't come . . . stay where y'are. Je*sus*!"

He turned away, gagging, and left the beetles to their voracious, useful work in the dry cave where spirals and human hands had been painted in ocher on its walls by people who had visited there long before, different people altogether, but who had at least one thing in common with the corpse now lying in the cave: the busy and formal choreography of dissolution.

Wheeler A. Fitzhugh was nonplussed. An extremely complex negotiation with the National Science Foundation required his urgent attention, a major grant for continuing the research center's ecological baseline studies hanging in the balance. With the grant, the center would become the Southwest flagship in monitoring the early effects of global warming.

And the general counsel in Denver had just finished going ballistic about the gold mine. "Wheeler," she had said, "if you people down there actively dispute this, like this idea of having everybody start writing congressmen, then it's politics. Lobbying. And if someone in Washington gets pissed off, they can point out we don't have a legal right to be lobbyists, and the whole museum—not just the center—loses our tax-exempt status. So check with me before you do *any-thing* like that."

So the bitch in Denver was screaming at him, the National Science Foundation was waiting, and here he was, squiring a large, loud buffoon of an artist around the center.

Fitzhugh had emerged as one of those rare talents, an effective science administrator, after several years of relatively unproductive—some said unimaginative—research on army ants that had taken him to the rain forests of Mexico and Central America and then here to the Denver Museum's Desert Research Station up a forested canyon in the Peloncillo Mountains thirty miles north of the Mexican border in southwestern New Mexico.

Gradually, over three summers at the station, he had lost interest in ants, in the tedious work of field research, and had found more satisfaction in voluntarily assisting the aging director of the station with administrative chores. He had made himself invaluable and, three years ago, the museum had appointed Fitzhugh director upon the old man's retirement. Though a second-rate scientist himself, Fitzhugh understood and was awed by superior research, and was content to act on so many occasions as its midwife.

It was a complicated, even Byzantine kind of midwifery, playing the politics of grantsmanship for most of the hundred-odd students and their biological mentors who worked at the station every summer. But he was a patient and subtly manipulative man, highly successful, and he basked in what he took to be the admiration of his research-minded colleagues.

And now he had a serious problem on his hands, a threat

to the entire area by this French-owned mining company whom the Forest Service had given a permit to drill for gold, which meant they could wind up scraping off the top of the Peloncillos and could ruin one of the longest-running ecological studies in history. . . . And here was this *artist* the museum director had sent.

Fitzhugh knew little of southwestern art, nothing of the region's artists, but he could not imagine how this rough-hewn man standing beside him on the greensward could be an accomplished sculptor. He stood erect as a tree, his chin with its blond beard jutting upward, sniffing the air like a dog, opaque dark glasses glinting in the sun. For another, this sculptor seemed more like the sort who would be found operating a tractor on a farm somewhere, or maybe a bulldozer. Big beefy forearms, a round paunch hanging over blue jeans, a denim workshirt, and a dusty narrow-brimmed black cowboy hat that seemed too small for his big head.

Bowdre. T. Moore Bowdre. A redneck. And a blind redneck to boot.

"No, not boo. *Bo,* like in bow and arrow," the man had said when they first met a few minutes ago in Fitzhugh's office. And then he had broken into what apparently was this redneck's version of laughter. "Hah—hah—hah."

Now they stood on the grassy area around which the center's dormitories and labs were ranged, structures mostly built with logs, that were in turn surrounded by piñon forest. Bowdre was here on a commission, and one that Fitzhugh found to be little more than a diversion of money and time from the important work of the center. The director of the Denver Museum—his boss—had explained that a donor who would remain anonymous at least in the near term had decided to make a substantial gift, a gift in six figures, to the museum for the research center, but there was a proviso. It was that T. Moore Bowdre from Sante Fe, who was noted chiefly as a wildlife sculptor, erect near the station's entrance a monumental sculpture of his choice. So the redneck, whom Fitzhugh had certainly never heard of before, had a blank check to put whatever monstrosity he wanted on the station grounds, and Fitzhugh, like it or not, had to be welcoming.

Well, he thought, perhaps tolerant would be enough.

The man Bowdre had announced that he wanted to stay on the premises for a while, maybe a couple of weeks, to get the feel of the place, and Fitzhugh was trying to figure out where, in the crowded facilities, he could fit him—and without causing a fuss among the scientists. And finding a billet for him was all the more complicated by the silent woman who accompanied him, a broad-shouldered woman with jet-black hair and the face of an Indian. He had missed her name, didn't know if she was his wife or just some kind of Seeing Eye companion. One room? Two rooms? He would have to winkle out the connection and arrange things gracefully. She was now across the green, poking around in the cab of the pickup they had come in.

"Well, Dr. Fitzhugh," Bowdre said. "Let me explain to you about that."

Fitzhugh cringed inwardly. The self-importance of the man, he thought. A *pompous* redneck.

"I don't have a particular notion in my mind yet, but I've been doing a little bit of research—hah—hah—of my own. You boys here do a lot of work with insects, I understand, which is natural enough, there being so damn may of 'em and all. You used to chase around after army ants, right? Maybe we could put a column of giant bronze army ants out on a foray, streaming across the green here, might be a good thing for those children I hear over there to play on. It's just an idea. Probably not any good either. After a few days I'll have a better feel for it."

A young woman in shorts, sandals, and a tank top appeared beside Fitzhugh, a recent arrival from . . . Was it Cornell? Ornithology. Today doing her weekly administrative chore, answering the station's phones.

"Dr. Fitzhugh? Excuse me. It's the sheriff's department. They've apparently found a body in Skeleton Canyon. They want Dr. Armand. They want him to come."

"Where is he?"

"He's out in the field, Rustler's Canyon."

"Have someone get him," Fitzhugh said. "It's his specialty."

The young woman headed off at a trot and Fitzhugh said, as if to himself, "You never know, out here. You just never know."

"Do you mind if I ask you," Bowdre said, "what kind of specialist you got here that goes to look at corpses? A physical anthropologist?"

Fitzhugh looked up at the man with a new interest.

"No, Dr. Armand is an entomologist."

"An insect man?"

"Yes," Fitzhugh said. "A forensic entomologist. From Rutgers. Out here he works on beetles. He can tell how long a corpse has been dead by examining the insect fauna. The police here find him very helpful when something like this happens."

"Well, I'll be damned. I'd like to meet that guy."

"I'm sure you will," Fitzhugh said, watching Bowdre's companion walk toward them across the grass. She had to be Indian, the high cheekbones, copper skin. She wore a white blouse and gray slacks like someone from a city.

"She's . . . ?" Fitzhugh began.

"Half Hopi by birth, almost all Hopi by instinct and up-bringing. Father's genes must've been as potent as the Quaker army. Hah. Oh yeah, we only need one bed."

The Hopi woman smiled at Fitzhugh as she approached

and handed something wrapped up in cloth to the sculptor. He in turn held it out to Fitzhugh.

"It's a miniature of something I did in marble for a lady I know. Thought you might want to know what you're in for here."

Fitzhugh unfolded the cloth and discovered the bronze bust of an eagle, about seven inches high. Its head was bent downward to the side, the beak almost touching its neck feathers. An anatomist would, Fitzhugh saw at once, find technical fault with every detail except perhaps the fiercely intense eyes, but it almost seemed alive, inexplicably bespeaking the gesture of an eagle.

He turned it in his hands. "My God," he said.

"Really?" Bowdre said. "Eagles are kind of a Hopi god too."

Daniel Ascension was a man out of time, whose comprehension of things did not include an inkling of the ways, the thoughts, the aims, the procedures, even the reality of a world where people in air-conditioned buildings wrote down words that were supposed to make people do things, or not do things. In the minimal glimmer of understanding that had been given to Daniel Ascension, he could fathom no connection between people writing things down and other people doing them. Daniel had always simply done what he had been taught, and that was mostly by example—his kin performing tasks that he could understand as being useful and then imitate whenever needed—and by listening to men from the area tell stories when they squatted in the shade.

He had been up to the Hidalgo County seat, Lordsburg, a few times, where all the motels were strung out along Route 10, mainly because he'd been told by his friend, the deputy sheriff, that he had to go up there and sign some papers in the county office, which he had done. He hadn't liked it much and was relieved to be back in his house on the edge of the mountain with the big tank he had dug twenty years ago full of water with the cottonwood trees growing nearby. He didn't see why he had to sign some papers just to lead people on horseback around the mountains and canyons. He'd always gone out around, exploring, knew every cave and cranny of the whole bootheel of New Mexico by heart, even found the place where they buried those two guys who were supposed to be twin giants. And they were big. From the thighbones, he guessed maybe seven feet tall, which was unheard of in those days, more than a hundred years ago. He had covered them up again and hadn't told anyone about it but the deputy sheriff, his friend. That had been two, three years ago.

Now he was sitting in his friend's police vehicle, four-wheel drive, and the couple was in the backseat. He had liked the couple when they had come up to him in Rodeo, sitting at the bar.

"Are you Daniel Ascension?" the man had said, pronouncing the last part *own* the way that was right. They had hired him as a guide, the man and his lady friend, wanted to explore some of the old canyons. Horseback. They were from somewhere east, way back east, like Pennsylvania, was it? Maryland? One of those. They had asked Daniel about things that he knew, like how much it rains, and where you might see the wild pigs called javelinas, and things like that, and Daniel had felt good enough about them that he decided to show them one of his favorite places, a place practically no one knew about because the cave's mouth was tilted upward, so you can't see it from the canyon floor and you can't see it from the rim, it being in under the edge. You just have to be on the ledge itself. Must've been Apaches who used it a long time ago, Daniel was explaining, when he looked in and saw the rotting corpse, just about faceless, and had told the couple to back off. They had scrabbled down off the ledge to their horses and had made their way out of the canyon to Daniel's pickup and horse van, where, on the radio Daniel kept in the pickup to listen to the police reports, he had called his friend, the deputy sheriff.

It was hot, sitting in the police vehicle on the side of the highway in the desert, almost colorless now in the high glare of midafternoon.

"I don't see why we've got to sit here, Jimmy," Daniel said. "I told you how to find it. And these people here, they didn't even see it. I don't see why they can't go home anyway."

Deputy Sheriff Jimmy Snyder chewed on his large brown handlebar mustache and sighed. "Daniel, it's just policy. You yourself said you saw a big dent on the head. And that means homicide almost for sure, and that means that His Majesty the Sheriff has got to get his nose in on it before anything else happens, and that includes lettin' you and these people go home. He's gotta hear it from you folks himself. That's the goddamn policy, and I din't make it up, goddamn it."

"Well," Daniel said, "where is he?"

The deputy sheriff looked up at the roof of his vehicle. "Daniel, you been listenin' to the radio. They're tryin' to reach him, called every sheriff's department unit in the county to find him."

"Well," Daniel repeated, "where *is* he?"

"Daniel, you know as well as I do he's at any one of three places and none of those ladies has a police radio blaring in their bedroom, so the sheriff don't know anybody wants him till one of us knocks on the door and rouses his fat ass out of . . . oops, excuse me," Jimmy Snyder said, his eyes glancing up at the rearview mirror and the reflection of the couple in the backseat. The woman, a tanned and, to Jimmy's taste, stringy blonde of about thirty-five, maybe forty, had her hand over her mouth as if she were suppressing a cough.

The radio burped with static and a voice said, "Bingo. Found him in Animas. He'll be with you in forty-five minutes, Jimmy." Burp.

"Hallelujah, brothers and sisters," Jimmy said.

"Sheriff," said the blonde woman in the back, "do you mind if we step out for a moment? It's been . . . I'd like to walk around a little."

"Oh sure, ma'am. No problem." He gestured with his head. "About fifty yards over there, behind that big old yucca, there's a little gully, get your privacy. But watch out for centipedes. Some of 'em five inches long and mean as a snake."

"You've been awful quiet, Connie," Mo Bowdre said. "What's the matter?"

Connie Barnes was sitting on the small double bed in the little room with varnished log-and-mortar walls and one little window covered by a rusted screen. She had put some of her clothes into the drawers of a serviceable bureau that had no doubt come from the Tucson swap meet. Someone had made an attempt to strip it, but there were still flecks of green paint, overlaid by blue, and again by white. Archeology. It certainly wasn't her idea of home for a week or two—so remote, primitive. She felt completely out of place in this strange little room in this strange compound full of people with strange interests. She pulled a brush through her long black shiny hair. A guy who studies the bugs on corpses?

Unlike the Navajo, Hopi don't have an active fear of dead bodies, but studying the bugs on corpses was something, Connie decided, only white people—*bahanas*—would think up. She shuddered.

"Nothing's the matter," she said. "Just don't have anything to say yet. You seem kind of quiet too."

Mo shifted his weight on the bed. "Well, these guys here, they really know what they're talking about. Nothing like experts to put a damper on a bullshit artist. But we'll get used to it in a few days. That fella Fitzhugh, you think he'll loosen up?"

"He liked the eagle."

"Yeah, he did." Mo sat down beside her on the bed.

"This is Apache country, you know? Used to be," Connie said, drawing the brush through her hair in long languorous strokes. "The Chiricahua Apaches. Geronimo."

"That bother you?"

She smiled. "Oh, no. They never bothered us Hopi. Too far south. Anyway, all that kind of thing is in the past. Geronimo was one of the last Indians to give up. In Skeleton Canyon, near here, somewhere. Everybody kind of admires him. What are we going to do here, Mo?"

"Hang around. Have a vacation. Listen to the birds."

It was definitely not Connie's notion of a vacation spot, this cramped, dark little room, surrounded by forest, a tangled clutter of trees and underbrush, inhabited by God only knew what kinds of creatures, only a glimpse of the sky. Nothing like the vast ocean of blue overhead, the sharp lines of the distant horizon with its familiar silhouettes, the shadows of clouds moving across the pink and green and blue desert, the high, rocky yellow mesas of Hopiland where she had grown up. The few Apaches she had met here and there retained the aura of their tribe's old reputation—scary and, Connie thought, morose. Stranger even than the Navajos. Maybe it was from growing up surrounded by all these trees.

Sheriff Jack Knott pulled himself up onto the ledge and puffed out his cheeks. "Whew!" he said, hands on hips. The lithe young deputy, Jimmy Snyder, stepped sideways on a boulder and then up onto the ledge beside his overweight, florid boss. They looked down the rock-strewn trail at the tops of a straggly tier of cottonwoods eking out a living alongside the normally and now empty creekbed. They could hear footsteps below them.

"It's gettin' late," Sheriff Knott said, and took off his mirrored sunglasses. The sun was nearing the mountains over on the horizon, a rocky fortress of pinnacles and cliffs turning violet in the afternoon shadows.

"You know, Sheriff," Jimmy said, panting, "if you had a little more of a pattern, you know, like a regular schedule, we could find you quicker when something like this comes up."

The sheriff looked up at his deputy, his lower eyelids drooping. He stared at the younger man from pale hazel eyes, then turned his head and spat over the ledge. Breathing heavily, he said, "You know, Depitty Snyder . . . I could assign your ass to wearing a rabbit suit and make you Mr. Police Bunny . . . and send you around to all the damn schools in Hidalgo County so you could explain . . . to the little children all the nice things the sheriff's department does for them. I could do that right now, this very damn minute. . . . So you think about that."

The sheriff had arrived about a half hour earlier where Jimmy's vehicle was parked on the highway. Behind his mirrored sunglasses Sheriff Knott had ogled the blonde woman, quickly concluding that she was one of those bony-chested, skinny-assed broads who were too frantic in the sack and then were always complaining about one thing or another afterward, and he had also satisfied himself that the couple didn't know anything that was officially useful. He had instructed the other deputy, who had followed him from Animas, to drive the couple back to the town of Rodeo, where their car was.

The three of them—Sheriff Knott, Jimmy Snyder, and a silent Daniel Ascension—had waited another twenty minutes for the tiny little scientist, Armand, to arrive. Then another five minutes for the coroner, and a convoy of three four-wheel drives had proceeded as far into Skeleton Canyon as wheels would take them.

Sheriff Knott could not imagine how anyone would do what Armand did, plucking maggots out of corpses, but he had a great respect for the precision with which the little man had specified the time of death of several corpses that had been found in one stage or another of decomposition in the empty reaches of Hidalgo County over the years. Half the time they were wetbacks, hoofing it into the promised land, only to run out of steam and die of thirst and exposure. That's probably what they had here, though what some wandering alien bastard was doing up here in Skeleton Canyon was beyond him. Or maybe it was some asshole still thought there was a hidden treasure out here, the treasure of Skeleton Canyon. People from time to time had hunted around for it, there were little holes dug all over the canyon, but then they did the TV show about it and the place was swarming with greenhorn adventurers from the East, even Europe, for two years, and sure as hell, a couple of 'em had got lost and died of exposure. That's probably it, thought Sheriff Knott, another would-be pirate.

Breathing heavily and pale in the face, the little scientist, looking like a human ferret, appeared around a red boulder and clambered onto the ledge. He seemed distracted. Sheriff Knott heaved himself to his feet and said, "This way. Our boy Daniel is ahead of us."

They made their way around a bend and, where the ledge widened out, they saw Daniel, squatting on his heels looking miserable under the brim of his greasy, wide-brimmed hat.

"You have another look?" the sheriff called.

Daniel turned his head, his almost colorless blue eyes squinting at the sheriff. "I ain't lookin' in there, Sheriff. I already saw it."

Sheriff Knott lumbered over to Daniel and looked around. "Oh, there. Huh." He took a few more steps and, putting his big hands on the rock, leaned forward. He pushed his hat back from his forehead. Then he spun around to Daniel, face reddening.

"Well, Jesus Christ, that's a woman in there. How come you didn't say nothing . . . ?"

"A woman?" Daniel said. "A woman? Well, I didn't see . . . I mean, it was . . . I didn't see that. Just a dead person."

"Well, Jesus Christ, this is serious," the sheriff said.

Were there a God, professor Jeremy Armand had been in the habit of saying archly and in his quiet thin voice to the first session of each year's seminar on evolutionary theory at Rutgers, then one could say He (or perhaps one should say She) was an entomologist, and to be more precise a coleopterist, beetles being the most various of all the insects, and insects being the most various of all creatures. By contrast, he would point out, there was but one species of human being. So indeed, he would go on in his finicky and elaborate attempt to shock his students out of their complacency, it is highly likely that God is made not in man's image but in that of a beetle.

The students would smile openly, not because they were either shocked or amused, but because Professor Armand's seminar was a requirement for a bachelor's degree in general zoology, which in turn was a requirement to go on into graduate work in such practical matters as conservation biology or, more purely, ecology, both of which had become better-funded scientific professions just as the world was being more rapidly denuded of species and ecosystems to understand and conserve.

Professor Armand was held in some esteem by the students in his field at Rutgers, for he was known to be one of the world's leading coleopterists *and* evolutionary theorists, but they also all thought him a weirdo—ghoulish, what with his wide (and largely misunderstood) reputation for dealing with corpses. Armand, of course, was aware of this and took some delight in fending off any questions his students might ask him about his forensic interests, always explaining that he would, when it was time, interrupt the two-semester-long seminar and devote one session to tales of murder, death, and decomposition. In fact, that seminar was held in a lecture hall instead of the narrow confines of the auxiliary classroom in the library, and it was attended each year by several hundred students, often repeaters, some of them even driving up from Princeton, who came, as they said, to be "grossed out."

A lecture illustrated by slides; none of the students ever forgot it. More to the point, while many students did forget the precise and lawful order in which insects visit the corpse of a human or a pig or any such creature, they never in their lives forgot that they were mortal, part of the cyclical ongoing business of life, that they were brought together from disparate inert elements for a brief period in what might be thought of as an individual life span but to return into disparateness again. No one, Armand would point out, even during that seemingly orderly interval, was a closed system. By the end of the lecture, after the slides (mostly close-ups, which were less grotesque than wider-angled shots) and the tales of murderers in jail thanks, for example, to the discovery of an unexpected pupal form of a beetle in the ground surrounding a corpse, Jeremy Armand would wax almost poetic about the endless gyre of life and death and the biosphere, and the students—many of them at least—

understood and were humbled. In his odd way, Jeremy Armand was a bit of a mystic.

He had needed less than a half hour to take his measurements of temperature and humidity in the cave and to pluck his samples from the interstices of the body, from its surface, and from the ground around, and put them all in glass bottles with screened caps, all carefully labeled. The young deputy had given him a hand out of the cave and offered to carry his case full of writhing data down to the canyon floor. The sun, Armand noticed, had dipped down behind the mountains and the cloudless sky glowed pink.

"All right, Sheriff," he said. "I have everything. My guess—preliminary, of course—is that she died seven days ago, but I'll know more precisely in a few days. It looks like a nasty blow on the head is the cause of death. But that's the coroner's business, of course. It's all yours, Dr. Wilkins. It's all yours."

Wilkins grunted. One of three medical practitioners in Hidalgo County, Wilkins did not like his assignment as coroner (the county was too poor to afford a full-time coroner) but neither did he like playing second fiddle to this little bug man who insisted that he be first to examine any such corpse, lest the "fauna be contaminated." What did the little twit imagine, Wilkins thought, I've got bedbugs or something?

A half an hour later, after photographing the crime scene and poking around for information and evidence, Coroner Wilkins and the sheriff and his deputy began to haul the cumbersome body bag off the ledge down into the purple murk of Skeleton Canyon.

"Will ya hold up there, goddamn it!" wheezed Sheriff Jack Knott, who had the feet end of the bag and most of the weight, being downhill. He had reflected, while he and the coroner were snooping around the body, about how many people had died in this out-of-the-way gash in the Peloncillo Mountains over the years, but his philosophizing had soon given way to dismay at the complexities he faced. There had been no identification on the body. The state police would be involved, probably even the feds. Like most residents of this remote southwesterly corner of New Mexico—and there were less than a thousand in well over twice that number of square miles—Sheriff Knott had a highly developed streak of xenophobia.

"There's a whole lotta loose rock here, like to kill a man. Jesus Christ, *watch* it."

Loose rock rattled and clattered down the canyon wall ahead of the grunting, cursing procession, and a few nighthawks swooped with athletic gaiety overhead against the now vermilion sky.

Mo Bowdre listened with part of his mind to Wheeler Fitzhugh's explanation of how the research station had come to be, here in this well-forested canyon in the Peloncillo Mountains, a gift from the McCormack family twenty years earlier, how it had come to be one of the preeminent sources of baseline ecological data about the region, and so forth. He and Connie were seated in uncomfortable folding chairs in the center's cafeteria, a large low-ceilinged room with some forty small square tables for four, most of them full, Mo guessed from the hubbub around him. He heard a woman's voice say, ". . . so it's obviously another instance of forced extra-pair copulation. That's what drives the society." He heard another voice, a young man's, say, "I don't see why we just don't call it rape. I mean, if *I* did it, it'd be called rape."

"Shut up, Arnold," said the woman's voice.

"Hah—hah—hah," Mo said.

"I beg your . . . ?"

"Sorry, Dr. Fitzhugh, my ears are weird. I'm always hearing several things at once. These people at the next table. What are they studying?"

"Uh, jays. A long-term study of jays, altruism, and monogamy." Fitzhugh cleared his throat. "It seems that monogamy is more honored in the breach among many birds. It's got a lot of ornithologists in a tizzy."

"Well, I should think so," Mo said, sniffing elaborately.

"Oh," Fitzhugh said, "here's Jeremy. Dr. Armand, back from his detective chores. Jeremy, anyone we know?"

"Pretty far gone," said a thin, high voice. "A woman. They may have trouble identifying her. Seven days, I guess from the . . . oh, excuse me."

"Jeremy, this is Mr. Bowdre, you know the sculptor who . . . and this is . . ."

"I'm Connie Barnes. Hello."

"Get yourself a tray and join us, Jeremy," Fitzhugh said.

"Yeah, I'd like to hear about this stuff you do," Mo said, then under his breath as the little man walked away, "Now that I've finished eating."

"So you see," said the little man, "in the lab here we put the pupal forms from the dirt into the same conditions as in the cave—temperature, humidity, and so forth. Then they metamorphose into adults in, well, say two days. So we can tell how long they have been in the pupal stage. And knowing that, we can work backwards—we know how long it takes their eggs to hatch and so forth. And since they always get there an hour or so after death, we can pin down the date. My guess is that it was seven days ago, eighteen June, but the flies will tell me exactly."

"I'll be damned," Mo said. "Never heard of that sort of thing."

"It's becoming quite common. There are several of us. A man named Goff in Hawaii is one of the best known. Of course Hawaii is very different than here. Moist. Different insects. The process takes place on a rather different schedule."

Connie felt sick.

"I hear," Armand said, "that you're here to get inspiration for the sculpture you're going to make for the center. I hope this doesn't put you off." He laughed reedily.

"Oh, no—hah—hah—we got corpses here, rape at the next table. Place is crawling with inspiration. I'm told that this is as far north as a whole lot of Mexican species come. Maybe we could install a great big Mexican beetle out there." Mo cocked his head like a dog listening to something. Then he turned his face toward the director and said, "What's this about a gold mine?"

"It's a nightmare," said Wheeler Fitzhugh. "This French-owned company, Entreprises Métalliques, has asked for a permit to do some exploratory drilling on a piece of land just a mile south of here. And the Forest Service—this is all Forest Service land around here except for this property—says they can't refuse. If the French company finds it, you know, enough gold, well, it doesn't take much, the way they pulverize the rock and put in acid, and . . ."

Tuck Eddy held his meal ticket by the back of the neck with a thumb and middle finger close up below the jaws and index finger resting on its head. Deftly he scratched the lower jaw on the edge of a glass jar and the mouth gaped, two razor-sharp white fangs thrusting forward from bloated pink gums. A small drop appeared at the point of each fang, then an orange spray. That's a good one, Eddy thought, generous. Maybe a twentieth of a gram of orange venom in the little glass jar. Thanks, little brother, he thought, and gently put the greenish snake back into a plastic box with a few rocks in it, put the lid back on, and put the box on a shelf that contained some fifty such boxes.

He now had at least a full gram of venom, the equivalent of a full week's wages, once he'd freeze-dried it into a crystal and shipped it off to the laboratory in California. It was Mojave rattlesnake venom, prized by certain pharmaceutical and medical researchers because it attacks the nervous system, unlike other rattler venom that goes for the blood system, breaking down the veins. And Tuck Eddy had twenty Mojave rattlers, especially toxic ones that came from a relatively small area in the grasslands back of the town of Rodeo.

Lethal little bastards, but Tuck was yet to be bit by a rattler after twelve years of fooling around with them.

"'Night, gang," he said, turned off the overhead light in the small room, and closed the door. His leather-heeled boots boomed across the trailer's floor and, in the kitchen, he put the glass vial in the freezer, then fetched himself a cold beer. "'Nother day, 'nother dollar," he said out loud to no one.

He was presently living alone. It wasn't every day that a man with about a hundred snakes in his house at any given time came across a woman willing to share his life, though this place, with its research center up the canyon, was more likely to have snake-tolerant women than maybe anywhere on earth. And one of those rarities was on her way west, Tuck Eddy thought to himself: a grad student at the University of Pennsylvania and a research-station junkie after two summers. Into frogs as a specialty, but not averse to snakes, and one hell of a lay, no strings attached. Melissa Jenkins, calls herself Mel, kind of big, a bit bony, but no airs, no bullshit, nice attitude about the world: live for the present. What was that Latin phrase she liked to use? *Carpe diem.* That's it. Big black eyes in a round face, dark reddish hair, she called it auburn, crooked smile. Luscious memories that had sustained him many lonely nights during the past nine months returned, and Tuck Eddy could smell her now. From her little postcard with the Gary Larson cartoon on it—the one with the dogs tickling the guy and the guy's foot waggling spasmodically—Tuck guessed she'd be arriving day after tomorrow, and the fun would begin. Make that big old bed sing. She had said she was going to take her time driving, see some places along the way. She was looking for a little adventure, she had said.

Oliver J. (Tuck) Eddy, sole proprietor of Venom Enterprises, supplier of poison drained from a host of rattlesnakes, scorpions, and anything else that stung or bit, sat sipping his cold beer and thinking about Mel.

A few more years and she'd be some kind of professor. He wondered how many more summers she would want to shack up with a guy who had bombed out of college—too many books, not enough action—and had bombed out as a keeper of reptiles at the Tuscaloosa zoo. Couldn't get along with the bloated nitwit director who was always downplaying the reptiles, discouraging the breeding program ("It's really a question of marketing these things," the jerk would say), and carping at Tuck Eddy like he was some kind of lowlife. So one day Eddy had said to himself "screw this" and took off in his dying Dodge pickup, loaded down with about twelve snakes and the few other things he owned, including the beginnings of a Rolodex of laboratories and zoos and collectors that he had copied from the zoo's administrative office, and made it west all the way to the bootheel of New Mexico, where, he knew, there were more kinds of snakes than Custer had Indians and maybe he could make a decent living off them. And it wasn't bad, Tuck Eddy thought to himself, though it would be even better once he had supplemented it according to plan. He yawned luxuriously. Tomorrow he would take the day off, head back out to Skeleton Canyon. He'd already loaded his gear into the Jeep. Get an early start, beat the heat.

•　　•　　•

Daniel Ascension sat smoking on the rickety wooden porch of his ramshackle house, greasy hat brim shutting off from his view the countless stars that hung in the night sky above him. He was profoundly disturbed, saddened the way a child can be when it begins to perceive that childhood is ending. He had been upset by the corpse he had found, but it wasn't the first dead body he had seen, not by a long shot.

What really bothered him was the place it had been found, the cave in Skeleton Canyon. The sheriff had said there were footprints in there, two sets of footprints, made by those jogging shoes people were wearing. One set matched the shoes the woman was wearing. In all the times he had been to that cave over the years, even when the canyon got so popular with the treasure hunters, he had never seen a single human footprint in its sandy floor, or any other sign of human disturbance. He had, without thinking much about it, assumed that he was the only person who knew about the cave.

He had liked to ride over there every now and then to sit in the utter silence and look at the petroglyphs on the wall, and imagine what it would have been like to be the first person to have ever seen the cave, and the canyon outside. Some old Indian. But now it was obvious someone else had known about Daniel's cave all along. It wasn't the same anymore.

Probably, Daniel thought, he'd never go back there. There were a few other places, more caves up in the Animas Mountains on Gray Ranch, where he reckoned nobody had been but him since the Indians left, but they weren't as good. And now the ranch was owned by those conservation-minded people, some kind of group run by a beer maker's son who did ranching and, it was said, wrote poetry or some damned thing. Said they didn't mind if Daniel poked around some of his old haunts, but Daniel didn't know how long that permission would last. You can't tell about people like that. He stood up and his cigarette made an red arc through the night and glowed in the dust. The screen door slammed behind him.

Jeremy Armand flipped the light switch and two long fluorescent bulbs flickered on over the bench in his laboratory. He leaned over and peered at the little glass vials he had brought back that afternoon from the cave in Skeleton Canyon. Each was filled with sandy dirt from the cave floor and each contained, under the dirt, a small dark form that would become precisely on schedule a blowfly. Nearby, other similar vials contained various kinds of beetles, most of them from his research site in Rustler's Canyon up in the mountains, a beautiful assortment, Armand thought, some chiefly Mexican, others chiefly northern, as was the case with so many creatures in these mountains. He would attempt to create small breeding colonies in the lab so as to determine precise life-span data for each species while at the same time determining each species' ecological requirements in the field.

Beetles, he thought again, are the canaries in the mine. Subtle shifts in beetle populations could be the litmus test of environmental change. But the morons, the public, could be made to worry only about pandas and lions and tigers, not the refinements of nature. He looked again at the Skeleton Canyon specimens, smiled, and turned out the light. The data would show that the woman had died seven days before. He would be able to issue a report to that potbellied redneck, Sheriff Knott, in three days. He walked the familiar path through the trees to his cabin in the forest about fifty yards from the main compound. Once inside, he poured himself a cognac and began reading the proofs of a monograph he had written the year before for a German journal in which he had reorganized the taxonomy of the eucmenid beetles of North America.

. . .

Wheeler Fitzhugh listened to the cheerful plash of water in the sink from the two old faucets with their knobby porcelain handles. It was a small bathroom, even cramped, with the little pentagons of white tile popular in the twenties, and it had been added on to the log cabin that had squatted on the creek's bank since Geronimo's time. The original cabin was now one of two bedrooms in the house of the Desert Research Center's director, one of the perks, a free house, that made up for a salary that was unexciting but enough, Fitzhugh thought, to put a bit aside each year for his special investments, and a beautiful house after all. He listened to the two streams of water, one never ending in the Peloncillos' only perpetual creek just outside, dancing over the rocks. The other one—recently the shower and now the basin faucet— served the needs of the woman newly arrived. Fitzhugh lay naked on his seven-foot-square water bed admiring, as he had ever since he could remember, the wondrously changeable configuration of his genitalia, noting as well the fine flatness of his abdomen, not bad for a man in his forties.

"Fitz," the woman called from the bathroom. "Where's the toothpaste?"

"In the drawer on the left," Fitzhugh said, smiling, thinking that right there, in his bathroom, was Mexico's, if not the world's, leading specialist in American desert plant associations, Dr. Vera María Madero, currently in the midst of a two-year appointment to the University of Arizona in Tucson. After a bit more splashing of water, she stepped into the room clad in nothing besides her thick and silky long black hair. "I am so glad to be back," she said in her measured and formal English, reaching out to switch off the lights. He heard a rustling sound and the bed's center of gravity shifted pleasantly. "How I have missed you," she said, and he felt her hands exploring. "Did you miss me?" she asked, the hands now brazen and insistent. "Oh," she said.

"How nice. The richnesses," the woman intoned, "oh, yes, the beauties of this blessed world, they are ours for the taking . . . oh, my dear, we belong . . . We have things to do, no?"

Deputy Sheriff Jimmy Snyder and his boss, Sheriff Knott, sat in Sarah Knott's kitchen, bottles of Coors Lite making little puddles of condensation on the red-and-white oilcloth that covered the kitchen table. Sarah Knott had retired to bed an hour before.

"Gin," Jimmy said, laying out his cards in three neat fans.

"Goddamn it," Jack Knott said. "That's three in a row."

"They're your cards," Jimmy said with a grin.

"I hate this."

"Yeah, losing's for shit."

"Watch your language in this house, boy. That's a Christian woman in the other room. No, I'm not talking about cards. It's the feds. I hate it when the damn feds've got to get involved. State cops are bad enough, but the damn feds—that dude that called? He said that one of their agents, field agent of some sort, may be missing, wonders if our corpse may be her. Jeez, what'd that bug doctor say? Seven days? How the hell do you lose a field agent for seven days? Anyway, this guy said he'd be coming around tomorrow morning. First thing. We better pack this up, get some sleep. Be ready for a visit from Their Holinesses, two little men in business suits, wearing neckties, you see if I'm not right. It's like they crank 'em out with some kind of stencil."

"Jack?" Sarah called from the other room.

"Well, good night, boy," the sheriff said, hoisting himself off the wooden chair, puffing out his cheeks. "Duty beckons. See you tomorrow. Damn neckties."

Connie Barnes woke up abruptly, with none of the usual drowsy fog surrounding her like a warm blanket, and sat up in the unfamiliar bed. Mo stood by the window in a pair of orange shorts, his back to her.

"There's a trogon out there," he whispered. Connie winced inwardly, imagining some ugly forest beast snooping around.

"What's a trogon?"

"It's a bird. Green and red, something like a parrot. Listen."

Connie sat in bed, listening, and presently she heard a distant *co-ah*.

"That's got to be a trogon. C'mere. Maybe you can see it." He moved aside from the small window, and Connie stepped across the little room.

Co-ah.

"Do you see it?"

Connie craned her neck back and forth, one hand holding

her long black hair away from her face, seeing only trees in the predawn light, different kinds of evergreen trees.

"No, I don't see it."

"That's too bad," Mo said. "It's a big deal seeing a trogon. Mexican bird mostly. Birders come from all over the damn country to see the trogons. Keep looking. It's called the elegant trogon. Used to be called the coppery-tailed trogon, but they changed its name."

"Why?"

"Indian-rights people objected . . . hah . . . hah," Mo said, putting a big hand on Connie's warm back end. "Hah . . . hah, oh, hoo, you sure fell for that one." Connie snuggled against the big man. "Say, whatever happened to your Hopi modesty?" he went on.

"I left it in Santa Fe." She rubbed his large round stomach.

"Co-ah," Mo said, a fair imitation. "The mating call of the coppery-tailed Hopi."

"Co-ah," Connie said. "Breakfast isn't for another hour."

"Don't mind if I do," Mo said.

By seven-thirty the sun had disposed of some thin clouds to the east of Lordsburg, New Mexico, and when Sheriff Jack Knott hauled himself out of his cruiser in front of the Hidalgo County Sheriff's Office, he knew it was going to be a scorcher. Hundred degrees easy by noon. There was an unfamiliar vehicle in the small lot, a green Chevrolet with Arizona plates, and a guy in it. Dark hair, light blue shirt, jeans—he had one knee propped up on the dashboard and he looked like he was asleep. Sheriff Knott strode over to the car and stood by the window, hands on his hips, gut thrust forward like the prow of a warship. The dark-haired man, maybe late thirties, opened his eyes, blinked, and glanced at the paunch, and the shiny leather belt and holster, about a foot from his face.

"This ain't the smartest place to loiter, boy," said the sheriff.

"You Sheriff Knott?" the man asked.

"I am. Now—"

"I'm Collins."

The sheriff blinked behind his mirrored sunglasses. Collins? Name was familiar.

"Larry Collins. FBI." The man held out his wallet and let it flip open. "I called you last night." He had a rough, nasal voice, an accent like you hear on TV cop shows they make in New York City. "I'd like to see that body you found."

"Yeah, sure," Knott said, thinking that this was the goddamnedest-looking FBI man he'd ever laid eyes on, looked like some kind of—what? Like some guy on the sidewalk in one of those TV shows. No wonder he hadn't connected this character to the name he had written down on the pad by the phone. He was glad he hadn't made a little bet with his deputy about the neckties.

"So, do you mind if I get out of this car?"

Knott backed away. "Come on," he said. "Get us some coffee, get acquainted. Something I'd like to know," he said over his shoulder as he strode toward the door. "How is it you boys'd be missing an agent for a whole week? Don't you people have to check in regular?"

"Well, Sheriff, some of us don't. Operate on our own on some assignments."

"Like you? Here," the sheriff said, holding the door of the building open. "Go ahead. To your right. You up to something in Hidalgo County?"

"Over in Arizona."

"Well, you know, Mr. Collins, it's a pretty hard thing to keep something secret in this part of the world. Lot of country here, but not too many people. Stranger sticks out like a blue steer. Specially Easterners."

The agent smiled briefly, showing crooked front teeth.

"Here," the sheriff said. "Turn here. Have a seat." He watched the agent slump down in the wooden chair next to Knott's wooden desk, an old oaken piece of territorial furniture that had served the local sheriff even before they named the place Hidalgo County.

"Coffee?"

"Yeah, black. Thanks. Then it's corpse time."

A coffee machine sat on a table in the corner of Knott's office, which a night deputy turned on at the end of his shift so that the sheriff wouldn't have to wait even five minutes for his first injection. He handed a mug to Collins, who seemed distracted. Sheriff Knott set his mug down on the old desk and settled into the chair, watching the agent. He was big in the chest and the shoulders, with a head of curly black hair, the sort it looks like you don't ever have to comb. Sure as hell doesn't look like an FBI man, the sheriff thought to himself.

"First time out here?"

"Nah, I was working on some stuff up north of here, New Mexico and Arizona, both. Some stolen Indian artifacts, you know, religious stuff. Hopi."

"Oh, yeah," Knott said. "I think I read something about that. Don't have any Indians down here. Just ruins. Most of 'em already been looted by pothunters. Most of our trouble down here, aside from the usual stuff, is wetbacks. And drugs, of course. We do a lot of work with the Border Patrol, DEA, that type a thing."

The FBI agent fidgeted in his chair, then said, "Listen, this coffee's too hot to drink. Why don't we go and . . . It won't take long."

Sheriff Knott cleared his throat. He didn't fancy looking at a corpse before caffeine was coursing through his veins. "It's pretty far gone."

"Yeah, well . . . anyway."

So Sheriff Knott led the agent down into the basement and the small cold room that served the county as a morgue. He fussed with latches and locks and then slid the heavy metal drawer out and managed to look elsewhere while Collins lifted the cloth and peered.

"Ah, shit," Collins said. "Put her away." He turned and went out, ashen under the veneer of a light tan. Knott closed her up, locked the drawer, and followed the agent, whom he found standing at the bottom of the basement stairs, balled-up fists in his back pockets. "That's her," Collins said. "I'd bet a year's salary on it. We'll have to ship her to Forensics in Washington to make it positive, but that's her, sure as hell. Same hair, same body size, frame. Shit."

The two men stood by the stairs, heads down.

"God *damn*," Sheriff Knott said. "You sure hate losin' one of your own." He puffed out his cheeks. "Well, let's go up and talk about this. I guess you'll be workin' in Hidalgo County now too. Now, you can count on this office for any kind of assistance . . . we got some boys know the country like the back of their . . ." The sheriff kept talking, seeing that the agent was in turmoil.

A molten white sun lifted up above the insubstantial, two-dimensional mountains and immediately began heating up the back of Tuck Eddy's already red-brown neck. It was going to be a scorcher, he thought, over a hundred by eleven, hotter down in the canyon, much too hot for a snake, but he wasn't after snakes. Squatting on his heels beside his Jeep, Eddy gulped the last half inch of lukewarm orange juice from a paper carton and pushed his straw hat up off his forehead with a thumb, shading his neck. The Jeep was painted an electric pink and grievously scarred. Tuck had bought it from the Pink Jeep Tours people up in Sedona, Arizona, where good-natured guides took tourists out on the red-rock cliffs and told them old cowboy movie stories or explained about geology and botany, rocks and trees, and tried to make them feel both excited and at home in a world produced by some cosmic Henry Moore. Tuck Eddy knew the feeling, all that soaring red rock made a man feel like he should kneel and whisper.

He'd bought the Jeep for just a little bit more than two thousand dollars two years ago and had found reason not to get around to painting it some more normal and explainable color. You could spot Tuck Eddy's Jeep for ten, fifteen miles out on the desert, like an ad for the dedication and perseverance of Venom Enterprises.

The Jeep's shadow stretched far out across the pale pink rimrock, the low sun having turned it into an elongated spirit lying across the land. A thinner shadow shot out across the rock like an arrow as Eddy stood up with a grunt. "Knees," he said out loud. "Knees." And to himself he thought: proof that God didn't have the whole plan in mind. He tossed the empty juice carton into the back of the Jeep and vaulted into the seat. The key jammed, then turned, and the Jeep's innards growled obediently and they lurched toward the edge of the abyss.

"Eee-hah!" Eddy hooted, steering between two boulders and over the side.

At a forty-five-degree angle, an open Jeep seems almost vertical, and last year, when Tuck Eddy had taken Mel, the big, angular redhead, over the side like this with no warning, she had shrieked with laughter. "You barbarian," she had sputtered. "You'll kill us both."

He grinned now at the memory—and the anticipation. Mel was coming, oh, God, she was a-coming, maybe tomorrow, god *damn*! The right front wheel lurched over a rock and the Jeep jerked and swayed, inching down the arroyo, now all green and purple in the shadows, one of several skull-dry tributaries that descended into and gave birth to the eastern end of Skeleton Canyon.

In the back of the Jeep was a shovel, a crowbar, and a brand-new machine that Tuck Eddy had bought by mail from Sweet Home, Oregon, for $599.95 plus postage. That was a lot of money for Tuck Eddy, but the machine had everything—including ground reject controls, depth controls, and headphones, so when he found what he was looking for, everybody within six miles wouldn't hear the machine's joyous electronic shriek. All the gear clattered on the metal floor with each slow-motion heave and twitch and sigh of the Jeep. The engine snarled and whined, and Tuck Eddy, tossed from side to side like a rodeo rider, was in personal, ass-rattling paradise. *Pow. Whap*, said the Jeep's anatomy in response to the warts and wrinkles of Mother Earth, and "Go, mama!" Tuck Eddy whooped.

But the Jeep stopped with a jerk and a squeal of metal criminally wronged, and the engine barked and died, and the floor shift handle rattled violently under his hand in a dying spasm, and there was a stifling silence.

"Damn," he said into the silent, hot, immobile world. He peered down over the side of the left front fender, now with yet another welt in it where it was wedged against a big slab of grayish limestone as implacable as a born-again Catholic. Like a nun with a ruler. Oliver J. (Tuck) Eddy had had the best of both worlds in his upbringing, a Catholic mother and a drunk father who had found God, but a Baptist God. Having been a rope in such a sectarian tug-of-war, he had inherited a series of attitudes about the fundament of things that, like matter and antimatter, had met and annihilated each other, leaving a vague and tenuous cloud of guilt-laden, imperceptible pollution, a kind of metaphysical haze that settled every now and then over his otherwise clear vision. For the fleetingest second, Tuck Eddy wondered if it was his fault that the Jeep was hung up against this nunlike rock, but he rejected the idea. Instead he switched off the ignition, stepped out onto the nun's head, and leaped off to the rear.

"Damn," he said again when he saw the right rear wheel turning slowly six inches off the ground. He looked around, up at the rimrock ten feet above his head, then at the wheel hanging there immodestly in the air, like you got your fly open at the dance and your underwear is showing.

It was dead quiet in the arroyo, still and windless, cool in the shadows. Eddy reached into the the back of the Jeep and hoisted his shovel and crowbar onto his shoulder, and in his other hand carried his Treasuremaster 600 (Series 2) metal detector like a high-tech weed eater.

Later, he said to himself. Later, mama.

And he set off down the slope, looking for a likely spot on the sides of the arroyo, itself so minor a factor in the clawlike network of gullies and mini-canyons that fed into Skeleton Canyon that it had, so far as Tuck Eddy knew, no name. He could think of nothing more exhilarating—a feature of the land big enough for a man to disappear into but too trivially obscure to have caught the attention of the world's carto-graphic busybodies.

Almost virgin, he thought, eyeing the V-shaped, rock-strewn sides of the nameless arroyo.

Almost, he fervently hoped.

Briefly and graphically, the anatomical problems of the phrase *almost virgin* engaged Tuck Eddy's mind, but he re-minded himself that he was looking for something else on this hot, bright, promising new day—the sort of place so ob-vious that it would have been overlooked by a century of less observant men, the sort of place a ragtag bunch of panicked Mexican bandits would have stashed thirty-nine gleaming bars of silver.

There were, of course, several versions of the tale. The most compelling held that the banditos on mules were smuggling the thirty-nine bars of silver from Mexico to some destination in Arizona. Probably they were taking it to some heady market like Tombstone and crossed what is now Gray Ranch, five hundred square miles of grassland and mountains, and headed for what would come to be called Skeleton Canyon, through which ran what already was known as the Smugglers' Trail. Meanwhile the Clanton brothers somehow got wind of the shipment and hid on the canyon's rim. The banditos, fearing that something was up, stashed the silver near the canyon or somewhere in it, and proceeded, no doubt assuming that they could pass unscathed through any confrontation since they obviously had no silver or anything valuable with them. But there had been no face-to-face confrontation, no chance to display their empty pockets, their empty saddlebags, and shrug. The Clantons had simply opened up from the rim and shot down all of the Mexicans. Finding that there was no silver, they left the bodies lying on the ground to become the canyon's namesake, and the brothers went on to fame and the glory of God at the hands of Wyatt Earp and Doc Holliday in the squalid little enclosure called the O.K. Corral.

There were variations, of course. Some had it that it was another local outlaw, Curly Bill Brocius, and *his* boys who had shot down the Mexicans and actually laid their hands on the thirty-nine bars of silver, only to find that it was all too heavy to tote, so they buried it somewhere in the canyon and then got themselves killed before they could get back for it. Yet another version held that they got almost as far as Rodeo when their animals gave out, so they stowed it in an abandoned mine shaft, and got killed before they could come back for it.

In any event, the tale of the lost treasure of Skeleton Canyon, in its varying details, had fired the imaginations of generations of treasure hunters and other romantics, and Tuck had lately become one of these. After all, Bill Cavaliere, a former deputy with Hidalgo County and no swinger on moonbeams, had told Tuck that *he* thought the silver was out there waiting to be found, and that was enough for the snake man newly arrived in the land of dreams.

The other basic story—the dry and soulless version—was much the same but for the suggestion that the banditos were hauling about four thousand dollars in silver coinage, that they didn't bury it but had it in their saddlebags when the gunfire rained down on them from out of the blue. The Clantons then grabbed the coins, hightailed it over to a cabin in the foothills of the Chiricahua Mountains, split it up, and blew this treasure within a month in the saloons and bawdy houses of Tombstone. People like Tuck, brains aswarm with self-replicating hordes of treasure virus, could dismiss the prosaic account out of hand without thinking twice about it. Not to do so was to confess in the depths of their souls that the world was doomed to be a bore.

So, recently, Tuck had been exploring the implications of the first version, in which the Mexicans buried the treasure themselves. He had tried to put himself in the minds of those anonymous wetbacks and, with his snake-collecting permit from the U.S. Forest Service, had probed the arroyos, the washes, and the caves of Skeleton Canyon whenever time permitted. Not one of his friends or acquaintances knew what he was really up to when his pink Jeep was gleaming on the rim or rumbling around the canyon floor, a commercial on wheels. Nor did Tuck Eddy know about the legalities of searching for treasure on federal land or taking it once he found it, and he wasn't about to look into all that.

He was two hundred feet down the arroyo from his stalled Jeep and the sun was high enough now to lay a brilliant

•

stripe of light along the upper edge of the arroyo's western slope. Except for the crunch of rock under his boots, the silence was palpable.

Though he knew the rattlers were still lurking among the rocks, he had the familiar sensation of being the only living being left here in the center of the universe, the very core of the innocent creation. He stared at the arroyo walls and took two steps downward. He looked again, put down the Treasuremaster, tipped his hat forward, and fetched a Camel Light from his shirt pocket. As he lit the cigarette with a green disposable gas lighter, he continued to stare at the arroyo wall, at three large pink rocks each about three feet from one another, which, from his particular vantage point, gave the illusion of being a cross.

"Sweet Jesus," he said. The Mexicans. Hagridden with centuries of Catholic superstition, always on the lookout for some sign that they were not doomed, lost, cast out, hopeless, any sign, any familiar symbol, however improbable . . . Perfect. He drew heavily on the cigarette and ground it out under his boot. Then he leaned down and picked up the butt and put it in his shirt pocket.

"*Madre mío,*" he said in pidgin Spanish. "*Oh, sí, vaqueros.*"

He started up the slope, jumping lightly from rock to rock, shovel and crowbar over his shoulder, Treasuremaster swinging in his other hand, his chest pounding with elation. Reaching the first rock of the illusory crucifix, he set down his tools and peered at the ground. Far below, from somewhere down the arroyo, he heard the sassy trill of a canyon wren. Nice timing, brother, he thought. He leaned on the rock and looked over it at the sand behind.

"Damn!" he said out loud.

On the patch of red sand behind the rock were six footprints, probably only a few days old, the clear imprints of a pair of jogging shoes. Tuck felt as violated as a Sabine woman and he began to sweat profusely. The arid air of Skeleton Canyon sucked up this unusual moisture and left Tuck Eddy shivering before his cross.

The gas station nearest the Desert Research Center was in the town of Rodeo. And the Rodeo gas station, like everything else in town, gave the impression of having satisfied itself that the technical achievements of the 1950s were ample to its needs. Three old gas pumps stood stolidly in the dust outside a modest storefront, their round heads white and expressionless.

Connie Barnes, seated behind the wheel of the pickup, described the situation briefly to Mo Bowdre, who, as usual, sat erect in the passenger seat, his dark glasses facing straight ahead.

"D'you suppose they've got unleaded gas here?" he asked.

Connie squinted at the pumps. "Yes. They do."

"Self-serve?"

"It doesn't say. I guess we wait. For a few minutes anyway." It was getting hot in the truck.

"No rush," Mo said.

The storefront screen door slammed and bounced and a man in a straw cowboy hat and a blue shirt walked around the rear of the truck, appearing at Connie's window.

"At your service, ma'am. Fill 'er up?"

Mo exploded in laughter.

Connie looked at him, then at the attendant.

"What are *you* . . . ?" she said.

"What am I doing here?" asked Special Agent Larry Collins of the FBI. "Just passing through. Thought I could be useful."

"Oh, sure," Connie said. "Something's—what's going on?"

"I'm surprised you're here, Collins."

Connie faced the big man. "No you're not. What's going on?"

"Posing as a gas station attendant? Sure, fill 'er up, boy. See, Connie, Collins here has gone underground. He's after the oil cartel."

"Regular or supreme, ma'am?" the agent asked, crooked teeth shining through a grin.

Connie put her hands up before her, palms out, fingers spread, and quivered. "Eeeee," she said, a Hopi sound usually denoting trouble.

"I'll fill it up," said the agent. "Then we can go somewhere and talk. This tub takes leaded, right? When are you gonna trade in this guzzler for something from the twentieth century, huh, Bowdre?"

Connie sighed. Collins, she thought, the impetuous oddball FBI agent who had blown into their lives the summer before, tracking down the stolen Hopi deities, which, in the end, Mo had found, along with the killer of Walter Meyers, the gallery owner in Santa Fe . . . The whole thing, including Mo's involvement in the first place, being what people had said was an impossible series of coincidences . . . and Mo had laughed and said, "Well, they do call this the Land of Enchantment, don't they?"

But this. Collins out here in the desert. At this particular gas station in the middle of nowhere. This, Connie knew, was no coincidence.

A few minutes later they were headed north on Route 80 through the San Simon Valley, a wide swath of brown and gray scrub sweeping up on both sides to the base of mountain chains that had begun to look insubstantial in the morning glare. Mo sat in the middle, seeming all the more enormous, with his too-small black cowboy hat down over his forehead, while Collins fidgeted by the window, talking in his nasal New York accent, his right hand gesturing like a pinwheel in an intermittent breeze.

"See, after I turned over those Hopi gods to the tribe—officially—Washington figured I was some kind of hotshot in this stuff—you know, crimes against the Archaeological Resources Act—so I've been up in Flagstaff chasing pothunters until this thing came up."

"This thing?" Connie said.

"Yeah. Wait, let me tell you. It's—well, complicated. You know anything about Pre-Columbian art?"

"Like Aztecs?"

"Yeah, Aztecs, Mayans, Olmecs—you know, those guys who made the huge stone heads, look like Africans. But this is Aztec, this deal. Some guys, Mexicans, have been running some new Aztec stuff out of the country, up here. Violation of Mexican law, U.S. law."

"New Aztec stuff?" Connie asked. "What, fakes?"

"New *found*. See, the big Aztec city, Tenock-something, I can't pronounce it, it's all c's and t's and l's—anyway the Spanish leveled it and built Mexico City right on top. A whole lot of stuff was simply buried, lost. Four hundred and fifty years back. Back in the Seventies, they found the main pyramid, under the subway or some damn thing. Now, apparently, somebody started digging below his own basement and found a cache of the stuff. Untouched. A treasure. Anyway, I'm getting ahead of myself."

The gray scrub flashed by outside the pickup, the highway smacking the trees rhythmically. Hot air buffeted them through the windows.

"Where are we going?" Connie asked.

"Doesn't make any difference. Just drive. A new piece, a gold cup with some kind of jaguar on it, turned up in a Canadian dealer's place, the Mounties confiscated it, the dealer weaseled out, you know innocently holding his bill of sale, all bullshit. It's hard to nail these creeps. You know that. But the experts had never seen this particular piece before, so— anyway, the Mexican cops and archaeologists finally figured out that it was a whole new find, a really big deal, a tomb of a merchant or something, not royalty but big. And some guy was looting this stuff right out from under his own base-ment, but nobody knows where. A while ago, the federales got a tip. The stuff was being taken out the country through here."

"Here? What kind of tip?" Connie said.

"Well, I'm not supposed to talk about the tip, but here, this part of New Mexico and Arizona." He waved his hand at the landscape behind them. "It wasn't real clear, but maybe through the research center. So to show solidarity with our Mexican brethren, the Bureau got involved, assigned me to the case. We already had one American agent working on it."

Collins paused and looked out the window at the desert.

"You already knew this, Mo?" Connie said. She suddenly felt as if she were underwater.

The big man nodded.

"What is going on?" she demanded.

Collins leaned forward and looked past Mo. "I needed someone at the research center. I'm not the type, you know, pretend I'm some kind of scientist. Anyway these guys all know each other. You can't just march in there and say you're a big ace in the field of frog mating behavior or whatever. They know."

"Eeeeee," Connie said.

"So I thought of Bowdre here. I mean, you know what he did about those stolen gods, that stuff. Brilliant. So I—"

Connie hit the steering wheel with the palm of her hand. "He's a—a *civilian*. How can the FBI send a . . . ?"

Collins shrugged and looked ahead through the wind-shield. "The Bureau doesn't, uh, know about it."

Connie was silent.

"I went to the director of the Denver Museum, the outfit that runs the center. Told him what the problem was. Told him he'd have to cooperate or get his whole place tossed. Told him we had a free-lance guy. So we cooked up an anonymous donor with a couple of million to drop on the center, no strings, except that the donor wanted a Bowdre sculpture near the entrance to the place. So here you are."

"Mo, you knew *all* this?"

The big man nodded.

"Why didn't you tell me?"

"I wanted you to hear it from Collins. You wouldn't have believed me."

A few scruffy low houses were visible on the glared-out land up ahead. "We're almost at Route 10," Collins said. "Turn around and head back south." Connie slowed the pickup, pulled off on the dusty shoulder, and stopped. The cab immediately filled up with motionless heat.

"What are these things worth?" she asked. "Like that gold cup that was confiscated."

"Worth?"

"You recall," Mo said, "that Connie is a certified public accountant, master appraiser of Indian jewelry. How much was the guy selling the cup for?"

"He had it marked at a million two."

Connie bit her lip. Some world, she thought bitterly, where a cannibal merchant's cup is worth five times a set of Hopi deities—gods. As if reading her mind, Collins said, "You know, gold antiquities, it's like turning on the switch in the greed closet. People go—"

"Sure," Connie said. "How dangerous is it?"

"Well . . . It could be dangerous, that amount of money involved." She stared at him. "It is dangerous," he admitted. "We've lost one agent. A woman."

"A woman?"

"Yeah. They found her yesterday in a canyon. Up here. I mean back there. Not in Mexico."

"Oh," Mo said, as if waking up from a nap. "There's a scientist at the center, a forensic entomologist, if you can imagine that. He's going to figure out the time of death from the insect fauna on the body."

Collins shuddered. "I heard. Guy named Armand. Man, that must be a weird place, that center."

"Excuse me," Connie said, "but don't you think this is real irresponsible, sending a *civilian* into . . . ?"

"Hey," Collins said. "All he's gotta do is hang around, sniff, listen, see what turns up, keep me posted. He agreed—"

Connie started the truck with a roar, slammed it in gear, and violently U-turned on the highway. She leaned forward and fixed the agent with black eyes.

"I'm a civilian too," she said through her teeth. "And *I* haven't agreed. You two are acting like a couple of kids and I don't like it. Not one bit."

Twenty minutes of silence later the pickup swerved into the Rodeo gas station, pulled past the upstanding-burgher gas pumps, and came to a dusty stop. Mo sat hugely in the middle of the seat, his little black hat down even further over his blond eyebrows.

"Mother Earth?" Mo said. "May I have a word with you?"

"I'm outta here," Collins said, opened the door, and headed for the storefront. Over his shoulder he said, "You know where to reach me."

"Is he really trying to pretend—"

"A gas station attendant? No, no. Hah. He's working out of Douglas, down by the border over in Arizona. Say, look here, I'm—"

"Don't say you're sorry."

"Oh no, I'm not sorry. I was bored. This seemed . . . And of course it's a new place and—"

"And you need me as your Seeing Eye dog."

"Well—"

"You should have told me."

"I know I should."

"Is there more I don't know?"

"More?" Mo said, heaving himself over to the window. "Nope, nothing yet anyway. So do you want to do this?"

"I don't know yet."

"Well, you've got the high ground now—hah—hah. For a while. I know that."

"It could be dangerous. It is dangerous."

"At most we'll be on the fringe, like Collins says, just sniffing."

"The place gives me the creeps."

"All those bug people?"

"No, all those trees up there."

"Ah, the forest primeval. But that's where we came from. Knuckle-walked our asses out of the forest, stood upright like timid little bears, and said hey."

Connie turned the key and the pickup shuddered and roared. "Sure. We came *out* of the forest. Onto open ground. At least that's the white man's version. Where to?"

Mo smiled broadly. "So I can continue to hang my jeans on your doorknob?"

Connie said something in Hopi.

"What?"

"It's a Hopi word. It refers to the endless meddling and tricks of the coyote."

"There are coyotes up in those mountains, around the center," Mo said. "In the trees."

"There's one in this pickup," she said, putting the truck in gear. She smiled in spite of herself.

•   •   •

"Oh, I get it," the young woman said. She was seated in a big wicker chair in Wheeler Fitzhugh's office, long brown legs crossed. One foot waggled irritably up and down, encased in a worn red-and-white Reebok. Her arms were tightly folded over her chest, and a childish frown, almost a pout, pinched her forehead. She wore a pair of shorts—cutoff jeans—and a red World Wildlife Fund T-shirt with the ubiquitous panda symbol looking sad and bewildered, peering over one of her slender forearms. Her hair was straight, blonde, and thin.

"I get it," she repeated. "I'm just disposable merchandise, a handy little roll in the hay, till Señorita Cactus shows up with her mariachi tapes."

Fitzhugh hated this, hated himself for having given in two weeks ago when he knew Vera Maria was coming. He knew at the time it would be trouble, nothing but trouble, trouble, trouble, and for what? A few rolls in the hay, as the girl had said, and with an inexperienced undergraduate, with big blue eyes that now glared at him. Since his wife had left a year ago, no longer interested in moldering in the boondocks, and had returned to the university life, Wheeler Fitzhugh had bedded a couple of eager young biologists, but this one had evidently expected more than just an enjoyable dalliance. How unenlightened, he thought.

"But—" he said.

"But? But what?" the young woman said, her voice rising in pitch. "*But* nothing." She stood up and leaned on his desk with both hands, staring at him. A string of blonde hair fell over her face and she swept it back angrily. "I could have *your* butt on a sex-discrimination charge, tell everyone how women students get to do shitwork around here unless they ball the director. That kind of stuff doesn't fly, even out here in Nowhereville."

Fitzhugh was dumb with fear and anger—fear at the perfectly plausible threat, anger at the injustice of it. She, after all, had given him a come-on, the long looks from her dewy sapphire eyes, then turning up next to him in the cafeteria line three meals running, the eager, rapt listening to his every word, the casual touch, the innocent bump, and then standing before his desk with a languid smile and then came at him right over the desk. . . . My God, Fitzhugh said to himself as the girl climbed onto his desk.

"But I'm not going to do that," she said. Fitzhugh stared as she unbuttoned her shorts, standing in red-and-white Reeboks on his desk, on his papers. She can't want . . . Fitzhugh thought, and he watched dumbly as she pushed her pants down and squatted on the desk before him, and he watched in stupefaction as the yellow stream made a puddle on his desk, on his papers. He stared as the warm liquid spilled into his lap. He stared as the woman pulled up her shorts and hopped backward off the desk.

"Piss on you, Fitzhugh, you prick," she said, and turned to the door. He stared as she paused before the door, her back to him, her head cocked like a bird. "A little prick," she added, and the door slammed and warm piss dripped in his lap.

Thirty seconds later Wheeler Fitzhugh began to laugh, only partly in relief at how lightly he had gotten off. Everyone, he thought to himself, at one time or another wants to piss on the director. He couldn't stop laughing.

"I'm going over," Special Agent Larry Collins had said. The crewcut Border Patrol chief in the Douglas, Arizona, office had frowned. He had a neck and head that seemed to form a single pink cannon shell. He held his chin, a double, drawn back into his neck, enhancing the illusion of a piece of military ordnance emerging from his tan collar.

"You know what it takes to get authorization from the Mexicans for a federal agent?"

"Hey, Chief, gimme a break. Unofficial, you know? DEA guys go back and forth like tennis balls. Our agent was in Mexico, man, she checked in from there, then she's found dead in some damned cave in New Mexico. Obviously—"

The cannon shell frowned again. "Yeah, obviously." He glanced sharply at Collins. "So what was she onto?"

"Hey, Chief, it's FBI business."

"Don't you give me any of that Bureau pigshit, boy. You're standing here less than two miles from the international border between the U-nited States and the Republic of Mexico, and you want to cross over that border, and that border is *my* business, I don't give a rat's ass if the enn-tire Justice Department says otherwise."

Collins smiled. "You own the border, huh?"

"This here two-hundred-mile section of it, I do, you damn right."

Collins explained about the Aztec cup, the apparent looting of a new tomb, the tip that pointed north to the Peloncillos.

"... so she must've been tailing some one of these guys, on their way, see?"

"So it seems," said the cannon shell. "And you think you'd be better at following her trail than the federales, huh? How long you say she's been dead? How's your Spanish, huh? *Habla español?*"

"Just an ugly American tourist," Collins said with a grin.

"You got it partways right." A small crinkle in the cannon shell's surface bespoke a smile. "I never heard of you. You was never in this office, never seen you. They catch you, you're just some unauthorized wild hair of an FBI agent."

"You got that partways right, Chief."

"They put you in one of their jails, you'll wish your ass was made of Kevlar."

"I thought with free trade and all . . . A new era."

"Same old era for the Mexican penal system, boy. It's called the Dark Ages. Now get outta here before I change my mind. One piece of advice."

Collins, halfway to the door, stopped.

"My guess," the cannon shell said, "is that they'd've come over in New Mexico, probably around Antelope Wells, over the other side of Gray Ranch. Otherwise why'd they end up in Skeleton Canyon? Skeleton Canyon is the old Smugglers' Trail, back in the old days."

"Thanks, Chief," Collins had said, and now, two and a half hours later, he was pushing eighty down New Mexico Route 81, a straight ribbon of two-lane highway between the carnivorous teeth of two mountain chains, headed due south. Off in the distance Collins had spotted the occasional ranch houses, miles and miles apart, and nearer the highway he had seen a couple of old metal windmills, motionless against the windless sky, like old sentinels each watching over its own rusting round tank of water. In the endless, colorless scrub, he had not seen a single cow. The middle of nowhere.

Ahead, a squat little collection of buildings signaled that he was about to arrive in Antelope Wells, a name attached to nothing more than a border crossing, a break in the fence line that stretched away forever. He slowed down and in a minute was parked alongside the chain-link fence near which was what he took to be a wooden corral. But a corral for what? Ahead a highway sign read ROUTE 81. MILE 0. He got out and stretched, walked over to the official-looking brown stucco building of the Border Patrol, and went inside, returning to his car in less than two minutes. He eased through the checkpoint and stopped after another fifty yards at a run-down one-story building that was the only human structure anywhere in sight in the Republic of Mexico. He entered a room that had been painted green sometime around the time of the conquistadores and saw a dignified old man in a jacket and tie seated behind a battered metal desk with a plaque that said ROBERTO GUTIERREZ. The silver-haired man greeted Collins with a smile.

"Señor," he said.

Collins gave him his name and said he was going to visit Mexico for a few days.

"*Habla español?*" asked the old man.

Collins shook his head and Roberto Gutierrez shrugged.

"In Chihuahua," he said, "in the south, there is much English. A lot of Amish people, your Amish people, going there to farm. Very—ah—industrious people."

"The guys on the other side over there told me you've been here a long time," said Collins.

The old man beamed. "Forty-seven years I have served my gobernment. Forty-five here. At this desk."

"That is a long time."

"*Sí*. I am supposed to retire three years ago. I sent the gobernment, in Mexico City, the forms, but nothing happens." He gestured with an open hand. "Paper. It all gets lost. I have to go to Mexico City myself. But I can't." He smiled. "I have to be here."

"You mean . . . ?"

"Seven days a week for forty-five years." He smiled again. "They were sending an assistant, but he got killed. Car crash on his way to this place. Just down the road." He looked across the room at the wall. "A great shame."

"How much traffic is there through here?" Collins asked.

"Oh, maybe six, seven cars a day into Mexico, five come out. It's very peaceful here. One day I will put my head down on this desk and die"—he laughed conspiratorially—"and my gobernment won't notice for months, years maybe."

Collins laughed and wondered if Mexico operated in a different time zone. Like maybe a century or two off.

"Señor Gutierrez, have you seen this woman come through here in the past week, two weeks?" He held out a black-and-white passport-type photograph. The old man's eyebrows lifted.

"*Policía?*"

"She's a friend."

"Oh. A friend." He stared at the photograph. "No, señor, I have not seen your friend, coming or going."

"I was going to meet her in Nueva Casas Grandes, but her phone doesn't answer. I thought maybe she had decided to go back to the U.S."

"Oh, señor, she could still be there. The phones—" He shrugged elegantly and smiled. He stood up and put a trim old hand forward. "Good fortune, Señor Collins. I've enjoyed meeting you. I hope you enjoy your visit to Mexico."

Collins shook hands and stepped out into the heat and into his car. The steering wheel burned his hand. He looked south. The blacktop stretched off into a heat haze that seemed a thousand miles away, and on either side of the road as far as he could see was nothing. A featureless plain baking in the mid-afternoon sun. A great place, he thought, to pick up a cold trail. On the other hand, it was action. Movement. Collins hated sitting around. It wasn't his style. Informed guesses, then action. Put a full-court press on 'em. A police friend of his, Tony Ramirez of the Santa Fe PD, had once accused him of throwing darts as an investigative technique. It had served him well so far. Pretty well anyway.

He started the Chevy and headed south into a land as startlingly unknown to him as it had been to Cortés.

Forty-five years in one place, at one desk, in the middle of nowhere. Collins couldn't imagine it.

•   •   •

Jeremy Armand stood in his lab, arms folded across his chest, thinking politics—academic and sexual. The Mexican queen had arrived again. Fitzhugh would perhaps be distracted, inattentive perhaps to some necessary administrative activities. He could see at least one side of the attraction. The woman was stunning, with her head of shiny black hair, skin that sometimes looked almost lavender. . . . But she was too tall for Armand's taste, perhaps five-nine. He couldn't imagine what she saw in Fitzhugh, who tended to be pompous. Nevertheless, they had adhered like magnets from practically the moment she had arrived at the center last summer for her first visit. Right after Fitzhugh's wife had walked out on him. Now the presumably hot-tempered Mexican was back and Armand wondered nastily if the director would remain in her good graces. It was common knowledge that he'd been banging that stringy-haired kid from Michigan State the past couple of weeks. As Armand was well aware, it was next to impossible to keep much of anything secret in so intensely collegial and at the same time crowded a place. Academics were such gossips, he thought, not for the first time in a career in which he had managed to maintain an opaque veil of privacy around himself. He wondered what Fitzhugh would do about the girl now. Probably, Armand thought to himself prudishly, it would better behoove the director to think with the organ that lay between his ears, rather than the one between his legs.

Armand bent over and peered one last time at the glass vials of sand from the cave in Skeleton Canyon. He left the lab and walked briskly through the trees to his cabin, the comfortable if simple one-room place that was one of the perks that came with so long an association with the center. Fifteen years, fifteen summers at least part of which were spent here at the center, advancing the cause of science in these Spartan conditions, so far from the amenities, the beautiful things, of civilization.

But then . . . Someone had left his mail in a little wooden box next to the cabin door. An issue of *Science* magazine and a letter. He recognized the handwriting on the letter, a colleague, doing fieldwork this summer. The postmark said EL PASO, TX. Armand smiled and went inside. He was thinking about early retirement.

By the end of the day, Tuck Eddy had dug more than two dozen holes in the harsh ground of Nameless Arroyo. He had gotten over the shock of seeing the footprints—so? Some hiker. And indeed, where the footprints passed through the rocks was the only other logical path for someone walking down the arroyo except along its very bottom, where the going was no easier. The site of the cross had not been tampered with, just walked by.

He had also determined, to his embarrassment and dismay, that the battery pack for his Treasuremaster 600 was exhausted and that, however brilliant his leap of imagination had been across a century and back into the old Catholic hang-ups, Tuck had apparently been wrong. After patient digging and scraping that had gone on until well past the time when the sun passed over the arroyo, he had found nothing. "Nothing ventured," he had said, "nothing gained."

During the afternoon he had pottered around lower down the arroyo, then headed back up to extricate his pink Jeep. It had been about 4:30 when he had managed his way out of the arroyo and headed west, well in sight of a man with a pair of binoculars about a half mile away and two hundred feet up above the scrubby forest floor in a square metal room mounted on a metal tower. The room was reached by climbing 238 metal stairs, and it was furnished with an iron-frame bed, a tattered easy chair, a metal desk and desk chair, and a large bank of radio equipment. All around were windows, providing a view of mountain range after mountain range, stretching away like rows of ripsaw blades to the horizon.

Down below, a sign on a chain strung across the metal stairway said KEEP OUT. PROPERTY OF THE UNITED STATES FOREST SERVICE. DEPARTMENT OF AGRICULTURE. It had been another drought year, the forest was like tinder, and the Forest Service had reactivated the old lookout tower. The man in the tower watched the pink Jeep disappear from sight.

What the hell was that boy doing in there? he thought to himself. It's that hairy snake hunter. But there ain't none around during the hot part of the day. Scorpions, maybe. Eddy. Tuck Eddy. He had weird interests, that boy, no telling what he'd be looking for. The man in the lookout tower put down his binoculars and picked up the phone to make his routine report.

"Oh," Mo Bowdre said, seated at one of the small square tables in the bustling cafeteria. "You're the venom man. I've heard about you. That's a pretty interesting way to make a living. Why don't you sit down, join us? This is Connie Barnes."

"Pleased to meet you," Tuck Eddy said, and set his tray down on the table. His plate held a small hillock of meat loaf and potatoes. And a side order of macaroni and cheese. "Are you with the center?" Connie asked.

"No." Eddy laughed. "Free-lance all the way. A lot of these guys here call me a bounty hunter, but I'm tolerated. 'Specially when one of 'em finds a rattler in his bed or whatever. I come here for dinner whenever I get tired of my own cooking. Not that this here is what you all hote queezeen. The cook kinda favors starch. He don't know how to cook a steak without turning it into charcoal. Anyway, one of the fellows here's givin' a slide show tonight. About his trip to

Belize. You gonna stay to see it?" Eddy forked a large quantity of meat loaf into his mouth. "Whoops," he said indistinctly.

"Don't mention it. It's a common manner of speaking."

"Well," the bounty hunter said, recovering, "he ain't much of a photographer, so he has to talk a lot. It should be interesting to hear."

"No reason not to stay for it," Mo said. The three of them ate in silence. Around them voices rose and fell like light surf.

"You know, Mr. Bowdre . . . ?"

"Mo. Please. People call me mister and I get gerontological spasms in my soul." He laughed his raucous laugh.

"Yeah, okay, Mo. I saw one of your things once. Up in Santa Fe last year. Bunch of horses rearing up all tangled up. Man, I don't see how you do it."

"Very slowly," Mo said. "I don't see how you can make a living milking snake venom. What do you think of that, Connie? See, she's Hopi."

Connie smiled. "I guess you have something in common with our snake priests. Did you ever see one of the Hopi snake dances? Before the priests had to close them down to non-Indians?"

"No, but I sure have read about 'em, seen the old pictures. Now, I'll tell you, I been working with rattlesnakes for twelve years, never got bit, but you wouldn't catch me wandering around with one in my mouth like those guys. Whooeee."

"Maybe you don't treat 'em like spiritual brothers," Mo said.

"Can't say I do. Can't say I'd even know how. But I treat 'em fair. When I catch one and take it home to milk it, I keep it several days, feed it. Don't want to turn 'em loose with no venom in this cruel world."

"That *would* seem a bit cold-blooded, wouldn't it?" Mo said. "You ever go collecting in Skeleton Canyon?"

"Oh, sure. Practically anyplace around here there's a snake or a scorpion, I been there. Skeleton Canyon I know real well. Why?"

"I'd like to go there sometime. I've heard about the place. It catches my fancy. I hear that there's a lot of outlaw history connected with the place. I have a family interest in out-laws."

"You do?"

"Yes, my great-uncle Charlie played a role in the—ah—Lincoln County Wars."

"Charles Bowdre? Billy the Kid! Hey, jeezus, are you . . . ? Wow."

"As you can imagine, the family is terribly proud."

Tuck laughed, then frowned. "You know, they found a body over there yesterday. In Skeleton Canyon."

"Hah—hah—"

"Mo, that's not funny," Connie said sharply.

"No, no, not that. I was overhearing a little snippet of girl talk from over there." He gestured to his left with a nod of his head. "The word seems to be out that the director, at his most heroic, is no more than five inches long. Oh, the life of the intellect. Well, anyway, maybe I could persuade you to take us over there sometime. To Skeleton Canyon."

"No problem. Say when." Tuck laughed. "You know, I wouldn't be surprised."

"About what?"

"About Fitzhugh. He's got a Jaguar."

"What, a captive?"

"No, a Jaguar car, a big sports car. And you know what the psychologists say—the longer the sports car, the shorter the guy's . . . well, excuse me, ma'am."

"It's Connie. And I think I know what you're talking

about. The Hopi have a saying about that too. What kind of car do you drive?"

"A secondhand pink Jeep."

"Oooooh, hah—hah—hah. Now, what the hell do you make of that, huh, Connie? I think I'm going to like this man."

Three

Into the black world of wakefulness, Mo Bowdre came with a twitch of remembering, slippery recall of mountain green, anguished lavender and blue in farther-off ragged land forms on the horizon, the pink and ocher spray of soft, undulating grassland, intimate orange bloat of a mallow flower, sighs of yellow and purple, snakeweed and aster against fading gray green on dusty roadsides, velvet breaths of late summer. Glimpses of the tarnished gold of dawn skies against black mountain vertebrae, the world turning tangerine, then the coppery red of a new day. . . . Oh God, oh God, how he wished . . . But he awoke in obsidian blackness next to the warm landscape of his companion, silky, his beacon in a world now gone, remembering the palpable clatter of the wind on the ruffled, ragged feathers of a charcoal-brown eagle glistening, spreading its huge shadowed wings with a turn of its oceanic eye, to take so slowly and uncaringly to the air.

Oh, sorry, he had said in one way or another.

Mo had come around a ledge in the desert on foot, only a boy, not that the eagle cared about the ages of man, so determined was it to be itself. It had lifted awkwardly into the blue-black crystal of the sky to become a speck of such enormity that the boy had felt, just for a moment, that he too might one day be a god.

Then Mo remembered, as usual, the abrupt flash of light in the mine, a moment of horrid orange, and only then the thunder, and the wayward, madcap plunge into the dark, the oddly painless moment of recognition of a world forever without color. How, he had wondered, could a world speak but in color, in light? How could the world now sing to him? Only in oafish, cumbersome, humiliating density. And for a long time, the world had not sung, but instead croaked, and T. Moore Bowdre heard no music. But from some small twangy place in his soul, he began to play for himself, on an increasingly insistent banjo of anger, a bluegrass cantankerousness. Slowly laughter returned to the diminished world, a world without light or color except what could be recalled, a world that lay outside him, but with enough left inside in memory and imagination and sheer greed for living. He made a quiet treaty with fate and quit feeling sorry for himself. He took up sculpture in a kind of defiance. Everyone thought he was mad, and he was. He made a name for himself locally, and then he met Connie.

It had happened when he knocked over a plastic cup of white wine in the gallery in Santa Fe. Naturally Frazier, the gallery owner, was off smooth-talking fat cats and everyone else was smooth-talking one another, a little nervous, all of them, about what to say to and about the big blind redneck sculptor so suddenly thrust into their scene. So, having spilled the wine, Mo had headed for the rear of the room—room? It was a hundred paces to the back wall—and had stood there with what he thought was probably a proper, shit-eating grin on his face, and he had heard the voice, obviously an Indian voice from its soft lilt.

"A lot of people here. That's real good."

She had introduced herself, and he, for the first time in several years, felt somehow at ease. With nothing more than a voice.

"I'm going to say something that'll sound outlandish," he had said.

"What's that?"

But a cheerful couple had presented themselves, wealthy buyers from Tucson, and he had said the right things to them, evidently, but he didn't remember that part of it because he felt as if someone had turned on the sun. This voice brought colors to him dancing—glints of gold and copper, lavender, the silvery frost on blue green, starbursts of yellows and veils of purple, the color of deserts, dancers, and now he could listen to the regular breathing of this miraculously devoted person lying beside him, this singular sleeping woman, and yet again Mo Bowdre was astonished by the dawn.

Sheriff Jack Knott stared at the ceiling of his office, not noticing the gray chipped paint in the corners. He was staring beyond such mundane matters and heavenward, where he imagined his soul commingling with that of the long-suffering Job. The phone receiver was as small as a toy in his thick red hand, and he leaned forward belligerently, elbows on his desk.

"I've told you all that I'm gonna tell you because that's all that anyone needs to know right now at this point in our investigation . . . No, that's *Sheriff* Knott . . . Yes, goddamn it, of course I'm in charge of the investigation . . . I don't care what *The Albuquerque Tribune* thinks *it* knows, this is a local matter under local investigation here in Hidalgo County where the homicide occurred and we . . . No, I told you,

there's no reason to think that woman was a federal agent . . .
No, we haven't identified her yet . . . Jesus, okay, I'll tell you
again, she was in her early thirties, red-haired, five-eight . . .
Well, how many red-haired people you ever met who weren't
Caucasian, for chris . . . Look, sonny, I ain't defensive, I'm
just tired of talkin' to you tight-assed little urbanites think
you know more than we do down here in Hidalgo County. You
know, Albuquerque isn't such a big city either, compared to El
Paso . . . What'd you say your name was again? . . . Yeah, I
keep a list . . . Bendel? *The* investigative reporter of *The
Albuquerque Tribune*? You only got one? Jeez, I got twelve men
on this homicide and this is just little old Hidalgo . . . Shit."

Sheriff Knott looked at the receiver and hung it up. Deputy Sheriff Jimmy Snyder was grinning at him.

"Let's see," the young man said. "There's me and you and
ol' Gentry and then . . . ? Who are the other nine, Sheriff?"

Jack Knott glowered up at the deputy. "You about nine
inches from putting on that rabbit suit, boy. I get so sick of
these smartasses from up there, Albuquerque, calling down
here for dirt as if they didn't have all those gangs shooting
each other to pieces every night, bunch a drunks plowin' into
each other, they got guys with forty-one DWI arrests still
driving on the goddamn streets. Well, goddamn it, what're
you doing to forward the progress of this investigation,
Depitty?"

"Just waiting for orders, Sheriff."

Sheriff Knott took hold of the mug of coffee that was the
only thing on his desk except for a manila folder. The coffee
was cold, and instead he opened the folder, revealing the
sickly color of a faxed memorandum.

"See this?" he said. "It's from Washington. It says this
here woman was named Melissa Jenkins. Graduate student
from the University of Pennsylvania. Biology. Was out at
that desert center the last two summers, left a couple weeks

ago to drive out here again. Came from Camden, New Jersey, parents both deceased, has an aunt who's been notified, no other relatives."

"But didn't that FBI agent say she was one a their people?"

Sheriff Knott looked up, exasperated.

"Yes, that's what he said."

"Well?"

"Well, what? So the FBI recruited this woman from graduate school to be an agent, doesn't that tell you something?"

"No, sir. Not yet it doesn't."

Sheriff Jack Knott permitted a smile to creep open, revealing yellowed teeth.

"Well, son," he said expansively, "I'll tell you. What it means is that the FBI knew a while ago, maybe even more than a year ago, they had to have someone on the ground. You know, an insider in that research center. And that person they had in there got herself killed. So you might just as well get your ass over there and find out who this lady named Melissa Jenkins knew, who she hung out with, what she was *doing* over there last summer. See?"

The deputy shifted uncomfortably.

"But, Sheriff, isn't this a federal investigation now?"

"Depitty," the sheriff said, taking a deep breath, "I've decided that a rabbit suit ain't good enough for you. Now you get your butt over there to that research place and figure out a way to find out what I want to know or I'm going to hang you by the *cojones* from the courthouse flagpole and tell people that you got caught sending money to the Sierra Club, you hear me? This is *my* investigation too."

"But—"

"Do it, boy. Don't worry none about jurisdiction. Just try and look important."

The deputy left, shaking his head, and Jack Knott scowled at the telephone on his desk. He hated the telephone. Hated the answering machine, and the fax, and all the other finicky little machines with their little buttons, all attached to the telephone and attached to what had been a simple life before they'd invaded the world with all this techno crap. He'd seen it coming when they made those little portable radios pounding with rock and roll, driven his daughters into the twilight zone, heads bopping like a bunch of Africans. The end of the world as God created it. Now he had to answer the machine-received call from that bullet-headed bastard in Douglas, Arizona, the Border Patrol Napoleon, a pain in the ass if ever there was one.

He punched out the numbers on the pink piece of paper and waited while the idiot buzzing completed its cycle.

"Yeah?"

"It's me, Jack Knott. So what do you need today?"

"Nothing you can supply. But I got some information for you. What's it worth?"

"Whatever it's worth, it's worth."

"You know that wild hair of an FBI agent, name of Collins? He's gone to Mexico. Headed right through your rinky-dink county. Yesterday. Antelope Wells. Sounds like some kind of vengeance trip, you know these FBI guys, they all think they're some kinda Eliot Ness. Some agent got killed. Izzat the same as that woman you boys came up with over in Skeleton Canyon?"

Jeezus Christ, thought Sheriff Jack Knott. Probably the whole thing is on *Unsolved Mysteries* already.

"You figure this has something to do with me?" asked Bullet-head.

"Everything has something to do with you, doesn't it? I mean, you got the only piece of a two-thousand-mile border where anything goes on, don't you? I mean, damn, Godfrey, you *are* the center of the universe, aren't you? Now why don't you butt out of my investigation?"

"Now, Jack, you just tell me if there's any little thing the Border Patrol can do for you. I mean, you don't sound too good there, boy."

Jack Knott slammed down the phone. He just purely hated it when the feds got involved in his patch. And it wasn't even eight o'clock in the morning.

The mouse writhed, hanging upside down, its nervous system seized up with fear. It hit the ground, feet flying, scrabbling into the corner against the glass, and the viper struck. The mouse never felt a thing except panic, or so Tuck Eddy said to himself for what was not the first time in twelve years of murdering mice.

"There you go, Molly," he said, and put the lid back on the aquarium, fondly contemplating the ridge-nosed rattlesnake, now with a mouse tail protruding from its perpetually grinning mouth. The state reptile of Arizona, but this was a subspecies he had caught over on the Gray Ranch a week earlier. Illegally, of course. It was on the federal and state endangered-species list, and if anyone from the Fish and Wildlife Department knew he had it, it would be jail time for old Tuck, but he just couldn't resist. He slid the aquarium under a table that supported three stacks of plastic containers, each filled with one or two snakes, and let the old and faded calico tablecloth fall over it. He didn't even want Mel to find it. She might be devil-may-care about a lot of things, but he didn't know what she'd make of him breaking the endangered-species laws, and he didn't want to find out. He wouldn't have to feed the snake for another month, and Mel didn't really spend a whole lot of time in this back room, so he figured it was safe enough. The crown jewel of his private collection.

He thumped out of the room and across the cluttered living room to the kitchen, where he poured himself his second cup of thick black coffee from a blue metal pot that simmered on the stove. God, what awful coffee, he thought to himself as he slurped from the edge of the mug. Ought to get myself one of those Mr. Coffee jobs, have real coffee and not this slop. But it does clear out the fluffballs.

He looked around the place. Cluttered but not messy. No dirty dishes in the sink. He wanted the place to look right for Mel when she came, which should be today, he reckoned. Maybe tomorrow, he thought with dismay, but probably today. Today, he repeated to himself, prayerfully. The old dial phone on the kitchen counter rang, and he thought: that's her, calling ahead from Lordsburg, maybe. He picked up the phone and he heard a woman's voice say his name. But it wasn't her voice.

"This is Connie Barnes," it said, and the round copper face of the big Indian woman flashed in his mind.

"Yeah, this is Tuck Eddy, how're you this morning?"

"Mo asked me to call you. He was wondering if he could take you up on your offer today or tomorrow." Her voice had a funny lilt to it, pleasant. But what offer?

"Uh—" he said.

"Going to Skeleton Canyon."

"Oh, yeah, I remember, sure. Well—today or tomorrow? Well, see, I'm expecting someone to show up today and I ought to—"

"Then tomorrow maybe? Mo's real interested in it, all the history, you know, the outlaws, Geronimo and all."

"Well, look, Miz—I mean Connie—today and tomorrow are both sort of, well, they're about the only two days this whole summer when—this person's sposed to show up today. But if she, if it's not today, then it's tomorrow, and of course

I won't know till— Say, I got an idea. You need to go today or tomorrow?"

"We were hoping—"

"Okay, tell you what. There's a good ol' boy lives over near Animas. Name's Daniel Ascension. I hear he takes people out around, day trips, you know. Horseback. That's actually safer, you know, for a guy who can't, uh—see. This guy Ascension knows this place like nobody, grew up here. You could try him. Let's see, I even got his phone number here. Yeah, hang on—" Tuck Eddy riffled through some papers till he found his Rolodex, and twisted the handle. He read out the number and said, "Give him a call."

The woman repeated the number and thanked him.

Tuck hung up the phone and stared into his coffee with an itch of suspicion. He had recognized the type, the country boy who got himself educated, could slip in and out of it, from redneck to—what do they say? urbane?—and back to redneck. But he sure didn't seem like an artist, a sculptor. Being blind for one thing, but there was something else beyond that. He couldn't put his finger on it. And besides, what's he want to do going to see Skeleton Canyon when he's supposed to be thinking up an idea for some damn statue at the center? Maybe he wasn't really blind. Maybe he was a fed in disguise, a Fish and Wildlife spy, checking out the center, checking out the collectors, his collection. Oh Jesus, he thought, maybe he'd just better turn Molly loose. It was a felony or some damn thing like that, having her in the house.

For a long moment the felon's paranoia and the addictive greed of the collector vied for Tuck Eddy's soul and, as had the Roman Catholic and Baptist beliefs of his parents, canceled each other out, leaving him feeling feral and gritty. His feet were sweating in his boots, his socks were already clammy, and the day had hardly begun.

He wished Mel would hurry her ass up and get here.

•   •   •

"Damn," said Mo. His arms were extended straight down, fists balled in frustration. "That's not what I had in mind." He turned toward the window and felt the morning sun on his face. "I don't want to go horseback riding, led around by the nose by some damned credulous rustic."

"What's that?"

"A mindless hick."

"Didn't you grow up in the country?"

"Just 'cause you're a country boy doesn't mean you got to draw up the wagons of ignorance around you. You can be born in the sticks and get an education. You did, after all."

"You mean traditional Indians are hicks?"

"No, that's not what I mean, and you know it," Mo snapped.

Seated on the bed, Connie watched the big man twitch with irritation. In the little bedroom with its varnished brown-log walls, he seemed even larger.

"We could wait a few days. Tuck Eddy said he'd—"

"Wait, wait. That's all we're doing here. Waiting. Wasting my goddamn time." He turned to face her. "Hang around the damn cafeteria twice a day and try to overhear something. Gossip. Who's screwing whom. That's no way to conduct an investigation. We've got to intersect these people, find out what makes the place tick. But they're all a bunch of separate planets, all in their own orbits out there. . . . I figured I could get that snake collector going. . . . Damn."

Connie shifted on the bed and it squeaked.

"Maybe Larry Collins made a mistake," she said.

"What?"

"Maybe he *is* wasting your time, putting you out here to—what? Sniff around. Maybe you should call him, you know, tell him it isn't working."

The big man sniffed and turned again to face the window.

"What is it, about nine o'clock?" he asked.

"What's the matter, your time sense off?"

"Yes. Damn daylight savings time."

"It's nine-oh-five," Connie said.

"Well, why didn't you just tell me that?"

"Because I love to watch when you get in a grouch, you know? Are you going to call Collins?"

Mo stood silently in front of the window. He sniffed hugely and exhaled in a kind of sigh. Then he burst into laughter.

"Now what?"

He turned around again to face her, smiling, big teeth gleaming through his blond beard.

"My sweet little Indian-American princess, you are the most manipulative human being on the planet. Or are all you Hopi women like that? You know, you mess around too much with the mind of a man from the dominant culture, you get your ass in trouble. It's happened before to you people."

"So we're not giving up?"

"Let's see if we can find that beetle man, what's his name? Armand?"

Connie grimaced as she stood up from the bed and followed Mo out the door onto the grass. Two minutes later, having obtained directions from one of the students, Mo knocked politely on the door of the laboratory of Dr. Jeremy Armand.

"Yes?" The voice came through the door with irritation.

Mo opened the door and poked his head through. "Dr. Armand? It's Mo Bowdre. Wondered if I could come in, talk shop, you know. This stuff you do is absolutely fascinating. Of course, if you're . . ."

"Well, I am getting ready to go out to the field, but then, there's no immediate rush, I suppose. Come in. Quickly, please, I have a controlled climate in here. Oh, hello. Miss Barnes, isn't it?" The little scientist stood in the rear of the room, leaning back against a workbench. There was a row of small bottles on the workbench, each with a black rubber stopper and, inside each, what appeared to Connie to be a layer of white plaster plus tissue paper. Near the bottles were an umbrella with a crooked handle and what looked like a fishing net, the kind they use for landing fish, but it was made of cloth, not mesh.

"I've been collecting in a new area, looking for new species. Beetles. These are some of the tools of my trade. My sweep net." He held it up. "My beating umbrella." He held that up and said, "You put this upside down under a branch, say, and then beat the branch with a stick, and you catch all sorts of things. And then when you weed out all the spiders and others, you catch the beetles and put them in these killing bottles. Not very high-tech, is it? I mean, not what most people think of as science."

"Still using ethyl acetate in the killing bottles," Mo said, and he listened to a barely audible intake of breath.

"Yes, do you . . . ?"

"Took biology in college. Wanted to be a doctor. Medical doctor. But that didn't work out—hah—so I went into mining, despoiling the earth, till I saw the light, so to speak. Anyway, I'd like to hear more about this forensic stuff you do. I never heard of that before."

The little scientist pursed his lips into an O, as if about to make a pronouncement, and then smiled. Connie had been trying to think what animal Armand reminded her of and had settled on a ferret, but the smile made him look human.

"It's quite old actually. The first entomological evidence used in a court of law was in France in 1850. A couple was accused of killing an infant that was found mummified near their house. But a naturalist of the time poked around and found mites and flies and old pupal cases that proved that the infant had died before the couple moved there. They got off, of course. That's most of our work—estimating the time of death. There is a regular schedule, as I mentioned the other night. First come the flies—blowflies, flesh flies, window flies—they all look something like houseflies, about the same size. The eggs hatch in very short periods, a day or two in most species, and then the vermiform larvae begin to go to work."

"Vermiform?" Mo asked.

"Legless, like little worms."

"Maggots," Mo said.

"Exactly. And they then go into the ground nearby to pupate. And that takes various amounts of time, depending on the species. So I simply collect the pupae from the ground and let nature take its course. Then there are the beetles, another line of reasoning." He smiled again. "There may be as many as ten families of beetles that show up for the party. Rove beetles are usually first—they're fliers. Would you like to see, Miss Barnes?"

Connie's stomach wobbled. "Uh—okay."

Armand crossed to a table that was lit by a fluorescent tube. There were several glass bottles filled with sand at one end of the table, and three open egg cartons, each compartment containing an inert beetle. Connie stared at them, slender black ones, round shiny ones, green ones. There was a sad beauty to them and, under her breath, she said a Hopi phrase.

"I beg your pardon?"

"Just a little, well, a little prayer. Hopi custom."

"Oh. Yes. Well, here is a rove beetle," Armand said, pointing to a slender black one. Then he pointed to a roundish one, mostly black but with yellow markings. "Carrion beetle," he said. "The green one here is a click beetle. They all come at different times, mainly to feast on the maggots. Usually the last beetles to show up are called hide beetles. They feed on the—ah—corpse itself when it's relatively dried out. There weren't any hide beetles on the body at Skeleton Canyon, which makes me think that she died about seven days before she was found. But the fly pupae will prove it unarguably."

"Any day now?" Mo said.

"Any day now. Any hour now. I've set the air-conditioning to create the same temperature and humidity as in the cave. The fluorescent bulb is variable too, to provide the same light." He gestured with a hand and smiled again. "Plus or minus, you know. Close enough. Soon we'll know for sure, and maybe it will be some help. There are other things we find every now and then. Some of my colleagues have been able to show that the corpse had died someplace altogether different from where it was found."

"How?" Mo asked.

"Well, in one case, it was quite simple. The body was found in a rural area—an abandoned farm, I think—but the entomologist found an urban fly species on the body. The urban fly had hitched a ride from the place where the murder was done. In another case, it had to do with mercury. Some of the blowflies had been reared in a mercury-free environment, while others, and the beetles as well, had high amounts of mercury in their tissues. And the place the corpse was found was a high-mercury environment. So it had to have been moved shortly after death. Of course, that kind of analysis takes equipment we don't have here."

"But you could tell if there was an urban fly or something like that, a wrong species?" Mo said.

"Oh yes, that's just taxonomy." Armand smiled again.

"Oh. No, there were no wrong species. Very straightforward. If that's what you were wondering."

"It's amazing," Mo said.

"Yes, nature is amazing. But I'm afraid I have to leave now. If it gets too warm out there, the beetles are more active, and then I make a fool of myself trying to pluck them out of the umbrella. Some of them are very fast."

Outside the laboratory, Armand paused and hitched up the shoulder strap of the canvas bag carrying his killing bottles. "I hope we can talk again," he said. "I'd like to tell you about my other work, a lot less grisly, but of interest, perhaps, to a former biology student."

"*Real* former. But sure. We'll see you around. Say, how many of you forensic types are there?"

"Entomologists? Oh, I'd say fifteen, twenty in this country. There are none in the Southwest, except when I'm here at the center. Nearest one is at UCLA. Fellow named Treadle. He keeps very busy with it." The little scientist headed to the parking area with a bouncy step.

Connie and Mo waited in the sun until they heard a car door slam and Connie said, "Well?"

"Vermiform larvae," Mo snorted. "Bleh."

"That's what I say." Connie looked around at the tall charcoal-green trees and sniffed the air. It had a dank, earthy smell. "This whole place smells of decay," she said.

"It's more acidic than you're used to, that's all. You like a more alkaline world."

"Like desert. Let's go to the desert. Maybe we can find someone studying centipedes. You know, something real cute."

A thin man in a cowboy hat and blue jeans faded to near white bent over and peered at the cylindrical rock, shadowed from the sun by the steep wall of the arroyo. Halfway down the east side of the rock was an abrasion, a recent one, and a thin streak of pink paint. Ride 'em cowboy, the man said to himself and straightened up, pleased. The sun hit his face and he pulled his hat brim down, and spat. He slung a Winchester .30-30 in the crook of his arm and began down the arroyo, making his way silently. The only sound was a distant insect hum and the occasional *chirt* of some canyon bird. Every few feet the man paused to look carefully at the arroyo walls rising up above him, loose red rock and boulders and slabs all still as death, any one of them ready, the man thought, to come loose and tumble down the sides, as they had all been doing for a long time.

After about a hundred feet the arroyo curved westward and widened and the sun lit the rubble in the dry streambed. The man picked his way down the streambed, pausing every few feet until, to his left, about thirty feet away up the side of the arroyo, he noticed darkened dirt around some big slabs of sandstone.

He climbed up the side and squatted by one of the big slabs, his wide hat brim shadowing his face. For ten feet on either side the ground had been disturbed, dug up and then put back, but without any attempt at disguise. Bootprints all over the place. People didn't usually get this far back up the canyon, usually just came to see where Geronimo surrendered, out near the eastern end, then went off. But this end of the canyon had gotten pretty busy lately, the man thought. First the woman. Now that snake collector. But he wasn't looking for snakes.

Treasure. No telling how many times he'd be back if he was bit by that bug.

The man stood up and looked at the disturbed sandy ground. Then he spat, scrambled down to the streambed, and walked silently back into the sun.

• • •

"Well, good morning," Wheeler Fitzhugh said cheerfully, walking across the grass. "How are you getting along? Getting a lot of good ideas?"

Mo stopped and Connie rested a hand on his arm. "We were just coming to find you," he said. "Thought we might go wander around a bit in the desert, see if there are some researchers we can get in the way of down there. Maybe you could tell us where we might find . . ."

Fitzhugh stopped and stood in front of these two alien beings. "Well, let me think. Yes, you might want to hook up with Dr. Madero, as a matter of fact. She's working up in . . . Good Lord, what's that?" A squad car rolled to a stop in the parking area. "That's the sheriff from Hidalgo County. What's he—" He spotted the man's handlebar mustache. "No, it's a deputy. Snyder. I wonder what he wants."

The deputy slid out of the car, looked around, and waved when he saw Fitzhugh. He trotted over.

"Good morning, sir."

"Deputy. What can I do for you?"

"Well, sir, I'm afraid we got some bad news. This morning we got an ID on that woman, over in Skeleton Canyon. It was—well, sir, it was one of your people. Least she was here the last two summers. Name of Melissa Jenkins."

"Jesus Christ," said Fitzhugh. "That's . . . How could that happen? She was due here today, tomorrow. What's—"

"Well, sir, that's who it was. Positive ID. And Dr. Armand, he said he thought it was seven days old. The corpse, that is. Anyway, maybe he knows for sure . . . ?"

"Not yet," Mo said.

Deputy Snyder looked at the big man as if he had noticed him standing there for the first time.

"We just left his lab," Mo went on. "He was explaining

all that to us, but there were no results yet. At least as of fifteen minutes ago."

"My God," said Fitzhugh. "This is—"

"The sheriff was wondering, sir, if there was anyone here we could talk to, you know, people who worked with her last summer, people who knew her."

"Tuck Eddy," Fitzhugh said.

"Sir?"

"The people Mel worked with last summer aren't here yet. The person who knew her best was Tuck Eddy. They, ah, she stayed with him. My God. He'll be devastated. Well, of course, we all—"

"Could I talk to this guy Eddy?" the deputy asked.

"He's not here. I mean he isn't part of the center. He's a snake collector, lives down the road about two miles. In a trailer, a big trailer on the north side of the road."

"I've seen it," the deputy said. "He got a phone?"

"Yes, yes, come with me, you can use the phone in my office. Excuse me. Jesus, this is terrible—" Fitzhugh, followed by the deputy, strode across the lawn toward the log building that housed the administrative offices.

Mo stood silently, sniffing the air.

"Well, I'll be damned," he said, "if this isn't one hell of a day already and it isn't even ten o'clock yet."

Jeezus, first it's the phone ringing, bust your ass to get to it, and it stops . . . Hope that phone wasn't Mel, but what the hell am I supposed to do? Now it's the door.

"Hold it! I'll be right there!"

How far into the boonies does a man have to move simply to guarantee a few minutes of peace. . . . Omigod, a cop car out there, Hidalgo County sheriff. Oh, shit, they got me. No, it'd be a Fish and Wildlife guy, not Hidalgo. . . . But what . . . ?

"I said, *hold* it, goddamn it! I'm *coming!* Jeezus."

*Maybe those enviros over at Gray Ranch didn't like me goin'
on their place, spotted me. Damn! What's the penalty for tres-
passing? Why do those twits get so damn smarmy about the place
anyway?*

"Mr. Eddy?"

"Yeah."

What is this, a boy scout in a sheriff suit?

"Tuck Eddy?"

"Yeah, yeah. What's the matter?"

"I've got some bad news, I'm afraid, and . . ."

*What bad news? Oh, jeezus, oh, Christ, how I hate the idea of
handcuffs, jail, huge fags. . . .*

". . . and I need to talk to you, maybe get a little help."

"You want to come in? Coffee? It's lousy, but it's coffee."

*Why does this kid in the sheriff's suit look so . . . faraway? I
can hardly hear his voice, what's happening? Okay, no coffee,
what? What? What's he saying, Melissa, no, what, what, no, it
can't . . .*

"No, no."

"You didn't know her?"

"No, no, man, I knew her, I knew her, you got to be
wrong, it can't be her. . . . No, listen."

*What's he saying? Not Melissa. Not dead. Not some corpse in,
what did he say? Skeleton Canyon. Oh shit, no, no. A week ago?
Where the hell was I? Oh, Christ, this boy scout is watching me
cry. Goddamn!*

"Hey, wait, wait a minute, okay, Officer? I'm . . . I . . .
Maybe you could . . . Maybe we could . . . Later, you know.
Like, like . . . Give me a minute, will you?"

"I'll wait in the car, sir. If you like. We can talk there."

"No, it's okay."

"I'm sorry, but we'd like to know anything you can tell us
about her. It might help with our investigation."

Anything I can tell him. Like the nearly marble-white skin up where her thighs . . . The big laugh . . . Like whooping when we made that water bed sway . . .

"Look, Officer . . ."

"I'm sorry. I'm Deputy Sheriff Snyder."

"I was expecting her today, maybe tomorrow. She sent me a postcard from Philadelphia. About a week ago I got it, said she was going to take a couple weeks driving out here, have an adventure or something. That's all I know."

"You knew her pretty well?"

Knew. Past tense. Shit, yeah, I knew her pretty well. She's gone?

"Yeah. I did."

"Can you think of any reason why . . . ?"

I can't talk to this guy. I can't talk to this guy.

"Were you aware that she was a federal agent?"

"*What?*"

"FBI. The sheriff's office in Hidalgo County is cooperating with the FBI in this—"

"What do you mean, an FBI agent? She's a herpetologist! Studies frogs, for chrissakes."

Was a herpetologist. Oh, man, this is . . . I got to get out of here. I can't talk to this guy. It looks like a mirror just shattered. What's going on? I can't hear him, but he's still talking.

"Look, Officer, I'm . . . Can you come back later, I'm not . . . I mean . . . I'm losing it."

He's heading for the door. Back in an hour. Yeah, fine, good. Waving. Car's gone. Where's that paint? Closet. Yeah, here it is. Six spray cans, fuck the ozone layer. Adobe, like mud, good color. Let's see now. . . .

Man, what has happened to time, there, no more pink Jeep. Adobe Jeep, goddamn but the sky is broken, like a mirror, dark, what's the matter? Mel. It can't be. Food, pots, bedroll, okay, okay, rifle, shotgun, shovel, ammo, metal detector? Yeah. Batteries charged . . . Got everything . . . Damn. The snakes. Take 'em. Let 'em go in . . .

Christ, no time, no room. Okay, guys, there you go, yeah, off you go, good luck. . . . You too, well, goddamn it, it's a chance, ain't it? Go on. Git. You, Molly, beat it. Aw, shit. I got to get out of here. Out of here. I can't talk to that guy. Can't talk to that guy. Can't talk . . . Crying again, damn . . . I hate this. . . . I can't talk to that guy.

"What do you mean, he's gone?" Sheriff Knott said into the microphone.

The radio behind his desk crackled with static. "His car ain't here. Pink Jeep. It's gone," Deputy Sheriff Jimmy Snyder said. "He was pretty upset but I didn't think . . ."

"And he isn't in the house?"

"It's a trailer." *Crackle.*

"I don't give a . . . He's not inside?"

"I . . . I can't get there."

"What d'you mean, you can't get there, Depitty? What the hell is . . . What's the matter with your voice?"

"Sheriff." *Crackle.* "I can't get outta the vehicle. This whole place is crawling with snakes. Must be fifty, sixty rattlers. Jesus, I never saw so many snakes. . . . What the hell am I supposed to do? This guy Eddy, looks like he let all his snakes go and took off."

"My God," the sheriff said. "Lemme think."

"I'm telling you, Sheriff, this really gives me the creeps." *Crackle.*

"What are they doing, Depitty?"

"Who?"

"The snakes, for God's sake, what're they doing?"

"Well, some of 'em are moving away, into the trees. But some of 'em are just, well, just sitting around in the sun. Like they're sorta dazed."

"Well, okay, you just set there, keep people away. I'll get someone down there to replace you. Then you go find this weirdo, Eddy. Shouldn't be too hard to find, he's in a pink Jeep, ain't he? I'll call the research center, see if they've got anyone knows how to catch snakes. And I'll call the state cops. Arizona, too, Cochise County sheriff. And you—don't you be telling anyone else that woman was an agent. That's up to the FBI. Jesus, boy, you sure do know how to make a mess."

Señor Gutierrez glanced at the clock on the wall and stood up. His back was tired from bending over the metal desk, finishing up his monthly report for the people in Mexico City, more paper to fill up some archive, paper that no one would ever read. From his forty-five years at this post, a mountain of paper noting the trickle of human traffic through this insignificant legal border crossing must have accumulated in some government warehouse. The work of a lifetime.

The old man stretched his back, put on his head a tan, small-brimmed Stetson hat, and stepped out into the white afternoon sunlight. Just walking from his desk into the dirt yard made his back feel better, and he walked out onto the road.

Far off to the south a heat haze hid the horizon, making a single, continuous pale blue realm from the distant earth and sky, an alchemy familiar to the old man. He watched a tiny dust cloud rise up from where the road disappeared into the blue. It danced wavily in the shimmering heat and Señor Gutierrez idly watched it grow, become more distinct. The sixth today, he thought. He saw the cloud resolve itself into dust and a greenish automobile.

Ah, thought the old man. That man, what was his name? Collins? With the photograph of the pretty woman. His missing *friend. Policía*, without a doubt, even if he had denied it. Perhaps this was Señor Collins, returning. Probably from the Drug Enforcement Agency. A pity that such a pretty woman should be involved in drugs. None of them came through here, the old man thought: why risk being seen, when the entire border was as porous as a sieve?

The car was now plainly visible—a green Chevrolet. It was Collins. In a half minute the car slowed and came to a stop in front of the old man, and Larry Collins stuck his dusty face out the window. He looked tired.

"Señor Gutierrez," he said, smiling, showing his crooked front teeth.

"Señor Collins. You are back soon. Only a day. Did you find your friend?"

"No."

"A pity."

"Yeah. Well, it was worth a try. It was nice meeting you, sir."

"The pleasure has been mine, señor."

The old man watched as the car eased to a stop on the United States side of the border and the curly haired man went into the adobe office building. And thinking to himself that, to God looking down, the affairs of humans must seem like the frantic and slightly ridiculous carrying on of ants, Señor Gutierrez went back into his building, took off his hat, and sat down behind his desk. He heard the Chevrolet's engine start up and listened to it fade into the silence of the day.

Mo Bowdre sat quietly, listening to the sounds around him, in the room that served as lounge area for the research center, a place where the scientists could gather before meals or during other idle moments. Mo had memorized the lay of the room, which was as jammed with comfortable sofas and chairs as a furniture showroom, and he inhabited a large easy chair near what was evidently a fireplace. He could hear the breeze rustling in the chimney, smell the vestiges of piñon logs burned several months earlier.

It was an hour till dinner, and sounds emanated from the adjoining cafeteria: the metallic clatter of pots, the slamming of oven doors, the occasional curse. And the lounge rapidly filled with voices—intense, edgy voices, some of which were already familiar to the big man.

Members of the research staff were instinctively herding together once each one, returning from the fieldwork of the day, learned that one of their own had been the victim in Skeleton Canyon. They were pulling their emotional wagons into a circle, Mo thought, here in a remote place where they have nothing but themselves, all of them engaged in a peculiar branch of a specialty that also served to set them apart from the normal run of people. An odd innocence. In their self-absorption, Mo thought, they don't even notice that I'm in the room, and he listened to the voices in the hubbub. . . .

"Well, no, I didn't *know* her, you know, like a friend, but I thought she was a lovely person. So enthusiastic."

"It's just horrible. To think . . ."

"What I can't figure out is what she was doing over there. I mean, that's hardly frog city over in that canyon."

"I thought she was nice, but there was something a bit, well, standoffish about her."

"Arnold, just because she was self-contained doesn't mean she was standoffish. She was gorgeous."

"Well, she *was* standoffish, shacked up down the road with that bounty hunter."

"Arnold, do I hear jealousy?"

"Come on, the guy's not one of us. He's a hairy redneck. What was he, a zookeeper or something?"

•   •   •

"Well, I hear that the cops are looking for him. Yeah, Tuck Eddy. I heard that he killed all his snakes and took off."

"Jesus. Killed all those snakes? He must have had a hundred."

"Imagine killing all those snakes. That's despicable,"

"Where's Bill Freeman? Didn't the bounty hunter used to work with Bill a little? He'd know about those snakes."

"I guess he's still in the field."

"Why would anyone want to kill her?"

"You mean the bounty hunter? The cops are looking for him."

"Why him? I thought they were lovers."

"Hey, lovers fall out, remember, Ingrid?"

"Screw you, Freddy."

"Up yours, Ingrid."

"Will you two quit that? This is a tragedy and you two are . . ."

"Well, I had the feeling that she was always sort of watching us all, like she was standing aside, studying us. Maybe she was a social scientist."

"She sure knew a hell of a lot about frogs for a social scientist."

"Well, I for one think there's something very peculiar about this. Jeremy said his guess was she'd been dead about seven days when they found her, which makes it nine days ago. But only last night I was talking to Tuck Eddy, right here in the lounge, before dinner, and he expected her to get here today. So what I want to know is what was she doing around here more than a week early."

•   •   •

"Hey, maybe Mel was really an undercover Fish and Wildlife agent and Eddy killed her when he realized she had the goods on him. You know he collected stuff off the register."

"That's pretty farfetched."

"Occam's razor. Simplest hypothesis that fits the known facts. That's got to be it."

"Look. There's that sculptor. Bowdre. Maybe someone ought to go talk to him."

"What for?"

"To be polite, for heaven's sake."

Mo smiled as the woman approached. "Mr. Bowdre, I'm Ingrid Freeman." Freeman, Mo thought. Wife of Bill Freeman, the legitimate snake man? "This certainly is an awful thing that's happened. I guess it's not the best time to be thinking about a sculpture for the place. Such a gloomy time."

"Please call me Mo. Yes, gloomy indeed. It'd probably be consoling to know the facts. Sounds like a whole lot of rumors are floating around this room."

"Oh, here's Wheeler Fitzhugh," the voice named Ingrid said. "He's got on his take-charge face. Maybe we'll get some of the facts anyway."

"People. People!" said Fitzhugh authoritatively. "Let me have your attention." The voice came from over on Mo's right and the room was suddenly as quiet as a class accustomed to receiving lectures. "I guess just about everybody's here. This is a terrible thing that has happened and I want to get everybody up-to-date on the facts before the speculation begins— which is unavoidable, of course. First, it was Melissa Jenkins whose body was found in Skeleton Canyon two days ago. She was evidently killed by a blow to the head. For those of you who weren't here last summer, Mel was at Penn, getting her doctorate probably next year. Herpetologist. *Rana.* A very promising career." The director cleared his throat.

"Dr. Armand guesses that she had been there for seven days when she was found. The results of his, uh, tests aren't in yet. She wasn't expected here till today, so no one knows what she was doing in the canyon more than a week ago.

"Now, today a deputy from the sheriff's office came to tell me this, and he wanted to talk with people who worked with her. Her coworkers last year aren't here, so I sent him down to Tuck Eddy's. Apparently Eddy freaked out when he heard the news, broke down, the deputy said. So the deputy said he'd come back in an hour. When he came back, Eddy's Jeep was gone and the yard was full of snakes."

"He didn't kill them?" a voice asked.

"No. Evidently just turned them loose."

"Well, that's tantamount to killing them," the voice said. "Most of 'em don't belong at this elevation."

"Bill Freeman and three of his students are over there now," the director said. "They hope to get most of them. Meanwhile the sheriff's department and the state police are looking for Eddy. He evidently cleared out for good, took most of his stuff. And that's all we know for now. There'll probably be some people from the sheriff's around the next few days and I ask you all to cooperate fully with them. Maybe they can . . . Well." He paused. "Of course, I'll try and keep you all posted whenever I learn anything."

The hubbub resumed, and Mo leaned toward the voice named Ingrid and said, "Are you by any chance related to this Bill Freeman who's out catching all those snakes?"

"Yes. He's my husband. He's herps. I'm mammals."

"Hah—hah—hah."

"I guess that does sound a bit strange," Ingrid said, and Mo was wondering what Freddy *was* when an eardrum-rattling scream filled the room.

"Jesus, what's that?" Mo asked.

"Fire alarm. Evacuate." Ingrid shouted as the horrid whine seared Mo's brain. "Let me help you."

Connie Barnes was brushing her hair in the cramped little bathroom, a towel wrapped around her, when she heard the distant whine. She ducked out of the bathroom, bare feet slipping on the moist linoleum, and crossed the small bedroom to the window. The sun had gone down and the surrounding, suffocating trees were shadowed, the parklike greensward now indistinct in the beginning dusk. She thought she saw a flame—fire!—in the direction of the main building, but then nothing. An illusion. Across the grass, people were issuing forth from the low-roofed main building, a buzz of voices. She picked out one—"this is a hell of a goddamn time for a fire drill!"—and hastily got dressed, minutes later striding across the grass toward the crowd. She spotted Mo easily, towering above the others, his black hat tilted down over his dark glasses, and noticed that a blonde woman about her age was holding him by the elbow.

"Mo," she called.

"Over here," he said. "Connie, this is Ingrid Freeman. She led me through the stampede. Where, as they say, is the fire?"

"I don't see any," Connie said.

"It must be a false alarm," the woman named Ingrid Freeman said. Connie noticed that she was still holding Mo's elbow, noticed she was short but with a more than ample bosom, and was grinning. She wore a T-shirt that also advertised the Denver Museum of Natural History with a drawing of a bighorn ram's head, faded jeans, and heavy-soled sandals.

"Ingrid here says her husband is herps and she's mammals," Mo said cheerfully.

"*Sciurus apache,*" said the blonde woman. "Apache fox

squirrel. Last time the alarm went off, it was one of them that got into the thing and set it off. I'll bet it's *Sciurus apache* again. You know, this is the only part of the U.S. where it occurs. Right here in these mountains and over in the Chiricahuas. I did my dissertation on it, a few years ago, still working on them—"

"False alarm! False alarm!" Fitzhugh's voice said over the buzz. "It looks like one of Ingrid's squirrels got into the system again."

"*My* squirrels," Ingrid snorted. "Makes it sound like I have my own private little herd."

The crowd began to straggle back toward the main building, and Connie noted that the mammalogist kept her hand on Mo's elbow, leading him back to the dining room. You don't lead the blind unless they ask you to, she thought proprietarily, and smiled inwardly: she recognized incipient jealousy in herself when she saw it. She trailed along, thinking that something called both fox and squirrel didn't make any sense. White people are strange, she thought. They name this fox-and-squirrel after the Apaches—and she'd heard someone mention an Apache pine the other day—when there are no more Apaches here. She stood in line in the cafeteria behind Mo, who was listening to the blonde woman talk about squirrels, and noticed that one of the young women in aprons serving up great ladles full of some kind of pasta had a round, flat Indian face. The server looked up at Connie and smiled, a beautiful smile, Connie thought.

"I'm Hopi," Connie said.

"Papago," said the young woman, smiling again. "Now we call ourselves Tohono O'odham."

"Desert people," Connie said, and felt better than she had for three days. And this grew into a true sense of well-being when the black-haired woman with the light brown skin seated by herself at a table smiled and invited her to sit down, introducing herself as Vera Maria Madero from Mexico.

"Wheeler told me you are Hopi," she said when Connie had settled herself at the table.

"Half. My father was a *bahana*, a white man."

"I've always been interested in the Hopi. I've read that you speak a Uto-Aztecan language." Connie nodded. "And that must mean that we are related somewhere way back. My ancestors have always lived in the valley where Mexico City is. They were Aztecs a long time ago, when the Spanish came. At least some of my ancestors were. A lot of my ancestors are Spanish also. We're all mestizos now." The two women laughed.

Connie intuitively liked this woman, so different from herself but in some inexplicable way—not merely racial—so alike. The racial connection was so far in the past, after all. At Vera Maria's questioning, she explained that the Hopi had emerged as a people from a place called *sipapu*, near the confluence of the Colorado and Little Colorado rivers. They had then gone off, a group here, a group there, into the four directions, and had wandered much of the world, until a kind of implosion had occurred—all the disparate clans beginning to migrate as if by command, by prophecy, toward the same place, the present Hopi mesas. Some of the clans had wandered to the south, far to the south, to places where there were great rivers, and then had returned. These might have been the Aztec relatives and they might have brought words, a richer language, which all the clans took to themselves.

"That," Connie said, "is how it might have happened."

"You believe this?"

"It makes sense to me," Connie said.

"The old Aztec story is not all that different. We wandered until we came to Lake Teotochniclán. And then there was a godlike figure, Quetzalcoatl, who left. Went across the sea, promising to return."

Connie almost gasped. "The Bahana," she said.

"What?" Vera Maria leaned forward with a smile broadening across her face. Her eyes crinkled with—what?—a kind of generosity.

"In our history," Connie said, "there was the White Brother, the Bahana, who arose with us into this world through the *sipapu*, and then left. He went to the east, promising he would return again one day with great wisdom, tools."

The two women looked at each other and giggled.

"So," Vera Maria said. "We two, we are on the cutting edge of our tribal destinies, yes? You with your Bahana, me with my Quetzalcoatl." They laughed again, not only in humor and camaraderie, but with a bit of nervous awe at the brazen and lonely steps they had both taken, for different reasons and at different times.

"What do we see in them?" Vera Maria said in a distracted way.

"Maybe it's what they see in us," Connie said.

Gone to ground, gone to ground, poor ol' Tuck, he gone to ground.

The voice was little more than a singsong whine rising from the gloom back around the dogleg of the old mine shaft. Tuck Eddy squatted on his heels like an owl, looking at the last red glow of day on the wall where the shaft turned and the ceiling got lower than his head and the walls got closer together.

Gone to ground, gone to ground, poor ol' Tuck, he gone to ground.

He had driven the Jeep into the more generous entrance of the mine, unloaded it, and brought his gear around the turn, to the very end of the shaft in this old played-out silver mine. He needed a den now that he was a nocturnal animal.

Gone to ground, gone to ground.

Well, maybe crepuscular too, he thought, as long as he stayed close. All these old mines around here had played out before they really got started. Mel. That had played out too, hadn't it? What happened? Why'd she got herself killed? What happened to me? Snapped. Crazy as a coonhound at full moon. But, he thought cannily, you can't be crazy if you know you are.

. . . poor ol' Tuck, he gone to ground.

The last red glow slipped away from the wall and Tuck squatted in the pitch-black mine shaft. He wiped his eyes with his forearm and took a cigarette from the pack in his shirt pocket. Not too many left, he noted. The flame from his green disposable lighter was hardly enough to light the rocks nearby. He hated the idea of running out of cigarettes.

Gone to ground, gone to ground, poor ol' Tuck, he gone to ground.

He knew they were out looking for him.

They wouldn't find him, not ol' Tuck.

Yes, they would.

They wouldn't think of looking here.

Yes, they would.

He was crying again.

Damn.

The Chevy plummeted south on Route 80. Ahead were the few lights of Rodeo. He wondered if there was a place open to get a cup of coffee. The hell with it. Get home.

He slowed down to forty-five and in seconds was out of Rodeo. He put his mind in neutral and followed the road as it curved into Arizona. Presently he saw on his left the sign that said SKELETON CANYON 8 MILES, and it vanished behind him. Home of the Smugglers' Trail of old. And maybe of new. He'd looked at the topo map in the sheriff's office. There was a dirt road that came close to the eastern end of the canyon, and another dirt road that led to it from from this side. Almost surely four-wheel-drive territory.

How had she gotten in there? If she was tailing someone ... Coming out of Mexico? Maybe that fat sheriff, Jack Knott, would be able to ... Tomorrow. Too tired to think. Think about it tomorrow. His eyelids drooped and, at seventy-two miles an hour, Special Agent Larry Collins's green Chevrolet left the blacktop and plowed deep into the sandy scrubland of southeastern Arizona.

Connie lay under the sheet, black hair cascading over her pillow. She watched as Mo methodically undressed and carefully hung each piece of clothing on the straight-backed wooden chair beside the stripped but unpainted bureau.

"You seem to have gotten over the green forest blues," he said.

"I had a real good time. Vera Maria is very interesting."

"She sounds it. Ingrid told me about her."

"Oh, you're in tight with Ingrid now?"

Mo paused in the course of unbuttoning his shirt and turned his head toward the bed. "She's just one of those talkative types, likes people to like her."

"That's not all she likes to have people do."

"Hah—hah—hah. In fact, she apparently did have a fling with some guy named Freddy some time ago."

"Did she tell you?"

"No, that one I picked up on my own sonar. But she filled me in on your Mexican friend, among others. World-class plant ecologist. Here in the U.S. on a two-year-appointment in Tucson. Came here last summer, and evidently within a week she was all over the director like iron filings on a magnet. This was right after Fitzhugh's wife stalked out." Mo sat down on the bed and began to take off his boots. "What'd you two talk about?"

"Mostly Hopi things. She's interested because the Hopi language and the old Aztec language are supposed to be from the same root. She's part Aztec. From way back, you know? When the Spaniards came."

Mo stood up and shucked his jeans and shorts and sat down on the bed again. "So you found a sister here and you're feeling more at home, huh? Does she speak any Aztec?"

"No, she doesn't. I had a feeling she was a little . . . well . . . I think there are parts of Aztec history she's not too proud of, so she has kind of funny feelings."

"You mean human sacrifices? Tearing the hearts out of guys on those pyramids? That old-time religion? Hell, that was all five hundred years ago. Bygones. But I do think it's pretty interesting we've got ourselves an ex-Aztec here in our midst."

"I guess there must be millions of ex-Aztecs," Connie said.

"Now that I'm a hotshot investigator with the FBI, I am defined by the word *suspicion*. Here, I'll get the light." He reached out toward the bed table and felt for the switch. "There."

"Mo?"

"Yeah?"

"Do you think you ought to take off your hat?"

"Is it . . . ?" He laughed. "Well, at least I took off my boots."

Four

Ramona Aragon, one of the few residents of Chiricahua, Arizona, which is little more than a railroad crossing off the road to Douglas, looked through the bleary eyes of dawn at the green Chevrolet parked in the sagebrush twenty yards from her kitchen window. What was it doing there, nowhere near the dirt track that led from the highway to Ramona's trailer? She noticed that the window on the driver's side was white, lacy . . . broken. It came to her that the car had run off the highway sometime during the night while she was asleep. She crossed herself and hobbled outside to inspect, fearing the worst.

She approached within a few yards of the vehicle and saw a black-haired head against the cracked window. Crossing herself yet again, she stepped up to the car and peered through the windshield at the man who sat slumped in the driver's seat, head lolling against the broken side window like death. But, she could see, he was breathing. Walking as quickly as she could, she returned to her trailer and called her great-nephew, Vincente, who worked in the county sheriff's department, waking him up at his home in Douglas. In less than an hour the ambulance and a sheriff's vehicle had come and gone with the man from the Chevrolet. A deputy had come in to thank her and say that a tow truck would come later to take the Chevrolet out of her yard.

Within yet another hour the medical staff at the emergency room of the county hospital three miles west of Douglas were heartened to see that Special Agent Larry Collins of the FBI had regained consciousness and knew who he was. He did not know what had happened or when. Retrograde amnesia was common enough even with a relatively mild concussion, and this man had a three-inch welt on the side of his head above the temple, suggesting that his head had hit the window with great force. The medical staff began to prepare him for a CAT scan to ascertain whether the agent had sustained a concussion or, far more dangerous, a cerebral contusion.

A serious agent from the Douglas office of the FBI, who had arrived simultaneously with the ambulance, listened to this explanation without comment, merely nodding his head, and went outside to his car to radio a report to his superior. An hour later he again listened without comment as the doctor explained that it had been a severe concussion, but had not caused any fracturing of bone or bruising or laceration of brain tissue. The patient was still experiencing nausea and dizziness and would have to remain in the hospital for at least twenty-four hours, and perhaps longer if his memory of the accident did not return.

"Your colleague has one heavy-duty skull on him," the doctor said. "I've seen less damage done to a head by a two-by-four."

The serious agent permitted himself a brief smile and thanked the doctor, thinking on his way out that Collins had struck him from the start not only as eccentric but a bit thickheaded.

"Sheriff, he'd have to be Al Pacino to pull off an act like that." Deputy Jimmy Snyder chewed his mustache. He felt as if he were fighting for his life. "I mean it was like seeing a balloon pop before your eyes. He could hardly breathe, he got all white, pupils dilated, I mean that was a man who was taken by surprise. Burst into tears, for God's sake, and he ain't the type. Anyway, why would he kill her? She shacked up with him last summer."

Sheriff Jack Knott was disgusted. He knew how fast matters of the loins can go sour, and he knew that if the Jenkins woman was an agent when she was killed, then she might well have been an agent when she shacked up with this snake man last summer, and furthermore if she was snooping around after something illegal over there at the center, she would have been better off living at the center, and not in some trailer full of snakes three miles away. So it stood to reason that whatever she was snooping around about, it had to do with the snake man. So he gets wise that she's an agent and, *bam*, dumps her in the canyon, a place he goes collecting snakes all the time.

"Depitty, I am not going to try to explain to you this whole thing because I think you are too dumb to understand it. And it was *real* dumb to let that man out of your eyesight. Now the son of a bitch has disappeared. God knows where he is, a suspected murderer on the loose, thanks to the leak you sprung in your braincase. Gimme the keys to your unit."

"What?"

"You're on the desk from now on till I decide what to do with you."

Stricken, Deputy Snyder handed over his keys.

"And get me the FBI office in Douglas on the phone."

Sheriff Knott sat at his desk drumming his fingers until the intercom buzzed. He picked up the phone and said, "Larry Collins, please. This is Sheriff Knott in Lordsburg . . . What? In the *hospital* . . . Yeah, yeah . . . Okay . . . Okay . . . Well, tell him I called after him, hope he gets well . . . Yeah." He hung up the phone.

"Shit," he said. He hated this. He had no choice except to kiss the ass of Godfrey Ryan, the bullet-headed bastard. He dialed the number in Douglas.

"Yeah?"

"Godfrey, it's Jack Knott."

"Say, Jack, you havin' a little bit of trouble these days, aren't you? Some kinda New Mexican jinx?"

"Look, cut the crap. I need some information. If you got it."

"You owe me, Jack. I don't owe you. Don't you remember, I told you about that agent goin' through your county?"

"That's what I'm calling about. What's he after?"

"Nothing right now. He's in the hospi—"

"I know that, damn it, but do you know why he was going through here to Mexico?"

"Yep, I do."

Sheriff Knott sighed. "Well, I got several related investigations going on over here, and I would greatly appreciate it if you would tell me what."

"It's smuggling, Jack. What else is there? But not dope. Pre-Columbian antiquities. Can you imagine? The goddamn FBI was working on this *e*-licit trade across the border and they weren't going to tell *me* about it. Till I wrung it out of that Collins's ass. Anyway, that's all I know about it for now. Now it's one of those deals, my people in Washington are talking to their people in Washington, and maybe one've these days I'll find out what the hell is going on across *my* piece of this goddamn border. Jeez. That nut ran for president, he was right. We ought to build a fucking moat hundred yards wide, but then we ought to fill it with nuclear wastes—"

"Godfrey, I am truly obliged."

"Stay in touch, Jack."

Sheriff Knott hung up the phone. He had run into that snake collector a few times, a real crazy bastard. So when the cops arrive, he thinks they know something—like he killed the agent. Or maybe just that he's smuggling stuff. So, given the chance by Depitty Snyder, he bolts. But where? What were the odds of him going to ground, sticking around? He sure knows the country well enough. Sheriff Knott contemplated in his mind's eye the precipitous cliffs and canyons of the Chiricahua Mountains across in Arizona, a huge area, maybe five hundred square miles, where a handful of Apaches had found ways to give one quarter of the whole U.S. army the slip for years.

That's where I'd go, he said to himself.

Mo Bowdre, sated with eggs, sausage, biscuits and gravy, and other wonderful things that were all, he knew full well, bad for him, picked up the receiver of the pay phone outside the main building and heard a dial tone. He punched out the number he had committed to long-term memory and listened to the buzz. A male voice answered, "Bureau." Another male voice said, "That will be two dollars and twenty-five cents," and Mo frantically fished in his pocket while the first male voice said, "Bureau."

"Goddamn it," Mo said, and jammed a quarter he had found into the slot.

"Bureau." The quarter clanked into the machine's digestive system.

"Hold on, hold on."

"Two dollars more, please."

"Well, goddamn it, wait." Mo dredged his pocket again and came up short. "I've only got one dollar."

"Bureau."

The phone line went dead and the machine disgorged Mo's quarter.

"What's the matter, Mo?" Connie asked, emerging from the building.

"Those boys at the Taco Bell Telephone Company want nine quarters in this Third World machine and all I got is five."

"Why don't you use your credit-card number?"

Mo beamed. "Damn good idea." He performed the transaction and listened again as the phone buzzed.

"Bureau."

"This is Bowdre. Can I talk to Collins?" He frowned as he listened to the agent on the other end of the line and then hung up.

"Now what's the matter?" Connie asked.

"Collins. Ran off the road last night, it looks like. He's okay, big concussion. Wakes up, drifts off. We better get down there. Maybe—"

"Yes, he is alone in the world, isn't he?" Connie said. "I'll get the truck keys."

"You don't have to do that," Wheeler Fitzhugh had said, sitting on the edge of the water bed after they returned from breakfast. "I mean, I really do believe in equality. You shouldn't—"

"In Mexico," Vera Maria had said, "we women of the educated class are beyond all that. We are so free, so equal, we do not find it offensive to do what used to be thought of as—what's the word?—uxorial tasks. I have to do my own—I might as well do yours at the same time." She had stood in front of him and bent deeply to give him a kiss on the forehead. "You see? I've run out of bras." She slipped away from him, laughing, and said, "So you go run the business and I'll do the wifely thing before I go out to the site."

Now, several minutes later, Vera Maria had put her own clothing and a pile of Fitz's from the bathroom hamper in the washer-dryer that took up most of a small pantry off the kitchen. She went back to the bedroom and opened the door to the closet, where, she had noticed, Fitz would absentmindedly toss a shirt, and indeed she found two in a heap on top of several pairs of boots. She picked the shirts up and noticed a sock in one of the battered and ancient pair of cowboy boots in the back of the closet. She shrugged, pulled the sock out, and the boot fell over. When she reached down to right the boot, she noticed a piece of paper in it. She picked it up, turned it over, and confronted a Polaroid emperor.

He was all gold, wearing what looked like a feathered headdress, huge round earrings, and a studded breastplate. He sat, one hand on his knee, a scepter of some sort in the other, his head typically far larger than human proportions would dictate. His thick lips were pulled back in what seemed a satisfied smile, revealing a row of large, even teeth, and his eyelids were lowered, giving him a contented look. It was very little like the fierce, almost grotesque representations one often saw. The gold sculpture had been brightly lit by a flashbulb, casting a sharp black shadow against the gray background stones. A magnificent piece, Vera Maria thought, even as her heart pounded and adrenaline rushed in her veins, making her breathless.

What was this photograph doing here? Why had it been made?

She stuck it impetuously into her shirt pocket, replaced the sock in the boot, and took the shirts into the pantry. A thought, the beginning of a hypothesis, struck her scientifically trained mind and a sudden chill made her shudder, the way the old women say it happens when a spirit of the dead comes too close.

Jeremy Armand pressed *Fn* and *PgUp* on his portable word processor and one last time checked the list of latinate names, times and dates, and the terse summary of the data. They proved within *scientific probability* that the date of death was the eighteenth of June, almost certainly early on that date, that is before dawn. He activated the old-fashioned dot-matrix printer and waited while it clattered out three copies of the two-page report, addressed to Sheriff Jack Knott, Hidalgo County Sheriff's Department, Lordsburg, New Mexico. He put one copy in a file drawer under his desk, folded another, and put it into an envelope, which he addressed by hand to Sheriff Knott. The third he plucked up and, along with the envelope, took with him across the grass to the building that housed Wheeler Fitzhugh's office and staff. Inside, standing in front of the secretary's desk, was Bowdre, the sculptor. God, he thought, the man is enormous.

"Three miles west of Douglas on Route 80," the sculptor repeated. "Thanks a lot. Old friend. Auto accident."

The secretary looked up and saw Armand.

"Hello, Dr. Armand."

Bowdre turned, smiling through his beard. "How're them blowflies doing?" he asked.

"On schedule," Armand said. "The data prove out my estimate."

"Science triumphs again," Bowdre said cheerfully, and left, reaching out to pat the door frame as he passed through it.

"Martha," Armand said, "I have to use the fax." He put the envelope in the outgoing-mail pile and went over to the fax machine. "It's my report to Sheriff Knott." The woman nodded, and Armand slipped the papers into the document hopper and punched out seven digits, standing with his arms folded across his chest as the papers ran through the system. The fax beeped and Armand took the disgorged report and walked across the hall to the director's office.

Wheeler Fitzhugh was bent over some papers on his desk, and Armand tapped on the door frame. "Wheeler?"

"Oh. Yes, Jeremy."

"Here's a copy of my report for your files," the little scientist said with a smile of satisfaction. "The data are remarkably clear. Eighteen June. Almost certainly before dawn. You may want to review it, but I already faxed it to Lordsburg."

"Oh, heavens no, Jeremy. You're the expert, the only one in a thousand miles who is capable of reviewing such a report." Fitzhugh smiled. "What is this, your tenth out here?"

"Eleventh."

"Well," Fitzhugh said. "That's a relief, to have something certain the police can go on, isn't it? And of course, it's very good for the center. Local relations. Thank you, Jeremy. As usual."

"Don't mention it, Wheeler." Armand sighed. "And now I can get back to *my* beetles." As he turned to go Fitzhugh made a thumbs-up sign, which Armand found odd. Uncharacteristic. As he headed across the lawn toward his lab, he thought it was as if Wheeler Fitzhugh were trying to demonstrate that he was "one of the boys." But, Armand thought, neither Fitzhugh nor Armand had ever been one of the boys, even when they had been undergraduates. People bent on being entomologists rarely are, the little scientist mused.

For the life of him, Mo Bowdre could not imagine how they do it.

Work in hospitals.

With all his experience in hospitals, he couldn't help but

think of them as little better than the gentle dungeons of the fourteenth century, with horrid men attaching leeches to your body—not the same thing of course, but surely the same presumed denouement. Death, that is. Not fair, not fair, oh, sure, Mo knew that, but he also actively sympathized with the legions who still today imagine hospital as an irrevocable step to the grave or crematorium. A lot of people do die in hospitals, he thought, and as a former med student, he knew that was more a matter of younger people wanting to unload the disintegrating aged than a problem of medical practice. God knows, they couldn't save his vision, but there were other parts they had saved.

No, what he couldn't imagine was how they put up with the stench of the place. Going every day to these supposedly antiseptic halls and rooms full of sterilized equipment, one's olfactory system drenched in disinfectants . . . and worse. He had long since been grateful that the Texas medical school had determined his inadequacy. Even before the accident, even before he'd had to rely on the other senses to a heightened degree, but certainly when he had had to lie there like some enormous tub of lard, scared to move, Mo's nose had told him that a hospital was . . . Doctors, he thought, nurses, all those people, we could do them a big favor. Sever the nerves between their olfactory sensors and the brain. What would they miss? He had read somewhere long ago that Chinese barefoot doctors use their noses to sniff out problems, but he couldn't remember any practitioner from an American medical school sniffing the potentially distraught seams and crannies of his particular temple before providing some prescription or another.

Mo was a hypochondriac, fearful of yet another outrageous blow, another sinister intrusion, followed by some doctor's cool, sympathetic explanation of the meaning of the alien list of numbers spat out by one diagnostic machine or another, adding up, manifestly, to an accelerated rate of organic de-composition.

A receptionist looked on her computer screen and said that Larry Collins was in Room 2A. They found the elevator and on the second floor made their way down the hallway, their heels sounding like SS troopers, the ammoniac atmosphere filling Mo's sinus cavities.

"In a list of my favorite places," Mo whispered, "hospitals do not figure."

"I know," Connie whispered back, and took his hand. She stopped them and steered Mo through a door. Mo could hear the regular breathing of a sleeping person.

"He's asleep," Mo whispered, relieved. "We can go. Leave him a note."

"Hey, Bowdre," Collins said in an oddly high voice.

"They said you were alive, but I thought I'd come down here and confirm it. I mean, how would they know? Who's sleeping in here?"

"I don't know his name. Some guy in the other bed."

"How are you?"

"I'll be okay, get out of here tomorrow."

"You sound awful. Weak. Concussion, huh? Loss of mem-ory. What have you forgotten?"

"How the hell would I know what I forgot? I forgot it," the agent said dreamily.

"How'd it happen?"

"I forget, must have fallen asleep at the wheel."

"Where were you coming from?"

"Mexico. I remember going to Mexico. There's chairs. Why don't you guys sit down?"

Connie pushed two little straight-backed cafeteria-style chairs up to the bed and Mo sat down, leaning toward the agent.

"Guess what?" Mo said.

"What?"

"We're getting nowhere in this investigation of yours, and it doesn't help having you lying here like a scarecrow without brains. When are you going to get them back?"

"I remember everything but the last, whatever it is, since I went into Mexico. It's a short-term loss, it'll come back."

"Do you remember why you were going to Mexico?"

"You sound like a cop," Collins said, his crooked teeth showing through a small smile. "Is all this going to your head?"

"Hah—hah— Oh. Armand's report says the body was found seven days after the—uh—"

The agent's eyes flickered. "Who hasn't seen dead bodies in this business?"

"What's that mean?" Mo asked, and noted that the agent had gone to sleep.

They walked in silence down the hall to the elevator. In the lobby Mo said, "Damn."

"Yes, it's awful, seeing him like that." Connie opened the glass door and the air outside was congealed with heat.

"Hot," Mo said. "Lost his damn memory."

"Well, just short-term, just for a while. This way." She tugged him once gently to the right, breaking the rules so Mo wouldn't walk directly into the fender of an ambulance that sat inert in the parking lot.

"He went down to Mexico for some reason . . . and he can't even remember why, much less if he found something. That doesn't help this investigation, not one damn little bit."

"Here's the truck, Mo. He's right, you know?"

"Right about what?"

"You're beginning to sound like a cop." She laughed.

"All I know is there's two agents assigned to this thing, and one of 'em is dead and the other is off in la-la land for God knows how long. So, for all I know, there's just me—

and you—investigating this." Mo stepped up into the truck and sat implacable in the seat, his beefy arms folded across his chest.

"So what do we do?"

"How the hell would *I* know, woman? I'm not a cop. I'm a sculptor, goddamn it."

From a distance Vera Maria could easily have been mistaken for a man, albeit a smallish one. Her hair was pinned up, encased in a chartreuse trucker's cap that said JIM BEAM in dark blue letters. She was dressed in baggy shorts, a matching khaki shirt, sleeves rolled down to cover her arms, and nondescript work boots. A white cloth, held in place by the cap, covered the back of her neck. Squatting on her heels, she contemplated the seedling growing before her from the rocky soil on the western slope of the foothills of the Peloncillos. The seedling was that of a birch-leaf mountain mahogany, *Cercocarpus betuloides*, not more than two years old, at the highest elevation she had ever found this species. In her rucksack were the devices she needed to measure soil moisture, temperature, and the other features that made this shrub just barely possible in such a place.

But she remained squatting, ecological considerations slipping away, replaced again by the image of the golden emperor. The same series of questions nagged her now as had cascaded through her mind when she stood before Fitz's closet gazing for the first time at the Polaroid. She had a sense that the figure in the photograph was about seven inches high, but why? There had been nothing specific in the photograph to show scale, like a coin or some other familiar object. Maybe something in the background. Gray. Was it rocks? Vera Maria pursed her lips, disapproving of her memory failure. But, then, it had been such a shock. . . . She would look at it again this afternoon.

If she was right about the size, it was worth a fortune. A million American dollars, maybe more.

But what was Fitz doing with this photograph? Why was it in his closet, stuffed in some old boot and covered with a sock?

There seemed to be only one conclusion. She would have to confront him about it. Tonight.

Or did she have to? She hated such confrontations. And why tonight? She felt a chill again, like the hand of death lightly touching her spine. She shuddered, reflexively looked over her shoulder, and stood up. The sand and rocks, almost colorless in the sun, rose up gradually to the east in the utter stillness and heat. She had never before, working in the field, had so eerie a sense of being watched. But there was no one, not even a bird, anywhere in sight.

Through the binoculars, the skinny man in the cowboy hat had easily identified the figure poking around the tree line as the Mexican scientist. Same one that was at the center last summer. He settled back against the boulder and watched her. He had thought to himself that it was a shame that a pretty woman would disguise herself to look so much like a man. Of course, her legs still had that thrilling curve to them, tan and silky the way a man's could never be, but all the rest was hidden under them ugly clothes. Shame, the man thought to himself, that a woman would hide all those curves and all that silky tan skin under a pair of men's military shorts, or whatever the hell they were, and a floppy shirt. A woman's ass, he thought, was a thing of such surpassing, breath-stopping beauty that it should be at least something you could guess at. Cover it up with those big shorts was a goddamn crime. He felt an unfamiliar surge in his groin and laughed to himself. Maybe I ain't so old after all, he thought. Maybe a last little fling here for old Oscar if

I can find him a nice brown ass like that one down there . . . Whoops.

The man ducked down out of sight and, with the simple athleticism of any desert animal, disappeared, making his way soundlessly through the arid land to his tower, which he mounted, all 238 steps, with a lightness of step one might expect from a twenty-year-old. Inside, he checked the clock: 4:30. He crossed over to the desk, pressed the buttons on the cellular telephone, and waited until the buzzing was interrupted.

"That Mexican one, she ain't paying attention to her work. Thinkin' about other stuff. Just squatted there near the canyon, lookin' off in the distance."

The voice on the phone said, "What about the snake man? See him?"

"That boy Tuck Eddy? Naw. What's up?"

"He took off. Disappeared. Police are after him."

"No shit. Now there's a boy could go to ground, lose himself. What's the problem?"

"Suspicion of murder. The woman in Skeleton Canyon."

"Well, I'll be switched."

"Keep your eye out for him. They say he lost his marbles, running loose like a madman. I don't want him in the way."

"If I was going to go to ground around here, I'd go over to the Chiricahuas. Like Geronimo and those guys."

"Yeah, good thinking. And Eddy may have blown his stack, but my guess is that he's shrewd enough to know that everyone will be looking for him there. So if he's around here at all, my bet is he's holed up somewhere in the Peloncillos. Fewer hikers and bird-watchers."

"Yeah, yeah. Okay. I'll look out for him."

"You're my eyes."

"Hell of a deal, ain't it. Take him out, right?"

"I don't want to hear about it."

There was a pause during which the cellular phone made a sound something like the passage of water over a rock.

"I said, I don't want to hear about it. From you or from that fat-assed sheriff. So do it right."

"What about the Mexican?"

"What about her?"

"Is she part of the problem?"

"Leave her completely alone, do you hear?"

"Okay, okay. I get the picture."

"You damn well better."

The skinny man turned off the phone and leered out of the windows of his metallic eyrie.

Eyes like an eagle, he thought.

"Maybe we ought to talk to a cop," Mo Bowdre said, and took a sip of golden beer. "Oh God, that tastes good." He was slumped in a large brown leather chair in the ornate, air-conditioned lobby of the Gadsden Hotel, the one jewel in the minimal tiara of Douglas, Arizona, where just after the turn of the century, the entrepreneurs of this border town built themselves a marble temple to boosterism. The vaulted stained-glass ceiling of the lobby was at least three stories high, held up by four marble columns decorated at the top with fourteen-karat gold leaf. The gold leaf was an after-thought, added in 1929 just as the national ceiling began to cave in, but the great tides of national affairs rarely reach Douglas, good or bad. The boosters' most notable extravagance had been an enormous bone-white Italian marble staircase that flowed like a bleached agate lava field down from the second floor to the lobby.

"Paul Newman," Connie said.

"Paul Newman? What are you talking about?"

"Well, I'm reading this brochure they have on the table. It says that the guys who made *The Life and Times of Judge Roy*

Bean stayed here when they were shooting. Wasn't that Paul Newman?"

"That was years ago, wasn't it?"

"He's cute."

"Still? Isn't he playing old men now?"

"You told me once how old you were. Your real age."

"You remember that?" Mo said.

"You told me."

"Yeah, but I talk about a lot of things. A lot of it's bull-shit."

Connie smiled. "I come from an oral tradition. I remember what people say."

"Damn," Mo said.

"So what are we going to do? You said something about talking to the police?"

"Maybe Tony'd have some ideas. Is there a pay phone in this lobby?" She walked across the lobby with Mo matching her step for step, giving the appearance not of a blind man but simply of a man wearing sunglasses indoors. Tony Ramirez, Connie thought, the quiet detective sergeant in the Santa Fe Police Department, and as close a friend of Mo's as any man Connie knew of. An unspoken mutual admiration society of two. An odd couple if ever there was one, but then, she thought, Mo and I are kind of an odd couple too.

"Here it is. I'll wait for you where we were sitting."

"This may take a little time," Mo said.

"Okay."

Fifteen minutes later Mo strode, erect and purposeful, with measured steps across the lobby. He stood in front of Connie's chair grinning.

"Tony thinks we're nuts—hah—hah—hah."

"We?"

"Me and Collins. Me to be here, Collins to have arranged it in what Tony, playing public official, says is 'an irregular manner.' I told him he should go to acting school if he wanted to pull off a bureaucratic act and he said he'd do some checking for us."

"Checking?"

"I gave him a bunch of names."

"Who?"

"Everyone we've met at the center. Some we haven't."

"They're all under suspicion?"

"Some more than others."

"Which ones?"

"If I tell you, you'll just remember. And I might be embarrassed later. Hah—hah. Let's go get some real food for a change, maybe a half ton of juicy dead cow, rare. Give us the strength to go back to starch city."

By four o'clock, a mountain of slate-gray clouds towered up, clinging to the crags of the Chiricahuas to the west, but the insistent west winds tore them away and hustled them tumultuously across the San Simon Valley. Led by errant zags of lightning, they came, turning the day dark, attaching themselves to the land in gray ribbons of rain.

The sky erupted with heavy artillery and suddenly it rained in the Peloncillos—large, widely spaced drops that made cuplike depressions in the dry ground, then a steady, drenching downpour that became tiny rivulets following the clawlike paths toward the canyons. Nearly black now, the clouds paused over the mountains as if gathering strength, replenishing themselves even as they lost their substance, then moved on to their next stop, the Animas Mountains, and the next, the Hatchets, where they would lose their charge and peter out. Some of the rivulets they left behind in the Peloncillos joined with others, and a few of these made their way into the canyons before vanishing into the sand. The world was pungent with the smell of wet earth and ozone, a fresh and metallic redolence that would last only a few minutes.

To the west the sky had already cleared and the sun balanced briefly on the jagged peaks of the Chiricahuas, making liquid jewels of the drops that fell from the mudstone ledge above Tuck Eddy's head. The storm had cleared his mind, washing away the terror he had felt building within him during the day of confinement in his lair and leaving him with a plan.

The rain is ol' Tuck's friend, he thought, ol' Tuck's friend. Now they'd started, he could count on these storms, regular as a train every afternoon, send everybody scurrying for cover, back to the center. If he kept to the rocks, and then to the grass, he wouldn't leave a trace. He could start to build his own society again. Man's a social animal, has to have *some* friends, for God's sake. A man all by himself is defenseless, damn near helpless. He knew where one of his friends was, knew just where to find it, out in the grasslands between Rodeo and the mountains. Long about now it'd be heading for *its* lair, one of two or three haunts, getting cool and sleepy, and Tuck would just go in there, and talk to it, and bring it home. Tuck wondered idly and not for the first time why they had named it for the Mojave Desert, which was a thousand miles away, when the most venomous form of it occurred only in this one little corner of the Chihuahuan desert.

Well, never mind.

I ain't no scholar. I'm a wildman. Bigfoot of the Peloncillos. Mowgli the Snake Boy, full of venom and vinegar.

They won't get ol' Tuck. No sir.

Wheeler Fitzhugh heard the shower running gaily when he walked into his bedroom. He poked his head around the door to the bathroom and saw Vera Maria's blurred body through the clear plastic shower curtain.

"Hi," he said over the sound of the water. "How was your day?"

There was silence. Then Vera Maria said, "Slow."

"Same here." Fitzhugh noticed Vera Maria's field notebook on the bureau. He opened it and flipped the pages to today's notations, spotting at the bottom of the page the familiar Latin name, *C. betuloides*. This was followed by an elevation—6,800 feet—and some map coordinates. Nothing else—no data on soil moisture, the other sorts of thing she kept track of. Must have found the shrub at the end of the day. She had the most amazing talent, Fitzhugh said. Almost like intuition. If he wasn't wrong, that was a remarkably high elevation for one of those shrubs.

He put his hand around the door again. "I'll see you over at the lounge," he said, and went to the closet to change into a fresh shirt. She might tell him about her find tonight. But probably she'd wait until she had completed her study. She'd go back to the shrub, work up the ecological parameters, and then hike that contour all around that peak, and then others, looking for more at that elevation. Intuitive and methodical. More good science from his center.

"Well, hi there, Mo."

Mo recognized the voice at once, of course—Ingrid Freeman, who was mammals, the squirrel lady. He was standing with his back to the mantelpiece of the big stone fireplace in the lounge, holding a cold bottle of Negra Modello beer in his hand. He'd brought two cases back from Douglas, not caring much for the thin stuff available for fifty cents a can from the center's supply. He smiled at Ingrid's voice.

"Hullo, Ingrid. How're the squirrels?"

"Squirrelly," she said, and put her hand on his arm. "You

have a good day?" Much as he hated it, Mo knew he would have to be led around again.

"Just fine, just fine. Went to Douglas, got some real beer. Ate two steaks for lunch. Say, did your husband catch all those loose snakes the other day?"

"They got sixty-eight. Must be another thirty got away. A shame. Bill had to go to Tucson for a two-day conference, so his students went back today to look around."

Leaving, Mo thought, Ingrid-who-is-mammals to try and bag herself a blind sculptor. What is it about me, he smiled to himself, that I got to brush 'em away like flies? "Ingrid?" he said. "Maybe you could help me out." He felt her fingers tighten slightly on his arm, like a tiny electromagnetic jolt.

"Of course, Mo."

"Well, there's an hour till supper"—another jolt from the magneto—"and I was told that there's a big old model of this part of the Peloncillos somewhere around here. I'd like to get someone to help me study it, get the lay of the land, you know."

"It's over at the other end of the room," Ingrid said, and the electric charge diminished, then rallied. "Let me take you over." She piloted him through the furniture and across the room, holding him firmly by the elbow. They stopped and Ingrid took his hand and slowly placed it on the round contours of a miniature mountain. Papier-mâché, Mo guessed.

"Now what's this?" Mo asked.

"It's the peak just east and north of the center." She pulled his hand down to the right and his fingers followed a widening little canyon. "There. Feel those little houses? That's the center. Now, this is the road down to Route 80."

"That's about three miles?"

"Right. Now"—she moved his hand again—"back to the center. Over here, just south of the center is the next canyon, Rustler's Canyon. Most of the main canyons around here run basically east-west, but this one is skewed some to the south and north. See? I mean—"

"Don't worry. A lot of blind people use the word for what they can feel or sense one way or the other. This is very helpful."

"Oh," Ingrid said. "I think that's lovely." She drew his hand from the canyon's mouth up the mountain until it disappeared in a splayed series of tributary arroyos. "Being sort of north-south, this one gets different amounts of sun on either side, makes for more ecosystems. A lot of us work over there. It's literally swarming with biologists on any given day."

"Tell me, where's Skeleton Canyon?"

"We'll get there," Ingrid said. "But first, just *north* of the center . . ." The lesson continued, Mo being guided with loving attention around the nooks and crannies of the Peloncillos, registering them in his brain like a three-dimensional projection screen, committing them to memory as surely as a soldier learns to disassemble and reassemble a weapon in the dark. Along the way, Ingrid took regular opportunity to bump her hip into Mo's leg or accidentally brush his arm with what Mo guessed were cantaloupe-sized breasts, almost literally emitting electromagnetic flares with every bump and brush. A flagrant sexpot, Mo thought, a man-eater, also thinking that a few years ago . . . Ah well. He dwelled these days in passionate monogamy.

"You know, Ingrid?" he said, standing back. "I think I know this place like the back of my hand. I'm really grateful to you for your kindly attention."

"Maybe we can do a refresher course tomorrow."

"A quiz? Say, I got a question. What's Freddy?"

"Freddy? Oh, Freddy Mervin. What *is* he?"

"Well, you're mammals. What's he?"

"Arachnids," she said, and Mo heard a distracted sound in

her voice. Like disappointment. "Spiders, mostly. Well, it looks like suppertime." Mo submitted to her guidance through the furniture emporium. At the door to the cafeteria she stopped and said, "Here's your friend coming." Definite disappointment in her voice.

"Thank you again, Ingrid. It's been wonderful."

"Maybe tomorrow."

"My quiz." He heard the woman move off and felt like a rat. He turned to face Connie.

"So, the squirrel lady strikes again," she said cheerfully.

"She was showing me the model of the mountains around here. Over there." He gestured with his head toward the back of the lounge.

"That's not all she was showing you."

"She's not my type."

"Hah—hah," Connie barked in a good imitation. "Vera Maria is meeting me here in a few minutes. You want to eat with us?"

"Yes, but the herps people asked me to join *them*. I think they want to lobby for a statue of a giant frog or something. I'm being wooed taxonomically."

Connie stepped close and, on her tiptoes, whispered in Mo's ear, "Remember, you make lousy squirrels." And, uncharacteristically for her in any sort of public place, she kissed him in the ear. "See you later."

"Hah—hah—hah."

Vera Maria had seemed distracted during much of dinner, not distant or cool, but from time to time her attention would wander, as if she had suddenly decamped to some other place for a few seconds, only to return with what was almost a visible startle. She had a pinched look, a tightening of the skin on her forehead. Connie wondered if she had a headache, and asked her.

"No, no. Forgive me if I have been—rude. It's nothing. A small personal setback. Nothing at all."

"If I can help . . ."

"No, no. Now you were telling me about some gods that were taken from your people."

Connie began to explain how she and Mo had become involved when Vera Maria again looked startled, as if she were waking from a dream, and smiled.

"Excuse me, I must interrupt. Maybe you can—help me. You said you were a CPA?"

"I was. Now I'm an appraiser. Indian jewelry."

"Is a CPA anything like a lawyer in this country?"

"Not much." Connie laughed. "We're honest, mostly."

The Mexican woman smiled. "Yes. But I mean in the way of—what's the word? *Privado de confidencia*?"

Connie was puzzled. "Yes. Client confidentiality."

"Can I hire you?" She reached around for her purse, fished around in it, and handed Connie a hundred-dollar bill. "Will this be all right for a retainer?"

"I don't understand. But sure . . ."

"There is something I want you to hold for me." She reached into her purse again and handed Connie a brown number-ten envelope. "See? Just this." She smiled, a bright smile that vanished as quickly as it had arrived. "Will you hold this for me? Just hold it?"

"Uh—" Connie glanced at the back of the envelope. It was sealed.

"Just hold it for me. Please. Until I ask for it."

Connie shrugged. "Okay." She slipped the envelope inside her shirt, and it felt warm against her skin.

"I'll be able to explain it all—later. A few days. Okay?"

"Okay."

Vera Maria seemed to relax. She told a long story about being chased off a research site in Sonora by a madman who thought he was Pancho Villa reincarnated, determined to rid the Republic of Mexico of the evils of European civilization, which included scientists. He and two followers had borne down on her suddenly one day on three terrible old plugs, and she had narrowly escaped whatever they had in mind for her by taking the high ground in some crags and rolling boulders down on them, the way the Apaches had when they were chased by Mexican soldiers years ago. It all seemed hilariously funny now.

F i v e

"It's that Papago lady. She must have done it."

"Did what?" Mo said, half asleep.

"Got the blue corn flour. For these pancakes. That's called solidarity."

"Pancakes are a bit solid too."

"Are you turning into a grouch?" Connie asked.

"Always was one," said Mo, masticating. "Even as a boy." He swallowed dramatically. "Did I tell you about the time—"

"Good morning." It was Wheeler Fitzhugh, sounding like a man running for the United States Senate. "May I join you?"

"I wish you would," said Mo. "Get me out of a tight situation here. See, Connie thinks I'm turning into a wizened old grouch, but it's just that I had funny dreams last night, and you know how you wake up with your dreams? Takes a few hours to grind 'em down. Anyway, sit down. I promise to be a good boy."

"Were you dreaming up a sculpture?"

"I was lobbied by the herps people last night. I'm thinking salamander. Say, you know, I was thinking, it must be pretty, well, hard being stuck out here in this place all year. You ever get out of here, get up to Lordsburg and live it up?"

"Simple pleasures are what we have here," Fitzhugh said, like brochure copy. "And there's no place I'd rather be in the world. But I do have to leave every now and then. We have a subgroup of researchers working out of El Paso. I check on them from time to time. Usually about every three weeks." He took a bite of something and Mo could hear his jaws working. "In fact," the director said, "I was down there— let's see, what's today—the twenty-eighth? No, it's the twenty-ninth. I drove back on the eighteenth. Twelve days ago. Time goes so quickly. Faster every day."

"El Paso, huh? You're not a Texan, are you?"

"No. Born and raised in Connecticut."

"Well, you know what we New Mexican–bred say about Texas. You step over the border and there's an immediate drop of thirty points in the Intelligence Quotient. I suppose you notice that when you go to El Paso. Hah—hah—hah. Well, it's a friendly rivalry, of course, until it comes to stuff like water rights in the Pecos and the Rio Grande, but us native New Mexicans just assume that Texans lost out when God handed out the brains."

Fitzhugh laughed politely.

"What sort of research goes on in El Paso?" Mo asked.

"Actually it's in the Guadalupe Mountains. Near El Paso. Comparative studies—we look at the same species there as some we have here. We're looking for indicator species for monitoring global warming effects on the Southwest. For example, Jeremy Armand's beetles? He has a colleague working on some of the same ones in the Guadalupes. Jeremy went with me last time. Bill Freeman too. We have the same thing going on with snakes. Also a number of desert plant species, of course."

"Now, that's just fascinating," Mo said.

"To us it is," Fitzhugh said with a sigh. "But it's hard to get the public interested. Which means it's sometimes hard to get Congress interested. Funding is tight, what with NASA sopping up the billions. Ah, Congress."

"Hell, those boys are dumber than Texans."

Sheriff Knott picked up the phone, punched out a number with angry stabs of his forefinger, and waited impatiently.

"Linda? Look, I can't make it today . . . Well, we got a manhunt on in this county . . . No, Linda, no. This is serious. I even deputized those cowboys in the sheriff's posse. Give 'em something else to do besides organize rodeos . . . No, Linda, it just wouldn't look right. I got to be leadin' the troops. And the feds're in it, state troopers, everybody and his damn uncle . . . Well, goddamn it, it ain't my fault . . . *Shit!*" He stared at the receiver in his hand and slammed it down. "Women," he said. "Sometimes it just isn't worth it."

Almost immediately the phone rang.

"Sheriff Knott . . . Look, Linda, I am sorry I used bad language . . . Yeah . . . Yeah. When it's over . . . Okay . . . Of course I do . . . Yeah, bye." He hung up, shaking his head, and leaned back in his chair. Waste of time, he thought. Seventeen cowboys roaming around the county, ten dollars each a day, waste of time *and* money. Real deputies all tied up on this wild-goose chase. He'd even given Jimmy Snyder a reprieve, sent him out on the hunt. But if that Tuck Eddy was anywhere in the Southwest, he was in the Chiricahuas, Cochise County. You could disappear in them hills like an Apache.

His mind strayed to Linda, down in Animas, and he saw her plump figure in his mind's eye, packed into those tight jeans like a teenager. She was beginning to get a bit long in the tooth, he thought, for jeans that tight, but then who isn't?

Damn snake man. Damn feds.

He thought of Collins, and pressed the button on the intercom. "Get me the hospital in Douglas." He waited until the intercom buzzed and picked up the phone.

"This is Sheriff Knott, Hidalgo County. Is Larry Collins still in there? . . . Till his memory returns? How long . . . Yeah, I understand. Okay, tell him I called, would you? . . . Thank you."

Poor bastard.

The sheriff heaved himself out of his chair, put on his hat, and left the office. On his way out he stopped before the young woman deputy at the desk.

"I'm going down to the Gray Ranch. Make sure they don't get all outta joint when we send some of the posse in there. Conservationists—strangest people on the damn planet."

The young deputy smiled. She had met one of the Gray Ranch assistant managers just the night before on the dance floor at one of Lordsburg's many motels, and hadn't found him strange at all. Quite the contrary.

Deputy Sheriff Jimmy Snyder stopped his vehicle alongside the pile of stones that commemorates the spot where Geronimo surrendered to General Nelson Miles in 1886, after a fairly long parley. It didn't make any sense to Jimmy. He could imagine the U.S. troops being dumb enough to parley here where there was no shade, stand around in their woolen uniforms in the hot sun, but he was pretty sure no Apache was that stupid. The old photographs of other such parleys he'd seen, like the one across the border in Mexico, they'd always been held in the shade of a stand of trees.

"Daniel? You think that's where Geronimo gave up?"

Daniel Ascension stared with pale blue eyes from under his hat brim at the pile of rocks. "No. It was over there. In the trees."

Well, that's settled, Jimmy thought. He drove a few hundred yards farther into the canyon, stopped again, and stepped out into the heat. He looked up at the canyon walls that loomed silently on either side. A single cloud, white as an angel, sailed across the blue-black sky and passed over the northern rim of the canyon, giving the momentary impression that the canyon rim itself was teetering toward him.

Wind from the south. Another scorcher.

The car door slammed and Daniel stood in the sun on the other side of the vehicle, shoulders slumped, face shadowed under his hat brim. "I sure wish we didn't have to go back there," he said.

"It's orders, *Deputy* Ascension." Jimmy Snyder felt good, happy the manhunt had brought about his reprieve, which he hoped would put the entire matter to rest. It sure would help if he and Daniel found the snake man, or even a trace of him. That'd show the sheriff how valuable he was. "Well, let's go," he said, but the two men stood for a moment, watching the shadows and the rocks around them. The silence was broken by a series of squeaky *chirts* from a canyon wren, annoyed by the intrusion. Jimmy spotted it just as it disappeared around a boulder, leaving the world as still as bone. They headed up the canyon. Daniel kept his shadowed eyes to the ground, looking for tracks in the sand between the rocks. They had a photograph of the snake man's bootprints, taken around his trailer after the snakes had been caught. A thin hope, the thinnest of hopes, Jimmy thought, keeping his less practiced eyes on the walls, the rocks, hoping however vainly to catch a glimpse of . . . something.

•   •   •

The skinny man saw a deputy sheriff and his companion from a half mile off as they clambered up out of an arroyo into plain view from the tower. Big heavyset deputy he didn't recognize. New. The companion looked like the Randall kid, one of the boys from the Frank Ranch over beyond Antelope Wells. They moved through the low trees in the direction of the fire tower. The skinny man put on his straw cowboy hat and began the descent to the ground. He was waiting for them, leaning against one of the stanchions that held up his eyrie, when they approached. The Randall kid was carrying a Winchester .30-.30, the deputy just his sidearm.

"Deputized the whole damn county, huh?" he said.

"'Lo, Ned," said the Randall kid. They shook hands.

Name is, what the hell—Jack. "'Lo, Jack."

"This here is Deputy Martinez. Just joined the force."

"We're looking for Tuck Eddy, that snake collector from over near the research center," Deputy Martinez said.

Not much manners on this one, the skinny man named Ned thought, so he didn't say anything. Just stood there leaning against the metal stanchion, and looked at the overweight deputy out of half-closed eyes.

"You know him?"

"Nope."

"He's five-eleven, brown hair—"

"I know what he looks like."

"You said—"

"I said I don't know him. But I seen him around."

"Keep an eye out for him. You see him, you call the Hidalgo County Sheriff's Office."

"Yes, sir, sonny."

The deputy glowered, and Ned smiled back.

"You got a good tracker here, Deputy. Knows the country. See you around, Jack." He turned and began the ascent. A few minutes later he watched the two men disappear into another arroyo, farther to the south. Bunch of stumblebums, he thought. If they thought they were going to flush the snake man by clattering around the canyons in broad daylight, they were even dumber than he had given the sheriff's office credit for.

Wheeler Fitzhugh had passed the word that morning to all the scientists that since there was a manhunt under way for Tuck Eddy, now under suspicion of being a murderer, the sheriff's office had asked that research in the center's various study sites be halted. Eddy was considered armed and dangerous—and off his rocker. However, Fitzhugh had persuaded the sheriff that it was important that the research not be interrupted, and that Eddy probably would not hide so near the center for the very fear of being spotted by roving scientists. So the sheriff had relented, with the proviso that the researchers stay together in groups of at least three for the next two or three days. In fact, Fitzhugh explained, the sheriff didn't really think Eddy was in the neighborhood, more likely over in the Chiricahuas, if anywhere in the region, but it was nevertheless wise to take the precautions the sheriff had decided upon, so he asked "all hands" to comply.

It had been years since Vera Maria had worked in the field with anyone. She couldn't concentrate with others around her. Their simple presence somehow interfered with the almost intuitive sense of the landscape that she found essential to her work. And having escaped from a number of tight spots in her career, the would-be Pancho Villa being but one such incident, she was not in the slightest bit worried about Tuck Eddy, the snake collector, whom she knew and believed to be really a very gentle man. She simply rejected the notion of him as a killer.

A loner by nature, today she had yet other things clawing at her that made her seek solitude—things she tried to put out of her mind but kept returning to. She had not had her

confrontation with Fitzhugh—out of a kind of despair? Or
was it fear? In any case, some unworthy emotion had immobilized her. Instead she had pleaded the onset of her period
and had gone to bed early—and she was angry with herself
about all of that. She felt craven. So she had ignored the rec-
ommended precautions and slipped off by herself, returning
to the place where yesterday she had found the seedling. Ever
methodical, she scribbled down the basic data in her notebook.

She stood looking down at the little shrub, almost sensing
the strained cellular effort it was making to survive here on
its species' upper frontier. She looked around at the sun-
drenched, nearly colorless rock face about twenty meters
north of her, the boulders at its bottom casting purple shadows. In the perfect stillness she thought she saw a lizard dart-
ing in the shadows. She watched to see if it would emerge
into the sunlight. There was the sound of a miniature breeze
gliding over rock, but nothing, none of the snakeweed and
creosote bush growing sparsely among the boulders, moved.
She looked back at the little shrub struggling to live, and remembered waking up the night before. A huge thunderstorm
in the middle of the night, God knew what time. The sound
of water rushing, Fitz cursing about the drainpipes, fumbling
in the closet, stomping out of the house, doors slamming,
and a chill came on her. The boots.

And that was Vera Maria's last thought before the projec-
tile struck and her mind exploded in awful orange fire and
she crumpled, instantly dead, on the hard earth, snapping the
little seedling off an inch from the ground.

Daniel Ascension stepped out of the shadows at the bend of
Skeleton Canyon, his eyes on the ground. They had prowled
several side canyons and were about a hundred yards from the
way up to the ledge where Daniel's cave was, where he'd

found the body five days earlier. It seemed a long time ago. Jimmy Snyder, walking four paces behind him, noted that Daniel had slowed down to a reluctant shuffle. Giving him the benefit of the doubt, Jimmy said, "See anything?"

Daniel stopped, eyeing the ground before him. "I just don't like this place anymore."

Jimmy stopped beside him in the glare and wiped his forehead with a sweep of his sleeve. "I know how you feel, Daniel, but we got to go look." He glanced up the canyon, up at the ledge where the cave was, and then down the rocky side of the canyon, noting a collection of boulders that had fetched up halfway down. He looked up along the dry creekbed, thinking soon the summer rains will have it flowing again, then—startled—he looked back at the pile of boulders halfway up the canyon's wall.

"What the—"

He ran up the canyon, leaping over the rocks strewn in the creekbed, and pulled up, gasping for air. He looked at the boulders. It was a slender forearm that reached up at a forty-five-degree angle from behind one of the boulders, with a hand hanging, inert but oddly elegant, in the air.

"Holy shit!" he intoned. Then he shouted, "Holy *shit*! Daniel!" He ran the rest of the distance to the boulders, scrambling up the incline toward the hand—a woman's—and stood looking down at the ruined body all askew, everything in the wrong direction, both legs obviously snapped, one of them with a white anklebone protruding from the torn flesh, skull bashed in, black hair matted with blood. The only visible part of her not scraped and broken and bloody from the fall was the arm with its elegant hand hanging in the air.

"My God, my God, my God." He looked up to the canyon rim, a hundred feet above. A creosote bush on the edge nodded in a sudden breeze and was still. He heard Daniel approach, loose rock clattering. He reached down and touched the woman's arm. It was still not cold, clammy. The hand wiggled slightly. He looked at his watch: 10:37.

"Aw, Jesus," Daniel said, and turned away.

"Daniel, can you get up on the rim from here?" Jimmy's breath was coming in chest-racking heaves.

"Yeah," Daniel croaked.

"Okay, get up there, and don't do anything. Just . . . if anyone shows up, keep them away from the rim, the whole area. Okay? Don't walk around or anything."

Daniel nodded and began to climb the slope. Loose rock clattered down the side in his wake while Jimmy Snyder, praying that other patrols were within its reach, thumbed the switch on his portable two-way radio. But the horror of the crumpled wreck of a woman broke over him like a wave of bile. He turned off the switch and threw up, bent over nearly double with the racking heaves. An eternity later he stood up and wiped his mouth with his sleeve, and turned the radio back on.

Within twelve minutes every official red light in Hidalgo County was blinking, three county vehicles were headed for the entrance of Skeleton Canyon, screaming along the desert highways. Sirens shrieked, phone lines and radios whirred and snapped with terse data. An FBI agent in Douglas, Arizona, opened a new electronic file, marked OPEN SKELETON CANYON, HIDALGO CO., N.M. with the date and a long file number. Equivalent files, satellite-beamed, immediately opened in Tucson, Albuquerque, and the J. Edgar Hoover Building, the grim temple in the federal triangle in downtown Washington, D.C. In a matter of moments nearly a hundred people knew of the death of this one woman, crushed by a one-hundred-foot descent into Skeleton Canyon, even before anyone knew her name.

Sheriff Jack Knott had gotten the word at 10:44, sitting in

his vehicle outside the office of the Gray Ranch. He had found, somewhat to his surprise, that the manager not only welcomed the deputized legions to search for Tuck Eddy on ranch property, but offered several ranch hands to help the searchers—for nothing. *Pro bono publico.* He hadn't needed to drive all the way down from Lordsburg; he could have simply called, said the manager. And please do just that anytime there was something the ranch could do for him. Pleased, Sheriff Knott had swung himself into the seat of his vehicle when the radio squawked and burped and the voice of the woman deputy in Lordsburg said, "Sheriff Knott. Sheriff Knott. Deputy Snyder reports dead body, female, Skeleton Canyon." Knott asked a couple of terse questions into the microphone and barked out a series of orders.

After driving slowly down the long graveled driveway to the dirt road that runs north-south almost the whole length of the ranch, he flicked on his siren and headed, flat out, for Animas, barely slowing to turn west on Route 61 and, again, south on Route 80 past the town of Rodeo to the canyon mouth—in all, a trip of seventy-five miles, which he made in less than an hour. Three other sheriff's vehicles were in the canyon, including Snyder's, and when Sheriff Knott made the last arduous five hundred yards on foot, it was just past noon and the heat was ferocious. The three deputy sheriffs, and two men from the Hidalgo County sheriff's posse, were squatting on their heels in the shade, smoking, when they saw the sheriff approach. They flipped their cigarettes into the dry streambed and stood up.

"She's up there, Sheriff," said Jimmy Snyder, gesturing with his head. "I'll take you up."

"Where's Daniel Ascension?" the sheriff asked, breathing hard after the exertion. "Wasn't he with you?"

"I sent him up to the rim. He's up there seein' that no one messes up any evidence that might be around. I told him not to walk around or nothing, just keep people away. She could've just fallen, but she could've been pushed, is what I thought."

Sheriff Knott stared at the deputy from behind his mirrored sunglasses, thinking that maybe a little demotion had caused this boy to recharge his brain a bit. "Let's go," he said, dreading the climb.

"She's real banged up, Sheriff. A real mess."

"Identity?" Sheriff Knott was nearly gasping for breath.

"Well, we didn't touch her or nothing, like look for her ID, but she looks to be one of those scientists from the research center."

"Makes sense," the sheriff said. He stood for a while, replenishing his lungs with oxygen, and stooped down to lift a corner of the cloth that covered her. "Jesus Christ!" He let the cloth fall back into place. "You'd hate to see that happen to your worst enemy." Then he lifted the cloth again and reached in, carefully plucking from the dead woman's breast pocket what looked like a reporter's notebook, long and narrow, with a spiral binding on the top, which he held delicately between his thumb and forefinger. He turned the front of the notebook toward Jimmy. "Can you read that?"

Jimmy squinted. "Let's see. It says V. M. Madero. Then it says DRC. Then it says 26 *junio* and there's a dash after *junio*."

"Well, sure as hell it's one of those scientists. DRC. Desert Research Center. Probably a field notebook of some sort. We'll have to let 'em know. My God, those people are having a hell of a time. But we'd best do our work first, then notify them."

Back on the canyon floor Sheriff Knott sent two of the four men back on the manhunt for Tuck Eddy and ordered the other two to wait at the scene for the coroner. "We don't need the bug man," he said. "Couldn't've been earlier than ten o'clock that it happened, if she was still warm when you found her."

He and Jimmy headed south to the vehicles, and forty minutes later they were on the canyon rim, standing beside Daniel Ascension, looking gloomily at an expanse of rimrock, ringed by low scrubby pine and oak.

"Shoot," the sheriff said. "You could run cattle over this place and there wouldn't be a footprint."

"It had to've been over there, Sheriff. 'Tween those two creosote bushes," Daniel said. Sheriff Knott thought that Daniel might just burst into tears, he looked so broken. Strange ol' boy, like a kid, but one of the best trackers in the county. Could find a ratshit in a hayfield, like some kind of intuition.

"Daniel, when're you gonna get a new hat? That ol' thing is so greasy I can smell it from here."

Daniel grinned. "It still fits good, Sheriff. When it don't fit, I'll get me a new one." Sheriff Knott thought he saw a shine in Daniel's sky-blue eyes.

"You boys go over there and see if you can see any sign. Scrape marks. Blood. I'm going to have a look at this notebook."

The two men walked gingerly over to the edge and squatted down while Sheriff Knott settled down on a rocky bench and opened the cover of the notebook. There were a few Latin words sprinkled around that the sheriff recognized as scientific names, but most of it was some kind of shorthand, with numbers and occasional scribbles that looked almost like abbreviations of words. Jesus, he said to himself, it's not only shorthand, it's Spanish. Madero. Maybe someone at the center can interpret it. There were two pages of gobbledygook under a heading 27—no doubt June 27—three pages under 28, and only a few lines under 29—today. He couldn't make any sense of it.

"You boys see anything over there?" he called.

"Just this one thing," said Jimmy Snyder. "You want to come over here and have a look?"

"Do jackrabbits like to screw?" He crossed the rimrock and stood behind the two men squatting on their heels. "What you got?"

"Daniel spotted this. Looks like a piece of mud that got jammed into the treads of those Reebok-type of shoes and then fell out." The sheriff leaned over and stared at the object that Jimmy Snyder was pointing at with a ballpoint pen. Since he was nearsighted, it was a small blur, maybe two inches long and curved, like an incipient question mark without the dot.

"You got a camera in your unit?" he asked.

"Yes, sir."

"Get it. Put a coin beside this, photograph it from four, five directions. We can see if it fits the shoes that woman is wearing. She was wearing some of them sneaker-type deals, wasn't she?"

"Or maybe," Jimmy said, "the treads on Tuck Eddy's boots."

"Don't touch it, it'll just fall apart. Dry as dust. Whoever this was, they was walking around in one of these arroyos after yesterday's rain."

Back in his vehicle, Sheriff Knott radioed headquarters to explain that he would next go to the research center. The young woman deputy there, who was only recently employed, was now feeling the exhaustion of only three hours' sleep, not to mention the unaccustomed need to field so many emergency calls and messages. She interrupted and said, "Sheriff? You got a call from a Larry Collins. Says he's a FBI agent but he spoke in, like, a whisper, so I figure it's some crank call."

"What'd he say?"

"Weird. He said he had a man in the center. That's what he said. I wrote it down here. A man in the center. He said you could talk to him. He said he's a sculptor named—let me see here—Mo Bowdre." She spelled out the last name. "I don't see why there'd be a sculptor at the research center, so I figure it's a nut call, but I thought—"

"What else did he say?"

"Said they wouldn't let him out for at least another day. Memory loss. I mean, do you get a lot of calls like this? The guy is in some kind of asylum! The whole county has gone crazy!"

"Hang in there, Deppity. You're doing a fine job," Sheriff Knott said into the mike, and turned off the switch.

There had been times, over the past couple of years, when Jack Knott had computed the idea of early retirement from the office of county sheriff. There was a lot of boredom, an increasing amount of paperwork, an increasing appearance of out-of-county police people in his affairs, mostly feds who seemed to think that the states and counties of this nation were nothing more than addresses, not jurisdictions with some right to take care of their own affairs. There were all these damn machines and electronic bullshit, enough to distract an honest man from an honest day's work, what with their incessant messages and requests. After all, he'd already built up a good pension, had simple needs—well, some of 'em weren't so simple to organize if he was supposed to be home cleaning hunting rifles all the time, and doing wood turning or some damn thing, while his wife Sarah hummed hymns in the kitchen, and Linda and the others . . . Well.

He could work it out, he thought, whenever he thought about retiring. But this was not a time for such thoughts. Something real had happened. A research-center scientist had been killed, turned out to be an FBI agent. The FBI was

looking into some kind of smuggling of pre-Columbian artifacts, maybe involving the center. Then the snake man had
gone bananas and lit out, same feller the woman agent had
shacked up with last summer. And now another scientist, another woman, winds up dead within a hundred yards of the
cave where the first woman was found. No evidence that anything happened but that she fell accidentally, but the evidence wasn't all in yet. Whole thing was juicy as a summer
peach. And now they got a man in the center. Well, I guess
I'm going to have to talk to this man Bowdre. In fact, here
I am, a local boy, Jack Knott, sheriff of Hidalgo County, New
Mexico, one of the least populated counties in the entire
United States, goddamn *authorized* to meddle directly in a
federal investigation. By damn. What did that actor say?

"Make my day," the sheriff said out loud, and turned the
ignition key on. As the engine roared he thought about
Jimmy Snyder. That boy, he did a good piece of work there.

When the sheriff's car pulled into the parking lot under the
trees at the research center, two young biology students,
whose administrative chores on this day were to look after
the children of the other biologists, speculated about whether
the cops had found Tuck Eddy. The children in their care
ranged in age from three to eight and were now rampaging
in a series of jungle gyms and rubber tires in the central
greensward. Older children, under the care of yet other undergraduates, were off on what was a real field trip, collecting
soil samples.

The young man from Fresno State said, "The guy's like a
snake himself. They'll never find him."

His partner of the day was an undergraduate from Princeton who achingly reminded the young Californian of another
Princetonian, Brooke Shields, but shorter. She said, "The
only way they won't find him is if he's in Canada, or Bolivia,

or someplace like that. Don't you understand, Dennis? There's no place to hide in this country anymore. So why else would the sheriff be here? It's got to be about Tuck."

"I'm telling you, that guy can vanish in this country. Just vanish. He knows every—"

"Dennis, that little boy over there just threw up. It's your turn."

"Bleh. I think I'll switch to business school."

"Wimp."

"Well, I'm afraid we got some more bad news here," Sheriff Knott said, sitting down in the chair in front of Wheeler Fitzhugh's desk.

"We've had a lot of bad news already these past few days, Sheriff. Now what?" The director sat erect and businesslike, hands folded before him on the desk. "Is this about Tuck Eddy? He wasn't with the center, you know."

"No, sir, but his girlfriend was, the one who was . . . Well, he's the only suspect in the case for now. . . . But this ain't about him. It's real bad news, I think. You got someone named V. M. Madero here? A woman?"

The man looked bewildered. "Vera Maria," he said. "Yes." He gripped the arms of his chair, like a man about to be ejected from a fighter plane.

"Well, I'm afraid I have to tell you that she is dead. She was found—"

Fitzhugh was on his feet. "What? *What?* Jesus—there's got to be—oh *Christ*!" He sat down, and Sheriff Knott thought he saw the man's eyes glistening before he bowed his head and held it between his hands. "Christ, Sheriff—"

The sheriff waited silently until Fitzhugh raised his head and let his hands flop onto the desk.

"How—what—?"

"Some men on patrol, looking for Eddy. Spotted her partway up the canyon wall, a little ways up the eastern end of Skeleton Canyon. She evidently fell from the rim."

"Fell? Vera Maria? She was like a mountain goat, sure-footed—"

"There wasn't any signs of what you'd call—we don't have a coroner's report in yet, of course, but it looked to us like she'd fallen off the edge, fetched up against some boulders. Pretty badly banged up. Seems to have happened a little after ten o'clock this morning. She was still warm when the deputy came across—"

"You ask around here, Sheriff, people will tell you she was surefooted as a mountain goat." Fitzhugh's eyes were fixed on the sheriff's, like lasers.

"Yes, sir."

"Surefooted."

The sheriff wondered if Fitzhugh had popped his cork. Maybe this Madero woman was more than just a member of the staff.

"Kinfolk?"

"Huh?

"She have next of kin? You give me the information, I'll notify 'em."

"She was from Mexico. My secretary—"

"I'll take care of it, Dr. Fitzhugh," said the sheriff, standing up. "I'll be wanting to ask some questions, of course, but they can wait awhile."

The secretary, ashen-faced at the news, supplied the sheriff with Vera Maria Madero's file and let him use her phone to call Lordsburg. He passed on the next-of-kin data and discovered that the coroner reported nothing inconsistent with a fall from the edge of the canyon—contusions, abrasions, broken bones, one puncture wound in the abdomen from which he had extracted a splinter, as if she had hit a branch, maybe a small tree, during the fall. No reason to think it was anything but accidental. Not the first person who had gotten too close to the edge in these canyon lands.

Sheriff Knott put down the receiver and went out into the anteroom, where he found the secretary, her shoulders hunched up, sobbing. He put a beefy hand on her shoulder and said, "This is a hard time. A hard time." The woman caught her breath and nodded silently. "It just doesn't seem fair, sometimes. What was it the feller said? Troubles don't come in as single spies, but in regiments. You know, I think Dr. Fitzhugh's taken this real rough. You got some coffee you could take him, or something?"

The woman nodded again and sniffed liquidly.

"One thing, ma'am, and I won't bother you anymore. You got a man named Bowdre here. Do you know where I could find him?"

Connie was sitting in the shade on the stoop outside their bedroom, humming a Hopi song about corn and butterflies. She was in jeans, Reeboks, and a red T-shirt Mo had bought for her. It said UP WITH DESERT RESEARCH and bore the likeness of a coatimundi, which Mo explained was a relative of the raccoon. Except for the one in the somewhat bedraggled zoo at the Ghost Ranch near Abiquiu, Connie had never seen a raccoon, and she had never heard of a coatimundi, but she thought it was cute.

A few minutes before, Mo had strode purposefully across the green to use the pay phone outside the cafeteria. Besides the twenty-odd little kids playing on jungle gyms under the eye of a couple of students down at the far end of the green, the center seemed utterly deserted. Mo was growing increasingly impatient—and discouraged. There still didn't seem to be any way to *plug in*, as he put it. He was calling his friend Tony Ramirez, in Santa Fe, to see if he had turned up anything interesting. She saw him turn the corner and head in her direction, black cowboy hat pulled down over his fore-head. That might be a good sign. At almost the same time she saw a cop emerge from the administrative offices—he wore a tan uniform, a large white cowboy hat, and a gun in a black holster perched on one of his wide hips. The cop—sheriff?—glanced at Mo, about fifty yards away from him, and began to walk in Connie's direction. She guessed it was a sheriff. He was a big man, not as tall as Mo, but heavyset and overweight, mainly in the stomach, which hung over the buckle of his belt. The two men were walking essentially along two sides of a triangle, getting nearer and nearer to one another as they got nearer to Connie. Occasionally the sheriff would glance over at Mo. Connie giggled to herself. The closer they got, the more often the sheriff snuck a glance at Mo, who, as usual, walked in measured strides with his dark glasses facing resolutely forward. Of course he was aware of someone else walking nearby, Connie knew, but he made no sign of it. With a last glance at Mo, now only ten yards away, the sheriff said, "Excuse me, ma'am, but I'm looking for a man named Bowdre. I'm Sheriff Jack Knott, Hidalgo County. You know where I can find him?"

"Hah—hah—hah. You want him dead? Or alive?"

The sheriff turned toward Mo. "You him?"

"Yep. Mo Bowdre. This is Connie Barnes."

"Glad to meet you, ma'am. Say—uh—"

"Mo," Mo said.

"Could I talk to you—it's about a police matter."

"Oh, I see what you mean. Well, Connie here, see, she's more than my better half. She's my eyes, and all."

"You're—"

"Blind as a mole. Anything I know, Connie knows."

Connie cleared her throat and smiled briefly at the sheriff. "You know a guy named Larry Collins?"

"Yes, indeed. Lying in the hospital trying to remember what happened to him."

"He said that you were his man in the center. You're on that smuggling—"

"We might want to have this conversation somewhere else, Sheriff."

"Yeah." He glanced around. "I suppose you're right. How about we meet at the saloon in Rodeo, say four o'clock? I've got some things I gotta do here. Another matter. We found one of the scientists, seems to have fallen into a canyon, Skeleton Canyon. Fatal."

"What?" Mo said. Connie looked up, wide-eyed.

"Terrible thing. A woman named Madero."

There was a low, rattling moan: Connie's head was in her hands. Mo stepped over toward her, and she got up and walked away, across the grass, still holding her head.

"It was her new friend, they hit it off right up front," Mo said.

"Shit," Sheriff Knott said. "These things are just goddamn awful. You think she'll—that meeting in Rodeo . . . ?"

"You know, maybe tomorrow would be better."

"Sure. Ten-thirty? At the saloon."

As the scientists drifted into the center from their fieldwork that afternoon, the news of Vera Maria Madero's death was greeted by almost everyone with an epithet, and silence. The normally talkative and gregarious scientists simply drifted off into private gloom. Melissa Jenkins's death—a murder and one that had been, in a sense, removed by the passage of time—had been shocking and mysterious, a matter to be discussed, to be thought through out loud, however depressing. Then, rapidly following that revelation, the disappearance of the bounty hunter had seemed mostly bizarre—suggesting that he was implicated in the murder, somehow making it all seem sordid as well as tragic. And still a cause for gossip. But this, a senseless accident, following on the heels of a murder—it was as if the gyroscope that kept this society from tumbling into free-fall had ceased spinning. People were stunned—like a third strike had been called—and went off into their own orbits of bewilderment and grief.

Many had come in early as the afternoon clouds threatened, and waited out the thundershowers in their rooms, assembling in the lounge only as dinnertime was at hand, saying little to one another throughout the meal.

It's like a big central spring has unwound, Mo Bowdre thought, sitting alone at a table, steadily chewing his way through a plate of pasta and meat sauce. Connie had returned to their room about twenty minutes after she had gone off across the green. She put a hand on Mo's shoulder and sighed. Then the Hopi sound signifying pain and trouble, so often repeated since ancient times: "Eeeeeeeee."

"Bad. Bad," Mo said, lost for words. "You want to eat?"

She sat down next to him on the bed. "No. I'll stay here. You go. I need to just—think."

So Mo ate alone, listening to the occasional murmur in the dining room. He heard Wheeler Fitzhugh bang on a glass and make an earnest attempt to be official and explain the circumstances of Vera Maria's accident, and listened to the muttered but somehow halfhearted expressions of sympathy for the director, and listened as the scientists subsided yet again into an astonished funk. Sated on pasta and the tasteless meat sauce, but thoroughly unsatisfied with himself and lightly cursing the ailing Larry Collins, Mo walked across the green to his room.

"I'm back," he said unnecessarily.

He sat down on the bed, put a hand out, and noted that Connie was lying on her back under the covers. "You know, once we've talked to that sheriff tomorrow, we can go," he said.

"Go?"

"Home. We're not accomplishing anything here ourselves. Leave it in professional hands."

"No, we've got to stay," Connie said.

"Huh?"

"That was no accident—Vera Maria."

Mo sat and waited.

"She wasn't the type to just fall off a cliff. She'd been in lots of tight spots, she was a—an outdoorswoman. She climbed mountains. Someone pushed her. It's part of the whole thing."

"But it could happen. An accident."

"No. Not to her. It's got to be part of the whole thing. That other woman."

Mo waited, but the woman said no more. Presently he heard the steady breaths of sleep. There was plenty more on her mind. And, he knew, he would learn what it was when Connie was ready. Not before.

Hopis, Mo thought, are weird.

Three hours after the sun had dropped below the Chiricahua Mountains to the west, Tuck Eddy, sweating profusely, returned to his mine and set his equipment down on the ground. He heaved and shifted a large rock, one of several he had artfully arranged to look like a natural rockslide, and which, he figured, obscured the mine entrance from all but the most penetrating examination. He moved two more and, gathering his gear, disappeared into the mine.

Inching his way down the pitch-dark shaft, he felt around for the flashlight in the back of his Jeep and, with its beam lighting the way, ducked at the dogleg turn and walked the rest of the way in a crouch. To the plastic box on a rocky ledge holding the Mojave rattlesnake caught the night before, he added two more boxes.

Just two of your garden-variety sidewinders, Tuck thought, but nice ones. He was beginning to feel like a family man again. He sat on the rocky floor and lit what was his last cigarette and said, "Well, boys and girls, ol' Tuck has a big decision here." He paused to exhale mightily. "Do I quit this bad habit, or do I break in the store in Rodeo?" He paused again. "You don't have an opinion on that?" Again he paused. "Hee, hee, guess I'll just try and lift some. Fetch you guys some mice on the way back."

Tuck finished his cigarette, ground it out on the floor, put the butt in his shirt pocket, and headed back into the night. He had to take care of his family, after all. He was a provider. A feeling of well-being suffused his very cells.

He was a man, a true man.

Had a little family to provide for.

And a purpose. A true purpose.

Whoever it was out here done that to Mel, well, that sumbitch was dead meat. Ol' Tuck, he'd be patient, find him.

Larry Collins couldn't believe it. Here he was in a hospital bed feeling woozy after—what was it now? Two days almost, with nothing more than a welt on his head, and he still couldn't remember what had happened. His mind strained to recollect those days. He had gone to Mexico. To pick up the trail of the agent. Melissa. Red-haired, call it auburn. Face gone. But her, sure as hell. Remembered the old Mexican gent at the border, Gutierrez, courtly old dinosaur. Then? Long road, heat, heat haze. Pink flowers cascading. Over a railing, wrought iron.

Collins's mind drifted. He was on a cement playground faced on three sides by the naked brick backs of buildings, windowless rear ends of tenements, turned away as if embarrassed to be seen in such a place. No nets, just rusty iron hoops, balls bouncing. Hey, honky. Hey, honky. Looking at the garbage spilled out of the Dumpster, balls flying. Hey, honky. Beautiful, clean, two points. Home. Home, now . . . Hey, what's this? *What's this?* All the blood. Hey, Mom? Dad? Get up. Stuff all fallen off the shelves, people standing around gawking. *Hey, didya call 911?* Shit. Sirens, always sirens, now they're coming here. To my dad's place. Hey, Dad, get up, will you? Mom? For Chrissake!

It was the old waking dream, intrusive. So now he was doing something about it. After the bad guys. Some bad guys. They're all the same. All responsible—an unknowing brotherhood over the aeons, all responsible—before and since—for his mother's body, holes in it, three holes in her breast, lying on the linoleum floor, and his father lying on the floor behind the counter, bleeding, a quizzical look on his face—like, why? Why's a fella like you doing this . . . ? The mouth open, a dark hole of concern, the little black one with the red coming out a few inches above, over his left eye. Saying *Why?*

So the college student changed course, chose the path of legal vengeance on the bad guys, any bad guy, got stiffed a couple of times for overzealousness—shit, he already knew from the streets how to give a guy a permanent limp without leaving a mark. Wound up in the desert, of all places, chasing other people's gods. Same thing. Our Father, who art in heaven, hallowed be . . . all it takes is two percent of the population to fuck up a perfectly good world. He wished he could remember what had happened in Mexico. All he could dredge up was a messy, run-down place and some pink flowers growing in profusion over a wrought-iron railing. Come on. Come *on*!

S i x

On a hand-painted sign outside its door, the Sidewinder Saloon in Rodeo boasted the longest stand-up bar in New Mexico, and Connie wondered who it had been who had gone around measuring all the contenders before proclaiming this one the longest. It was a relief to step inside out of the glare of midmorning, and it was indeed a long bar—almost fifty feet, she guessed, with three separate stations of beer on tap, and three separate arrays of bottles on shelves. On the wall above the bottles, running the entire length of the bar, was a row of muddy, amateurish oil paintings depicting desert scenes, cowboys on horseback, cowboys shooting at other cowboys, cowboys shooting at what appeared to be Mexicans, soldiers shooting at Indians, and, incongruously, a slightly overweight nude woman with greenish skin reclining awkwardly on some sort of sofa. Connie averted her eyes. There were what appeared to be hundreds of dollar bills pasted on the wall between the three arrays of bottles, and no bartender in sight. In addition to the bar itself, ten or so round tables were scattered around the room, and at one of these, near the wall at the right, Sheriff Knott sat reading a newspaper.

"This way, Mo," Connie said.

On the wall behind the sheriff was another nude, evidently the same model, sitting on a stool, looking at her knees with an expression of what seemed to be surprise. Connie looked around and saw at least four other unbecoming paintings of the same woman.

As she approached the table with Mo behind her, the sheriff looked up, smiled, heaved his bulk out of the chair, and said, "Morning. Thanks for coming. Have a seat."

Chairs scraped on the unfinished wooden floorboards and the three sat down, Connie taking a chair positioned so that she would not have to look at the woman on the stool every time she looked at the sheriff.

"Vern's running an errand. He'll be back soon. Get us some coffee, or whatever."

"Who's the—uh—artist?" Connie asked.

"Vern." He pointed over his shoulder with his thumb. "That's Vern's wife. She ran off about ten years ago with some guy passing through, selling Electroluxes or something like that. So Vern put these pictures he had done of her up on the walls. To get even. Makes for an interesting day-core. After a few years she came back, things hadn't worked out with the vacuum man, and she walked in here one afternoon looking to make up with Vern. Took one look at herself hangin' on every wall in the buff, guys at the bar all grinnin' and leerin' at her, and she took off again. Hasn't been seen since."

Mo chuckled, and the sheriff said, "The food here's as bad as the paintings. But it's a good place for a private meeting. Practically no one comes in here in the mornings, and Vern's hard of hearing. Too vain to wear his hearing aid."

A door at the far end of the bar swung open and a thin

man with straggly gray hair came around the bar and began to approach them.

"Coffee?" the sheriff asked.

"Both black," Connie said.

The sheriff held up three fingers, and Vern, smiling, turned and went back through the swinging door. "Well, Mister—uh—Mo, I made a few inquiries this morning. You're a sculptor, Santa Fe. Gonna do a statue for the center. Boy, that place sure has had a string of bad luck. Whoop, I don't mean you doin' the statue, of course. You went to UNM, wildlife biology or something like that, and then med school in Texas. You didn't last there very long, then kind of disappeared, till you turned up a sculptor. So none of that tells me how you're connected with that agent, Collins."

"Let me explain that to you, Sheriff," Mo said, and told him briefly about the previous summer, when he had wound up working with Collins and the Santa Fe PD on the recovery of some stolen Hopi gods, and how Collins had arranged to put Mo at the research center to sniff around about the smuggling of Aztec artworks.

As he finished, Vern showed up with three white crockery mugs of coffee and three spoons, all of which he set on the table with a single clatter, moving off to stand idly behind the bar.

"Well, that's pretty damn irregular, putting an amateur into a situation like this," the sheriff said.

"Two amateurs," said Connie.

"So what've you two amateurs sniffed out?"

"I'd have to say, just what you'd expect from amateurs," Mo said. "That is, nothing." Connie picked nervously at a fingernail. "Collins seemed to have some kind of bee in his bonnet, went off to Mexico. But now he doesn't remember what he was doing there, never mind if he found anything out. I reckon he was trying to pick up the track of that agent that got killed. By the way, I made some inquiries this morning too. Collins says we should cooperate with you."

"Did he tell you what makes the FBI think that the Aztec stuff has anything to do with the center?"

Mo sipped at his coffee. "Whew. Hot. He said they got some kind of tip. Wouldn't say what. Didn't mention any names—you know, suspects, people to look out for."

"He didn't mention Tuck Eddy?"

"Nope. You think . . . ?"

"Well, as soon as a deputy shows up, the man lights out. We got more than twenty men lookin' for him in this county, but he's probably over there." The sheriff gestured to the west with his head. "Some agents from the FBI are scouring the Chiricahuas, along with the Cochise County Sheriff's Department. And APBs and all that."

Mo leaned back in his chair. "So you think Eddy was doing the smuggling, the agent got onto it somehow, and Eddy killed her in Skeleton Canyon."

"That's the theory."

"Hard to imagine."

Sheriff Knott stiffened and scowled. "Why?"

"Well, as I understand it, the woman shacked up with him last summer, went back to graduate school—where is it? In Pennsylvania. Then shows up dead in Skeleton Canyon a week before she was scheduled to arrive at the center, and Collins seemed to think she had been in Mexico. When would she have gotten onto Tuck Eddy the smuggler, and how would he have known she was onto him? Maybe he just freaked out, snapped, when he heard she was dead."

The sheriff scowled into his coffee cup.

"Couldn't it have been *anyone* at the center?" Mo asked.

"I suppose so. Anyone who was actually there thirteen days ago when the woman was killed. The eighteenth. That leaves out a few people. I checked the center's log. Place looks like a damn commune, but they keep close track of what everyone's doing. Fitzhugh, he was in El Paso from fifteen to twelve days ago. Him and the bug doctor, Armand, and a guy named Freeman."

"Freeman's herps," Mo said.

"What?"

"Snakes. They're doing comparative studies here and in the mountains near El Paso. Anyone else ruled out?"

"Coupla students—they'd shipped 'em off to Tucson for some kind of supplies. But I think it ain't goin' to be students in this smuggling thing. Have to be a regular, guy comes each year."

"Well, that narrows the list considerably. Down to thirty-two."

"Thirty-one," Connie said.

"Oh, jeez," the sheriff said.

"Connie doesn't think that was an accident, by the way. She says that the Madero woman was too practiced an outdoorswoman to do something like falling off a cliff."

"Well, that's what a lot of people at the center told me too," the sheriff said. "When I told Fitzhugh about it, he kept saying she was surefooted as a mountain goat. But the coroner's report . . . He didn't find any sign of anything but a fall down a cliff, and neither did we. Searched around the rim. We did find some packed dirt, like it had come out of the tread of one a them running shoes like she was wearing. We'll check it out. But for now, it's an accident."

Connie fidgeted, picking at her fingernail again. "She and Fitzhugh were, you know, lovers," she said.

Sheriff Knott looked sharply at her and picked up his coffee mug. "I wondered about that. His reaction—"

"What do you mean?" Mo asked.

"You tell someone, like an employer, about an accidental

death, they—well, it was like he lost it there for a minute. Teary, repeated himself over and over—freaked out."

"Like Tuck Eddy, sort of?" Mo said.

"But Fitzhugh didn't light out," Sheriff Knott replied. He looked at his watch and grunted as he reached round into his back pocket and pulled out a thick wallet. "Gotta go. This has been real helpful. I got the coffee," he said. "And here's my card. Call me when you sniff out something else." He stood up. "You know, I suppose you're right about that snake man. But I'm going to have to keep all these boys marching around the damn landscape for a few more days. Can't call 'em off now when the feds are involved in the manhunt. Why, hell, they'd think Hidalgo County was see-cedin' from the damn Union." He put three one-dollar bills on the table.

Mo laughed.

"And sometimes I think that might be the right idea."

"Sheriff—" Mo said, sticking out a big hand.

"You should call me Jack," said the sheriff, shaking Mo's paw. "You were born here, New Mexico, right?"

"Lincoln County."

"I woulda sworn to it. Sounds like the Bowdres've gone straight after all these years."

"Well, see, Jack, we went and got ourselves redeemed."

Jeremy Armand sat in the passenger seat of his white Trooper while a graduate student filled it with gas from the unleaded pump. He was thinking about beetles when something odd penetrated his thoughts. There were two vehicles outside the saloon, one a sheriff's cruiser. It was a strange time of day for people to be at the saloon, even though Vern always opened it up at ten o'clock. People in Rodeo didn't drink in the morning, or at least didn't want to be seen doing so, and

Vern's food was terrible. So people generally stayed away until the sun was over the yardarm.

Armand saw the door open and Sheriff Jack Knott emerge, blinking in the glare. He put on a pair of mirrored sunglasses and stepped heavily off the wooden porch, got in his cruiser, and headed north up the highway like a low-slung predator. Armand studied the other vehicle, an old pickup truck. He recognized it as the sculptor's. Bowdre. That's odd, he thought. What would the sheriff have to do with Bowdre? Or vice versa? He had seen the sheriff around the center the day before, obviously in connection with Vera Maria's death. She had seemed to be getting chummy with the sculptor's companion, that Hopi woman. Maybe the sheriff was talking to her. One of the last people, probably, to talk to Vera Maria.

Or maybe it was simply a couple of redneck soul mates getting together to swap lies, but he doubted it.

The gastank flap slapped closed. The graduate student went inside to pay and returned, sliding into the driver's seat.

"Okay, we're off," she said.

Vern approached the table, carrying a coffeepot. "Refill?" he said. Connie nodded. He poured the coffee and wandered off with an amiable smile.

"You've been fidgeting around," Mo said.

"I've got a problem."

Mo waited, a big hand wrapped around his mug.

"Vera Maria. The night before she—died, she hired me."

"Hired you? What for?"

"For confidentiality."

"You'll be explaining this all in good time?" Mo asked.

"I told her I was a CPA and she asked me to hold something for her for a few days. An envelope. Like client confidentiality, you know?"

Mo sipped from his mug. "What's in it?"

"I don't know. It's sealed. It's real thin."

"You got it here?"

Connie reached in her handbag and pulled out the envelope. "Yes."

"Open it up."

"But—"

"Connie, the woman's dead. For all you know there's something in there that has some bearing on all this business. You could be withholding evidence."

"Mo—"

"C'mon. What else are you going to do with it?"

"Okay." She slit it open with her thumb and, with little more than the fingernails of her thumb and forefinger, pulled out a photograph. There was nothing else in the envelope, which fell to the table. She gasped.

"What, what?" Mo said.

"Mo, it's a photograph. Of a gold figure. Like an emperor or something. It's Aztec, Mo." She felt the exhausting surge of adrenaline, difficulty breathing.

"Can you describe it?"

Connie described the figure, the large head, the satisfied look, almost a smile, with regular teeth, the scepterlike thing in his hand. "It's got a real dark shadow of itself against these—well, they look like gray rocks. Like a flashbulb."

"What kind of picture is it?"

"What do you mean?"

"Is it a slide? A print?"

"It's a Polaroid, color."

"Well, you better just slip it back in the envelope. Give it to Jack Knott. If they got a junior-criminologist fingerprint kit in this county, they may be able to tell who took that picture. They'll probably think you did."

"I only touched the edge."

"Hey, we're getting good at this detective stuff."

"But why would she have this?" Connie said.

"We got to do some thinking about that. Meanwhile why don't you call the sheriff's office? See if they can radio Jack Knott and tell him to turn around."

Connie looked again at the photograph and idly turned it over. "Mo, there's a date on it. Someone wrote twenty-eight *junio* on the back. Isn't *junio* Spanish for June? It was a brown felt-tip pen."

"Two days ago."

Connie slipped the photograph back in the envelope, put it in her handbag, and stood up. "I'll call the sheriff's office."

"Mr. Collins, what are you doing?"

Collins hopped on one foot, his other leg tangled up in his jeans and a rush of nausea rising. He hopped again, managed to get his leg into the jeans, and turned. The little round nurse with blonde-gray hair and an astonishingly large nose for so small a person was standing in the doorway, half scowling, half smiling.

"I'm putting on my pants, Miz Furillo." He sat on the high hospital bed. Behind the white curtain, in the other bed, his roommate whose name he had never heard or bothered to find out was snoring gently. "Shhh. You'll wake up old Whosis. Next I'm going to put on these socks. Then my shirt. Then I'm going to go to the nearest florist and order a dozen yellow roses for you and all the other angels of mercy on this hall, and go back to work."

"Mr. Collins. The doctor hasn't—"

"He said when I remembered the days I blacked out about, I would be okay. I could go. So I remember them," he lied. "So I'm going."

"But the doctor is the one who—"

"Miz Furillo, I am a great big grown-up, employed by the

United States Justice Department as a special agent of the Federal Bureau of Investigation, and one of the things I happen to know is you can't incarcerate *me* in your hospital. I am well, I have my memory back, and those are the medical criteria that make it okay for me to go."

"Mr. Collins, can I tell you something?"

A black tunnel began to close in on him. He could see light at the end of it, light shining on the upper torso and face of Nurse Furillo.

"Yes, you may," he said, swallowing to keep from throwing up.

"You look very pale, Mr. Collins, and you put on your pants backward."

The narrowing light in the black tunnel shined on Nurse Furillo's exceptional nose for a moment, and as he said shit to himself it winked out.

"Wheeler? Is this you? It sounds like things are out of control down there."

It was the director of the Denver Museum, braying through the phone.

"What exactly is going on?"

Fitzhugh pictured the hatchet-faced man, scion of a Colorado mining fortune with a degree in paleontology from Yale. In his blue pin-striped suit. Probably with the harridan general counsel standing over him like one of the Furies. Scrawny woman with overlong legs, wizened prune.

"Things are under control, Prescott. Let me assure you of that. The sheriff and I had a long talk yesterday about our multiple tragedies here. Dr. Madero—a terrible thing—seems simply to have fallen to her death in some of the difficult terrain here. A truly tragic loss—to us all and to science. That fellow Eddy, who of course is not part of the staff here at the center, simply seems to have lost his mind and run off. It's not technically our problem, but of course we all know him and he's, well, part of the community. There's a manhunt in progress and the sheriff assures me that everything is being done. He's currently under suspicion in the Melissa Jenkins murder. They were—uh—close last summer. Her death is, of course, under federal investigation as well, and they simply do things their own way. Jeremy Armand has been helping, of course. Among other things, it's very good for community relations."

"Wheeler. I want to point out two things to you." Wheeler Fitzhugh stared at the ceiling.

"Yes, Prescott."

"Community relations may seem paramount to you, but neither they nor this kind of problem call forth the delight and confidence of the National Science Foundation, the House Committee on Science and Technology, our populist senator, Missus Geniviere Wilham, or Representative Olive Murphy. All of them have called me to inquire why they are reading in the newspapers in Washington, D.C., about two women scientists dying under mysterious circumstances. During, I might add, *your* watch."

Fitzhugh swallowed a gram or two of rising bile.

"Prescott, "he said. "We are doing very good science here. We have always—"

"The other thing I want to point out, Wheeler, besides the fact that all our allies are confused by events at the center, is that, in explaining them, you used the word *simply* three times. I do not believe they are simple, but nonetheless I want these matters resolved soon. And I expect more frequent reports. And no further surprises."

"Yes, sir, of course."

"And one other thing."

"Yes, sir."

"What is the museum's liability for the Mexican woman's accident?"

"Is this a concern of the general counsel?" Wheeler Fitzhugh asked.

"In fact, it is."

Insufferable bitch, Fitzhugh thought. "Tell her that Dr. Madero, like all the others here, signed the usual waiver. As that scrawny sourpuss knows, that's standard procedure here."

"Temper, temper, Wheeler."

"Prescott, we are dealing with a couple of tragedies here and—well, never mind."

"I know. It's very disturbing to us all. Call me tomorrow, or sooner if anything comes up. By the way, is that sculptor still there?"

"Yes, he is. Apparently he expects to be here another week."

"Oh. Well, take good care of him. This is a very significant donation, as you well know."

"Yes, sir." Fitzhugh hung up the phone, feeling gritty. One day, he thought, I won't have to put up with this kind of crap. The sooner, the better.

Ingrid Freeman stood in the shade, looking through binoculars at the pair of squirrels scampering, one after the other, in the branches of an Apache pine tree.

"Isn't a bit late for that kind of behavior?" asked the young graduate student who was standing near Ingrid, jotting down notes as she called out terse phrases describing the squirrels' activities.

"Yeah. It seems almost—hold it. They're copulating. No, it's a mock copulation. A dominance thing."

The graduate student made a note and looked hungrily at his mentor. The stories about her appetites were legion and much dwelled on by the students, as were the grand mammaries now putting a titanic strain on the buttons of her blue workshirt. Zoology's Dolly Parton, he thought.

"I wish I was doing that," he said.

Ingrid lowered her binoculars and took the graduate student's measure, as if seeing him for the first time. His face turned red. She put a hand on his arm and smiled. "That's fine with me, Tommy." He smiled back. "All you got to do is find yourself a female squirrel."

The student's face turned nearly puce, and Ingrid resumed her vigil with the binoculars. The squirrels leaped into a huge mountain mahogany, which reminded her of Vera Maria. She had been looking for them at higher elevations, to see if they might be an indicator species, their range changing with small changes in the climate. Some unframed question, a blurry sense that something was wrong, had been nagging at her like a chigger bite since last night when she had gotten over the first shock. It struck her now. What had Vera Maria been doing near Skeleton Canyon, which was hundreds of feet below the upper range of the birch-leaf mountain mahogany? Relieved to have found the question, but unwilling for the moment to think of its implications, she lowered her glasses and turned to the young student, who, she could tell, was squirming inside with humiliation.

Looking through the binoculars again, she said, "There's an old song, Tommy. It goes like this." And in a fair imitation of Linda Ronstadt, she sang, "I'm not saying that you're not pretty." She laughed and said, "In fact, you're cuter than hell. It's just you guys have seriously exaggerated my reputation. Don't take it personally."

Sheriff Jack Knott stared down at the square photograph of the contented-looking gold emperor lying in the middle of his desk. "Looks like he just had a nice meal of fresh virgins, don't it?" He continued to stare down at the photograph. "And you say this Madero woman gave you this to hold for her in confidence the night before she died?"

"That's right," Connie said.

"And you didn't know what it was?"

"The envelope was sealed. I only opened it an hour ago. At the saloon. After you left."

Connie had called the sheriff's office from the saloon in Rodeo and had been told that Jack Knott was unable to put off an appointment he had in Lordsburg, so they had followed after him and waited in the lobby till his meeting was over.

Now, using a pair of tweezers with a delicacy that was startling in a man with such large and clumsy-looking hands, he turned it over. "And there's the date on it." He slipped it into a plastic bag and buzzed his intercom.

"Yes, sir?"

"Come in here, Marlene. I got something here for Forensics to dust."

"You mean Eddie?"

"Just come and get this."

The sheriff sat silently behind his desk, his lips pursed, thinking. He looked at Mo Bowdre, sitting erect in a chair in front of his desk. Couldn't tell if the man was asleep or what—still as a rock, and just as expressionless. The Hopi woman was sitting motionless in her chair, a distant look in her eyes. The woman deputy, Marlene, came into the office and the sheriff nodded toward the plastic envelope, which she picked up and carried out of the room between her thumb and forefinger as if it were something unclean, like a urine specimen.

"Well, it sure looks like you found your smuggler, doesn't it?" the sheriff said.

Mo stirred. "It sure looks that way, Jack."

"Then why did they kill her?" Connie asked.

The sheriff cleared his throat. "Well, see, ma'am, it isn't—I mean, it looks like she fell off the cliff. An accident. I know you think elseways. But maybe this is all taken care of now. That agent, Melissa Jenkins, was onto her, she killed Jenkins, then shows up a few days later at the center with this here object she's gonna slip on to someone else, and by accident falls off a cliff and kills herself."

"It'd be nice that way," Mo said, "but there isn't a shred of evidence to make that believable. I mean, would you tell Collins that the thing is solved now?"

"We got that photograph."

"Why would she take a picture of the thing? If she was simply moving it along through some channel, why would she want a picture of it? Do I smell coffee?"

The sheriff stood up. "Yeah, let me get you some. Black." He poured the last inch of by now viscous liquid into a mug and set it on the desk near Mo's hand. "You could stand a spoon in that stuff. Been here since this morning," he said. "Well, here's another question. Why would she write a date on it? Maybe that was the date she was supposed to pass it along to whoever, wherever." He sat down heavily in his chair.

"Think about it, Jack. If you had an appointment to pass on something like this, probably worth a million dollars or more, would you have to write down the date? Chances are you'd be able to remember it in your head. That damn photograph just doesn't make any sense."

"Except maybe," the sheriff said, "as a sales device. You know, proof that she had the thing in hand. Somethin' like that."

"Then why entrust it to Connie? What was that all about?"

The sheriff grinned and looked at Connie. "You in the

smugglin' bidness, ma'am? Heh, heh. No offense. Forgive me for bein'—uh—a little lighthearted here." The woman's expression reminded the sheriff of an ancient mountain, beyond the scale of human follies, unreachable. Thick black eyebrows, almost touching, not in a scowl but in a permanent state of assessment, the way some people look at other creatures on the earth that have more than four legs. Eyes nearly black, unfathomable as a lake of oil. Seeing for two, of course.

Damnedest pair of people he'd ever met, just sitting there like a couple of—aliens? Relentless. He'd read about the Hopi, supposed to mean the peaceful people. Maybe what they meant was implacable people. Knew they were right and everybody else who saw things different were wrong. As for the Lincoln County sculptor boy, well, he could make a show of being less intense. But he was another ton and a half of damn grindstone.

"You studied biology," the sheriff said. "How do these people think?"

Mo shifted in his seat and said, "Hah—hah—hah. What do you mean?"

"Why would that woman have written a date down on the photograph?"

"They're trained to keep records, notes. Dates, circumstances. They spot something, they make a note of it. Write down everything. A lot of science is boring. Just making notes of a whole lot of things. Then you add up your notes, see if you've got a pattern." Mo took a sip of his coffee. "My God. That's absolutely—Jack, you ought to patent this stuff."

"What're you saying? About the notes?"

"Don't know that I'm saying anything. Except that you're dealing with methodical people. If they aren't methodical, they don't get published. They don't get published, they don't eat. It's a habit of mind. But none of this, the photograph, the date, makes any sense. At least not to me."

Sheriff Knott stood up and put his hands on his desk. "Well," he said, "I got something here doesn't make much sense to me. Maybe it will to you, being trained the way you was. It's what I guess you'd say is her last words."

Christmas lights. Strings of Christmas lights. The image of houses lined with Christmas lights, the eaves, the gables, all strung with Christmas lights. A street more like a suburb than the city. Everyone on the street put lights on their houses, like some kind of competition. They used to pass it on the way to his grandmother's place in Westchester County. Why am I thinking of that? Larry Collins wondered. He closed his eyes and tried to stare at the image of the street.

Purple.

Purple lights. A house lined with purple lights. No, not Christmas-tree lights. Neon tubing. Purple. Outlining the house. Inside the wrought-iron fence with the pink flowers. A long one-story house made of brown bricks, adobe, with archways, the whole place outlined in purple neon light. How to make a nice place ugly.

"That's what I thought," Collins said out loud. He sat up in the hospital bed. *That's what I thought when I saw the house.* It's coming back. I was there.

Beyond the curtain the old man snuffled and groaned in his sleep, and the agent lay down again. *Hacienda.* Some neon sign, blinking. Someone's hacienda. Whose? I was there.

Some old woman. He could almost see her, but she faded and the purple neon blinked stupidly and disappeared.

Shit.

But it's coming. It's coming.

•   •   •

"I'd like a dark beer," Mo said. "Whatever you got. The lady wants iced tea." He heard Vern amble away. They had returned to the Sidewinder Saloon in Rodeo to examine the field notebook. There were a few locals sitting at the bar exchanging stupidities, which Mo monitored desultorily with part of his brain while Connie read the strange foreshortened words and numbers out of the notebook.

"Does that make any sense to you?" she asked.

"Not a damn bit of it," Mo said. "Except those numbers. Maybe they're coordinates."

"Coordinates?"

"Yeah, map coordinates. Show where she was when she was doing whatever the hell it was she was doing."

"How do you know that?"

"What?"

"Where you are on a map."

"They got little machines, read off of satellites. They can tell you within a foot or two where you are on the map, how high, all that. I forget what they call those things. Maybe she had one. Maybe she just used a topographical map. That's probably it. Anyway, we should check it out."

"What about the rest of this stuff."

"It's gibberish to me," Mo said. "Maybe we can get one of the people at the center to translate it."

"Who?"

"Well, now, that's a good question. You know, according to those boys over there at the bar, the betting money is that the snake man is over in the Chiricahua Mountains. These guys got a fixation on Geronimo. Their grandfathers surely hated Geronimo because he killed a lot of white people. But these guys think he was a great man, fooling the feds and all for so long. If old Geronimo showed up today, they'd probably make him mayor of Rodeo, have a nice little xenophobic parade. How times do change."

Vern approached, set down the glasses, and wandered off.

"Mo, this is serious."

"Yes, it is."

"Then how come you're listening to those people and not thinking?"

The door of the saloon opened and they both heard Vern's reedy voice say, "Well, here's old Ned. Down from his tree house. Who's lookin' out for confragations?"

There was a murmur and Vern said, "What?"

"Goddamn it, Vern, if you wanta have a conversation, then put in your goddamn hearin' aid."

"Just trying to be sociable."

"Fire season's just about over," the man called Ned said in a loud voice. "All these thunderstorms wettin' down the place. What d'you boys hear about that crazy-assed snake man? Killed his own girlfriend, is what I hear."

"That's what the sheriff thinks, all those boys out there lookin' for him."

"You know, that snake man, he took up lookin' for the Skeleton Canyon treasure."

Loud guffaws.

"Yeah, he did. I saw him pokin' around in Skeleton Canyon the other day, diggin' holes. Crazy bastard."

"You see just about everything up there, don't you, Ned?"

"Eyes of a damn eagle."

Mo leaned toward Connie and whispered, "You hear all that? See? You just got to get in the rhythm of things."

Connie had no idea what he was talking about.

"Tell me those numbers again," Mo said. "The ones from her notebook."

"Those coordinates?"

"Them," Mo said, and committed them to memory.

•   •   •

"God*damn* it!" said the director of the Federal Bureau of Investigation. He slammed down the phone. "How the hell did we get into this?"

The two men seated before him began to sweat under their white shirts.

"Well?" the director insisted.

The older, and senior, agent shifted in his chair. "Well, sir, it seems that they put this man Collins onto a smuggling thing, pre-Columbian stuff from Mexico—and he's always been sort of a—"

"How many times," the director said, "do I have to tell you what I think of these free-lancers." He glanced down at the file on his desk. "This man has been disciplined twice for running off on his own. Goddamn it. He should have had a clone on this thing. A *clone.* Now he's got amnesia and no one in the entire Bureau knows what he's doing. And we've got a dead agent. God*damn* it, the man's a loose cannon."

"Sir, the people in Douglas are looking into the murder of the agent. And the budgetary constraints suggested that—"

"Wonderful. Wonderful." The director put his hands one on top of the other on his spacious and shiny desk. "Let me tell you, let me tell you *one thing.* The next time I don't want the budget to override procedure. Either we do it right or we don't get involved. You hear? And I want this man Collins under control. Or retired. Once he wakes up, that is. I want to know what the hell he knows, what he's doing, all that. Got it? Now get out of here."

Once in the hallway outside the director's office suite, the younger agent said, "That was two things he told us."

"Smart-asses," the senior agent observed, "wind up in places like Douglas, Arizona."

· · ·

Mo hated this. He knew that Ingrid-who-is-mammals had thrust her distinguishing characteristics at him in a most flagrant way. And he knew Connie knew that. He also knew what no one else knew, which was that for the most fleeting instant he had been, if not tempted, at least titillated. Reconsidering, he decided that the chances were that Connie knew he had been titillated.

Literally.

It occurred to him that it might be fun to have someone look up the word in the dictionary, see where it came from. Had to be from guys having strange women bump their tits against you. I mean, he thought, women have got to know what they're doing with their tits and if they bump them up against you . . . well, the hell with that.

Mo felt guilty for having faithless thoughts, however fleeting. He was wedded in soul to this alto-voiced Hopi woman who let him see the world's color and light through her simple existence at his side, the lilt of her voice, the perfume of her body, the aura of warmth that he could sense when she was five feet away. He felt no wanderlust, no unfulfilled need. Still, he said to himself, the reprobate, tits are tits, and immediately felt guilty again for the eternal, evolutionary nature of the human male.

"Two things," he said as he and Connie walked across the green to the dining hall. "The first is that I love you more than the sun or the sky. Now you don't have to respond to that because it's against your tribal wisdom to say anything so fatuously outspoken about the emotional side of life."

"I told you once that I loved you."

"Yeah, on a tape recorder. But I'll take what I can get—hah—hah."

"So what's the other thing?"

"What other thing?"

"That you want to tell me."

"Oh. Yeah. Well, I want to talk to that Ingrid Freeman woman again. Do you suppose you could guide me to her?"

"The one who's in heat?"

Mo stopped in his tracks. "Now, Connie, damn it, I told you I love you, and I mean that. You alone. Alone in the whole damn world. But this is an investigation, it's serious, and I got to check something out and that woman can help. So now, damn it, don't you be throwing some guilt trip on me like you Hopi women do."

Connie took his hand. "I think," she said, "all women do that. We watch you boys real carefully."

"Not just Hopi women?" Mo asked.

"Every woman."

"There is no redemption," Mo said. "I hear thunder. The afternoon storm is late today."

Tuck Eddy squatted in the mine shaft, impatiently watching the sky finally darken. He could hear the thunder building up in the west. Through a space in the rocks he had piled up at the entrance he could see about thirty feet of the other side of the canyon where, under an overhanging ledge, there was an abandoned eagle's nest, and white droppings on the rock below. Tuck had spotted the nest earlier that spring when he was out looking for snakes, a working nest, golden eagles, two eaglets, which meant one thing: practically nobody ever came here. A perfect place to go to ground, what with the long-abandoned mine shaft across the way, and in his mad passion to flee, it had come to him in some feral connection of neurons. Now the two white-headed eaglets had grown up and fledged, soaring around the mountains somewhere. Tuck was envious. He was getting tired of the nocturnal life. The thunder was moving closer, the sun gone. His mind drifted back to the silver. The silver bar he had found. First one and then the others. In all, eleven.

Goddamn it if he hadn't found the treasure of Skeleton Canyon.

At least, about a third of it.

He had been sitting in the back of the mine shaft, leaning against the rocky wall, absently scrabbling at the loose rock with his hand, waiting for the day to pass. Something sharp nicked his finger and he stuck it in his mouth, tasting blood. Oh shit, he had thought. Better find out what the hell that was. Some venomous critter maybe. In a matter of minutes he had unearthed a silver bar, about nine inches long, and his crazed mind had taken off like a rocket as he knelt before the wall, holding the heavy bar in his hand.

For a moment he thought about praying. But he didn't know which god to pray to.

Mammon, goddamn it. Mammon.

Oh, yes, Mammon, you good ol' sumbitch, lookin' out for the righteous, the workin'man, us salt-of-the-earth people . . . Oh, yes.

He dug. Ten more bars emerged, each adding to the elation of Tuck Eddy, who continued his anthems to Mammon, patron of the loyal and patient . . . the crazy. He hadn't been at all disappointed when the rock wall yielded no more silver bars. Eleven. More than enough, he thought, especially for someone who was probably going to get killed in this cave. He carefully stowed the bars back in the wall and covered them with loose dirt. What fun he could have had with all this silver and with old Mel, go to Rio, go to the frigging Maldives, buy a damn island. . . . Well. He wasn't done out here yet.

He crawled up to the entrance of the mine and waited for the end of the day, wondering if those old outlaws had seen an eagle's nest over yonder on the wall and had thought— same as him—that people probably didn't come here that much.

Then he heard them.

"There!" said a voice, and Tuck froze, staring wide-eyed from his lair. Oh shit, he thought. Oh shit. Ol' Tuck's a goner.

"We can get up under there," the voice said.

Not here, please, God, not here, Jesus.

Lights flashed outside in the canyon and thunder boomed instantly, clattering among the rocks.

"Christ, that was close!" shouted another voice. "Let's go." Tuck stopped holding his breath when he saw two men scramble up onto the ledge where the eagle's nest was. One, a fat guy, was wearing a sheriff's uniform. The other, stringy and young looking, had the unmistakable stamp of cowboy. Bowlegged. No ass whatever. It began to rain, softly at first, then in a torrent. Greenish light flashed, crackled, the skies snarled and exploded, and through the gray rain Tuck could make out the two men sitting with their knees pulled up against their chests, motionless. Looking across the canyon.

Right at him.

He didn't have a prayer. His knees were killing him, but he couldn't move. His nose itched, but he couldn't scratch it. He waited out the storm immobilized like a fawn, adrenaline coursing through the veins of otherwise inert prey.

The light show moved east and the rain turned to a drizzle. He watched the two men clamber down off the ledge and out of his line of sight. He remained still, breathing through his mouth.

"Let's get out of here," a voice said, and Tuck Eddy let out a long breath, fell backward to a sitting position, and stretched out his legs. Whoooo-ee, he said to himself. He'd be still another while before he went on the prowl.

"Ah, Ingrid. You promised me a refresher course on that model. Could I take you up on it?"

"Sure," she said, but with a trace of hesitation.

"Have you been introduced? Oh, yeah, you two met after the fire alarm." Mo felt the woman take his elbow and was resigned. He knew his way through all the furniture to the table with the three-dimensional map, having done it once before. "Does this model have coordinates on it?" he asked. "You know, like a topo map."

"Yes, it does," Ingrid said. At the table Mo reached out and put his hand on the model. Then, with his forefinger, he touched the place where the research center was represented by tiny little houses.

"We are here," Mo said.

"That's amazing."

Mo beamed. He gave out the coordinates he had memorized and said, "Take me there, would you?"

"Let's see," she said. "That would be"—she lifted his hand and put it down on some high ground—"right about there."

"Just north and east of this canyon here, let's see, which one is it? We aren't up to Skeleton Canyon yet, are we?"

"That's Salt Canyon. The next one to the north is Skeleton Canyon. That's amazing."

Mo beamed again. "And so," he said, running his finger up the canyon back to the high ground, "this is the place."

"What place?" Ingrid asked nonchalantly, but Mo could hear the tinge of suspicion beneath it.

"The place where those coordinates meet," Mo said.

"Yes, but—well, what about it?"

"Oh. Hah—hah—hah. It's a bit embarrassing here in this scientifically minded company. But, well, you see, I'm an artist. Artists do weird things, like go to—well, gurus, mediums, you know? And I went to one before we came down here, a nice old lady in Espanola, Hispanic, a *curandera* as well as a medium."

Mo heard Connie's mouth open.

"And she went into her trance," Mo went on, "and mumbled those numbers. I didn't have the faintest idea what she was talking about. Hah—hah—hah. But then, the other night, when you were showing me this model, I felt something—well, it's hard to explain—like electricity."

"Like that's your power place?" Ingrid said.

"Hah—hah—hah."

Connie stood with her hands on her hips and a smile on her face in their cramped little bedroom.

"Okay. What was all that?"

"What?"

"All that stuff, mediums, gurus." She laughed. "You should have seen the look on that woman's face when you started in on all that."

"Oh, did she shrink away in revulsion from the paranormal?"

"No, she looked up at *you* like some kind of guru." Connie giggled.

"Omigod. A fruitloop has infiltrated the bastions of reason. We're all doomed." Mo unbuttoned his shirt. "You know, this is all beginning to make some sense."

"Not to me," Connie said, and waited for the big man to go on, but he was silent, saying nothing more except, as he switched off the light, "You're my guru. You know that." And in seconds he was asleep.

Seven

"Say, there, *Doctor*, what's with the Mexican?" said the voice on the phone.

"I told you not to use any referent in these calls."

"Well, yeah, you did. You also told me to keep my hands off that Mexican. So?"

"She fell."

"Now, that's got to be bullshit."

"It's what the coroner's report says."

"That's got to be bullshit too."

"Nothing has changed. That's all you've got to know. Now, what about the snake man?"

"I ain't seen him."

"Keep looking. I don't want him around out there. We've got only a day or two."

"That soon."

"Yeah, that soon."

"And then . . . ?"

"Then it's a new route. This one is tainted."

•   ·   •

Connie woke up with a start. She had fallen asleep the night before with the photograph of the Aztec emperor in her mind, the grinning visage, drooped eyelids that gave him a mild and contented look. Like he had eaten some virgins, the sheriff had said.

Next to her, Mo Bowdre slept on his back. He too had a contented look on his face. Things were beginning to make sense, he had said. He was beginning to weave a tale in his head, as methodically as her uncles had woven her white cotton wedding robe years ago, and then the accompanying shroud that she would be wrapped in when she died and went off to be a cloud. She didn't want to think about that now, or about the husband who'd gone off to Winslow and got himself killed on the highway.

She thought about Mo, concocting a story that began with an insight as flimsy and as unknowable to other people as something peculiar he had smelled or heard or touched. She knew it was no use asking him. He would explain in good time. He's like us Hopis that way, she thought. A storyteller, not to be rushed.

But she also knew something, part of the story, that he couldn't know. She woke up knowing it. And she would tell him. In good time. She wished he'd wake up.

Ingrid Freeman sat at the table with her husband and one of his students. They were recounting the macho moments when they trapped a yardful of Tuck Eddy's rattlesnakes, but she wasn't listening. She sat hunched over, her hands wrapped around a warm cup of coffee, fretting. Ingrid had a devious mind, one therefore given to suspicion about others, and she didn't know to whom she should go with her insight that Vera Maria had not died accidentally by falling into Skeleton Canyon. The edge of the canyon was several hundred feet below the upper limits of the birch-leaf mountain mahogany. So that is one place she would not have been working. And if she hadn't fallen, then she had to have been dumped into the canyon. Ingrid wondered how to find out where Vera Maria had actually been working that day. The other woman, Mel. Had she been dumped too? If two women were murdered, both from the center, then they had to be connected. But how? It was too bizarre. But something awful was going on here at the center. And that was as far as Ingrid's mind—well attuned to the machinations of sexual intrigue—could take her into the depressing but somehow exciting corridors of crime.

She looked up as Mo Bowdre and his Hopi woman crossed the room, carrying trays. He had that silly black hat on, too small, and a leather vest as big as a sail, over a blue workshirt. The woman, she noticed, was wearing a white blouse and gray slacks like she was in a city. Ingrid was amazed at how easily he made his way, taking deliberate steps between the tables, keeping pace with the Indian like some fluid mechanical mountain. He looked so completely— what? Reliable. Maybe tell him. But why tell *him*? What has he got to do with it? A blind sculptor from Santa Fe. She watched him sit down.

God, what a hunk, she thought to herself. Too bad he's got that Hopi duenna.

Mo pulled his chair in underneath him and said, "You're all fidgety this morning, woman."

"I know part of your story, Mo."

"My story?"

"The one you're making up."

"Now just what are you accusing me of?"

"You said things are beginning to make sense," Connie said, and had a bite of blue corn pancakes.

"Oh. That story. Pass the maple syrup, would you? I'm going to give these pancakes another chance."

"You've got two stacks of them," she said, putting the glass syrup pitcher next to his hand.

"That's what I call giving 'em a chance."

"I know when that picture was taken," Connie said. Mo chewed.

"These things aren't all *that* bad," he said. "When?"

"Two nights ago. When the false alarm went off."

"In fact, these things are damn good," Mo said. "How do you know that?"

"Stop talking about food, Mo. This is important. Just eat and listen. When that siren went off, I looked out the window and I thought for a minute that I saw the fire."

"But there was no fire. It was a squirrel set off the alarm. That's what they said."

"An Apache fox squirrel," Connie said. "Well, how do you say? There was a fox squirrel in the chicken yard. I saw a flash. Everyone was coming out of the dining hall and the siren was still going and there was a flash. I thought maybe it was fire, but then . . . don't squinch up your mouth like that, Mo. I know what you're going to ask. The picture was made with a flash. Real dark shadow behind that emperor."

"But—"

"The shadow was on the stones."

"Stones?"

"The background. The stones were a funny kind of gray. Like a bluish gray. Like the stones the lodge building is made of. But most of the rock that I've seen around here is real reddish. So someone set off the alarm, took the picture while everyone was running out, and then turned it off."

Mo beamed. "Which means only one thing. Wheeler Fitzhugh. Fitzhugh was talking about the death of that agent, a report to the staff, and then he apparently left. And then he was also the one who came out and reported the false alarm. Our director, he of the heroic five inches, is photographing Aztec art. Interesting hobby." Mo took another large bite of blue corn pancakes, chewed, and swallowed. "Could you make these?"

"Mo—"

"Is he in here? Fitzhugh?"

"He just sat down."

"Okay. When we're done, take me over to him so I can tell him we're leaving."

Sheriff Jack Knott hunched over his old wooden desk, a mug of coffee in one hand and the phone receiver in the other.

"Well, look here," he said, his face going red. "We've had this manhunt on for three days now, and I swear to God we've been in every damn nook and cranny of the Peloncillos, and that snake man is nowhere to be found, not a sign of 'im . . . Some o' these boys can track a goddamn lizard in a hay-field . . . Damn right. I don't think that boy'd hole up over here anyway. Chiricahuas much more likely . . . And we been able to conclude over here in the sheriff's department that the snake man is not a prime suspect in the death of your agent . . . Well, is Collins up an' around? Well, that just leaves us in shit, don't it? Don't you boys ever talk to each other? . . . What I'm saying is that I don't see any point in keepin' this manhunt goin' for another damn day. . . ."

Sheriff Knott's face grew redder as he listened. "All right," he said, and hung up the phone. "Shit," he said, looking across the room where Deputy Sheriff Jimmy Snyder stood. "Smug bastards, those FBI. They insist the manhunt continue at least through today. They *insist*," he added in a prissy imitation.

• • •

Wheeler Fitzhugh sat alone at a table eating oatbran cereal, which he detested. The scientists, out of respect for his obvious grief, gave his table a wide berth, and that was fine with him this morning. He didn't want to talk to anyone. He had awakened before dawn with an erection and reached out for Vera Maria's body before all the events of the past two days cascaded into his mind, and he had first panicked, then grown furious, and now, spooning the tasteless dry meal into his mouth, he was feeling profoundly sorry for himself. And, to make matters all the drearier, now that windbag of an artist was headed for him, a big self-satisfied grin on his bearded face. For the benefit of the Indian woman at Bowdre's side, he forced a smile and said, "Good morning."

"Mornin'," Bowdre said. "We want to thank you for your hospitality these seven days."

Fitzhugh's heart skipped a beat.

"I figure it's time for us to go. I mean you folks've got plenty of trouble without the likes of me hanging around, gettin' in the way."

"You're—"

Bowdre put his big hands into his back pockets and rolled back on his boot heels, then forward. "Yeah, I think I've got it all figured out now."

"What?" Fitzhugh said. He felt the slight adrenaline rush subside as he waited for the man to answer. The smile behind the blond beard widened. Even the man's teeth were huge, like an enormous herbivore.

"Well—hah—hah. I believe I've got me the idea I came here for. The sculpture." Fitzhugh felt the tension vanish from the back of his neck and his shoulders. He smiled.

"And may I . . . ?"

"I like to keep these things to myself until the unveiling. But there's one thing you could tell me that would be real helpful. I want to kinda tie it into the local environment. You know this gray stone this here building is made of? I'd like to get some more for part of the sculpture—sort of a base, you know? Is it local?"

Wheeler sat back and pushed his bowl of oatbran away from him. I'm just not going to eat any more of that crap ever again, he said to himself. "No, not really. It came from a quarry over on the other side of the Chiricahua Mountains. It's a gray rheolite. Nothing like it nearby. I think the quarry is still open. Shall I . . . ?"

"No, no, don't bother yourself. I'll get after you when the time comes. Anyway, Connie and me, we just wanted to say goodbye for now, and thanks."

Fitzhugh stood up and managed another thin smile. "It's been a pleasure. I'm sorry that you were here under such trying circumstances. It's all very sad."

"Yes, it is," said Bowdre. "Well, we'll be on our way. Say goodbye to the others for us. We'll just fold up and slip off like the Arabs." Fitzhugh shook the enormous paw in front of him, and bowed slightly to the Indian woman. The two aliens turned and walked off, and Fitzhugh was suffused with relief. One less thread to think about in what looked like a raveling sleeve.

Dr. Arthur Ramos heard his name over the hospital's sound system and went to the nearest nurses' station. A pretty dark-haired nurse—new—smiled up at him. "Phone's for me," Ramos said, and the nurse held the receiver out. "Punch two-three, please. This is Dr. Ramos."

"And you're the attending physician for Special Agent Larry Collins?"

"Yes, I am. Who is this?"

"This is Special Agent Bowdre. I'm calling about Collins. Has he regained his memory yet?"

"He says it glimmers in and out."

"What's that mean?"

"I beg your pardon."

"What's that mean, glimmering in and out? Does he remember anything about his trip to Mexico?"

"Just snatches."

"Snatches."

"A building. With neon lights. An old woman. Things like that."

"So he'll be staying with you for a while?"

"Another day at the minimum. Probably longer. It was a very severe concussion."

"Thank you, Dr. Ramos."

Ramos handed the phone back to the nurse and smiled. "Thank you," he said, and heard his name called again. He frowned, and walked down the corridor to the waiting room. An old couple sat hunched on a small sofa in the corner, looking miserable. Near the window stood a tall man whom Ramos recognized as the expressionless FBI agent with whom he had discussed Collins's CAT scan the other day.

"Dr. Ramos," he said. "Can you give me a report on Collins?"

"Yes, of course, but this is very strange."

"Strange, sir?"

"One of your people just called and asked about Collins."

"One of *our* people?"

"Yes. I think he said his name was Bowden. No, Bowdre. Special Agent Bowdre."

The agent looked perplexed. "I don't get it," he said. "I don't know of any Bowdre."

Dr. Ramos shrugged inwardly, thinking how strange these FBI people are.

Mo Bowdre took the now familiar path across the green to his room.

"Special agent?" said Connie, walking beside him.

"Hah—hah."

"Isn't there some law about impersonating an officer?"

"Well," Mo said, "I didn't say special agent of what. Anyway, I *am* kind of a special agent. But Collins hasn't got his brains back yet. So he won't be any use to us." They walked on in silence.

"You will start telling me what's going on soon, right?"

"Yeah. Let's pack up and get out of here. I got to make some phone calls and that public phone is too public. I'll tell you what I'm thinking on the way."

"The way where?"

"Maybe we'll go camping for a night or two."

"This better be good," Connie said, thinking that it wouldn't be.

It didn't fit. No way the damn little squiggle fit. Not in the woman's Reeboks. And not in Tuck Eddy's boots. It meant that someone else had been up on that ledge over Skeleton Canyon. And that someone was not Tuck Eddy. It was, Sherriff Knott thought, either someone who had happened to be walking through there that morning before the woman fell, or someone who had pushed her. But it was not Tuck Eddy. Goddamn snake man just lost his gyro and went feral somewhere. But probably not in the Peloncillos. Stupid damn manhunt, out looking for a nut but not a criminal nut. Stupid damn FBI. He looked up at Jimmy Snyder.

"You're right, Depitty."

"So now what?"

"You got to get your ass out on this half-wit manhunt. Daniel here?"

"Yeah. He's waitin' outside. Doesn't like to come in this kind of place. Say, Sheriff, I had an idea."

"Congratulations."

"This don't mean she was pushed, but it means she might've been, right?"

"Right."

"And not all that far from where Daniel found that other woman, the agent, in the cave."

Sheriff Knott looked at his deputy. "Those prints," he said. "Get me those photographs from the cave, will you? Did we ever get a report from the FBI on what kinda shoes they were?"

"I didn't see it," Deputy Snyder said.

"Call 'em on the phone. Find out what's holding 'em up. Tell those smug forensic fags to get in gear."

"What about the manhunt?"

"You're relieved for the day. Tell Daniel he can go home. Tell him we'll pay him for the day anyway. Charge it to the damn feds." Sheriff Knott smiled with pleasure.

The phone rang and the sheriff picked it up. "Sheriff Knott." He listened and said, "Sure. Come on over. We don't have anything to do here today."

He hung up. "That fella Bowdre I told you about? He says *he's* got an idea too. Whole place is just full of ideas today. Now go get me those photographs." The deputy left and Sheriff Knott leaned back in his chair. Progress. Get this damn manhunt called off, get a lead on all this killing, solve the whole mess and . . . the image of Linda's aging but still round fanny, packed in her tight jeans, came happily to mind.

Route 80 stretched before them, straight as a rod, disappearing in a shimmering heat haze miles ahead to the north. On the right the Peloncillos rose up, almost feminine in their gentleness compared with the steep and forbidding fortress— the red turrets and pinnacles of the Chiracahuas about five miles across the colorless desert to the west. She was beginning to like the look of the place, at least from her vantage point out here on the desert. The trees in the mountains still made her claustrophobic. The pavement slapped the wheels, and the truck swayed and bounced as it sped over the road's slight irregularities. Mo sat erect on the seat.

Connie thought about the old Apaches, the Chiricahua Apaches, living on those crags, the last holdouts, the women going out to gather nuts and plants while the men went hunting. They didn't grow anything of their own, and she could hardly imagine that. She thought of her people's cornfields down on their desert, the cornstalks four paces apart in dry washes, waiting for a few timely rains as the summer progressed. She couldn't imagine the life of the old Apaches, nomadic, ranging over this land, down even into Mexico, raiding, fighting. They had finally lost, lost their land, hauled off to Florida or someplace, never to return here. She couldn't imagine that either, not having your own lands since before memory. She wondered what it might have been like to grow up an Apache woman. She remembered reading that if an Apache woman committed adultery, her husband could cut off the tip of her nose.

Yuck.

Apache women had also been warriors, fighting with the men when needed. Some of them had been especially fierce, as strong as the men. All the stories, she thought, the old stories of how it once had been and could never be again. I would have been one of them, she thought, the warrior women, and a hazy melancholy lifted.

"Story time?" she asked.

"I'm flying blind here," Mo said. "Blinder than usual. Fragments. One fragment is that photograph. Now there's only two reasons—actually three—why anyone would take a photograph of an object they were smuggling. One is some kind of foolish hubris—you know, pride, keep a record of your triumphs. Another reason is what Jack Knott said, a marketing device. You send a photograph along to the next guy up the line. Prove you've got what you said you've got. That works fine, especially if the other guy has to come a long way to pick it up. So the photograph was taken on June twenty-seventh. That's the flash you saw. And you'd have to guess that it was Fitzhugh who took it. So he's a smuggler. And your Mexican friend wrote June twenty-eight on it, so that's probably when she found it. Rummaging around his stuff. Now that date might be something like noting down scientific evidence. Habit of mind.

"So you've got Fitzhugh the smuggler and he's going to send the photograph off the next day, prove he's got the emperor, and Vera Maria finds it, takes it away. He figures that out somehow—maybe she confronts him about it, Aztec pride and all—and he goes out in the field and pushes her off the cliff." He paused and puffed out his lips. "Then he takes another photograph and ships that off to the customer." He paused again.

"But there's another reason why you might take such a photograph. Cold feet."

"Cold feet?" Connie said.

"See, say you've got this smuggling thing going somehow, but then you find that an agent of the FBI has been murdered, somewhere on the trail of these things. Or maybe you had to kill the agent yourself. Like a noose tightening. Things are getting too hot and you want to let the feds know a bit about what's going on so maybe they can stop it—without you gettin' nabbed. By the feds or by your colleagues in crime. Your Mexican connection, maybe. So you take a photograph to send anonymously to the FBI to let them know that there's this action at the center. Maybe that's how Collins got onto this in the first place. He was talking about some mysterious tip, remember? Maybe Fitzhugh's been screwing around like this for some time.

"Now, if Vera Maria finds this thing and asks him about it, he could simply say it's a photograph he took in Mexico or something. Wave it off. But she kept it, gave it to you in confidence. CPA. Sisters under the skin.

"So she would know that Fitzhugh was up to something, maybe weaseling to the cops—if she was already in on the deal, one of the team."

"No, no," Connie said, shaking her head. "Not—"

"She guesses that this was some kind of tip and so he has to kill her or she'll rat on him and he'll get his *cojones* chewed off by some Aztec thug."

Connie stared at the highway, disappearing under the hood of the truck. The wind roaring around the cab was hot, dry. "Close your window," she said. "I'll put on the air conditioning."

"Now, I can tell you don't like that much, implicating your friend in a nefarious scam against her very own ancestors. Well, there are still lots of possibilities here. Supposing Fitzhugh didn't know she had the photograph."

"But he'd want to send it to the customer, wouldn't he? And it's missing—"

"Suppose you saw the second of two flashes?"

"Huh?"

"Suppose by the time you got to the window, he'd already taken one picture. Then he took another, which you saw."

"Hubris?"

"Right, one for the customer, one for his ego. A little memento he could jerk off about in his retirement."

"But then . . . ?"

"Why did Fitzhugh kill her?"

"Yes," Connie said.

"We don't know that he did. Someone did, though."

"You're sure of that?"

"Yep. From the field notes. She was up on that high land above Salt Canyon that morning. Those coordinates were the last things in her notes. Why would she drop everything and suddenly nip off about a mile to the edge of Skeleton Canyon? Someone had to have hit her, probably killed her on that high ground and took her over and dumped her in Skeleton Canyon. Look like an accident."

"Why Skeleton Canyon?"

"Good question."

"That's where they found the agent."

"I know." Mo lapsed into silence. Up ahead, several miles off, Connie could make out a few low buildings that signaled they were nearing Interstate 10. A few minutes of silence later, she slowed on the ramp to let a semi rig thunder past, and pulled out onto the highway. The semi's back end bore an enormous full-color photograph of a Pepsi-Cola can, looking cold, dewy, and inviting.

It wasn't much of a story so far, Connie thought.

"Here's something," Mo said. "Whoever killed that agent, they didn't expect her to be found, hiding her in that cave and all." He was silent again. "But whoever killed Vera Maria did expect her to be found. Tossed her down there out in the open during a manhunt."

"So?"

"I'm thinking."

That morning Special Agent Larry Collins made his escape from the hospital in Douglas. In the middle of the night, the old guy in the other bed had died and the people had wheeled him out. He had heard one of the attendants piously say something about God's ledger, and after going back to sleep, he awoke with the picture of a ledger in his mind. A page of a

ledger. A list of names and dates. It was the book at the hacienda where guests signed in. *Melissa Jenkins, Philadelphia, PA,
USA. 17–18 junio.* That's what he had seen. He had found her
trail. And it had meant something at the time, but now he
couldn't think what. He lay thinking, perfunctorily ate the
bland breakfast they provided him, and at ten-thirty, when
there seemed to be a lull in activity in the hall, he gingerly
climbed out of bed and got dressed. He felt for his wallet.

Missing. Damn.

In some safe, with all his other stuff. His gun. He felt
dizzy. And naked. He stepped out of the room into the hall,
looked both ways, and strode purposefully toward a door
with a red exit sign above it.

Down the stairs, through another door, bright light from
the reception area—wow, bright—through the glass doors.
Hold on to the railing. Jeez, I got to sit down.

He made his way around the corner, sat down on the dusty
ground, and leaned back against the building in the shade.

Melissa Jenkins. June 18.

Sleep on it.

"I'm Mo Bowdre. This is Connie Barnes. We're here to see
the sheriff."

The deputy behind the desk had watched this enormous
blond man with a little hat and sunglasses walk across the
floor toward her, taking deliberate, measured steps. There
was something peculiar about how he moved, but she
couldn't put her finger on it. The woman with him looked
like an Indian. They made a strange pair, she thought.

"He's expecting you," she said. "It's through that door and
then two doors—"

"Thanks. We know the way," Mo said with a smile, and
turned to his left. They went through the door and down the
hall.

"Come on in," Jack Knott said. "Sit down. You been doing some sleuthing, huh?"

"Just thinking, Jack."

"Well, that don't sound too dangerous. Meanwhile we've come up with something interesting. About the Madero woman. And that snake man. On the ledge, up above from where she wound up, we found a coupla little bits of packed dirt, like from the tread of a shoe. They didn't come from her shoes—don't fit—and they didn't come from that boy Eddy's boots either. So someone else was walking around up there. Had to have been sometime that morning or the night before or the rain would've washed 'em away."

"That's very interesting," Mo said.

"What's more interesting," said the sheriff with a dramatic pause, "is that them squiggles of dirt do match the prints we found in the cave where that lady agent was found. Some fella in those Nike running shoes. So maybe the Madero woman was pushed. Now, the agent was sniffing around after that smuggling business, and Madero had that picture, so you'd have to guess that—"

"Same fellow, same motive. Both women knew too much," Mo said.

"Right. And it wasn't that boy Eddy. When he took off, he only took the clothes on his back. He must stink by now like a pig in—excuse me, ma'am. Anyway, I told the FBI that lookin' for him was a waste of time and money." The sheriff looked at his watch. "Say, it's eleven-thirty. I usually eat lunch early. Why don't we go across the street and get a bite. Talk over there. Inez's internationally famous greasy spoon, known the world over for a chili stew that'll clean out your sinuses for life."

"Sounds good, Jack. But I need to make a couple of phone calls first. Is there . . . ?"

"Empty office right across the hall."

When Mo emerged from the office twenty minutes later, the deputy touched his arm and said, "The sheriff and your friend went ahead. I'll take you over there."

"Mr. Collins! What are you doing here?"

Larry Collins was back in the Bronx, hearing the sirens coming closer, staring at his father lying dead on the ground. He heard someone calling him and fought through the fog.

"Mr. Collins? You have to wake up."

Collins opened his eyes and saw Nurse Furillo's astounding nose, about a foot from him. She was bent over, her hands on her hips.

"You look terrible," she said. "Can you get up? Walk? We're going to put you back in bed where you belong."

I've got to tell Bowdre, he thought. Melissa Jenkins, June 18.

"Mr. Collins?"

"It's okay, Nurse, it's okay. I'm coming. Gotta talk to my office. Give me a hand."

The little nurse pulled him to his feet, put one of his arms around her shoulders, and they wobbled around the corner and into the hospital.

"Phone," Collins said. "First the phone. Important clue in a federal crime, Miz Furillo."

Nurse Furillo was not one to think much about the regular heroics she and other nurses performed in the course of their duties, but the idea of being of assistance in a federal investigation suffused her with pride. She led him over to the reception desk, told the receptionist to fetch a wheelchair, and dialed the numbers the agent gave her.

"Collins," the agent said after a pause. "You got to get a message to a man named Mo Bowdre. Yeah, B-O-W-D-R-E. He's at the research center. Tell him Melissa Jenkins was in Mexico on June eighteenth . . . Yeah. If you can't find him, tell that sheriff in Lordsburg to find him and tell him . . . What? . . . No, I can't remember what's so important about it, but Bowdre will know. Make sure you . . . okay. Yeah." He hung up the phone as the receptionist wheeled up a chair. He looked at it with relief.

"Okay, Miz Furillo. I'm all yours."

Inez's Restaurant was a dark, cool place, windowless, and lit by a few hidden lights around the walls and candles in red glass cups on the tables. It reminded Connie of the restaurant where she and Mo hung out in Santa Fe, Tiny's, but it was smaller. The only noticeable decor was a series of exuberant bullfighting posters on the wall. She and Sheriff Knott were at a table in the corner. He had ordered coffee for both of them, and she had asked the waitress to bring a Negra Modelo beer for their friend who would be joining them shortly.

"There he is," the sheriff said, and stood up. "I'll go get him."

"Wait," Connie said. "I think he heard you."

The big man turned like a beacon, smiling in their direction, and walked across the room toward them with one hand out, touching and then moving around the intervening tables.

"That's damn amazing," the sheriff said.

Mo approached the table, touched the back of a chair, and sat down, saying, "Hello, Jack." He reached out his right hand and touched Connie's arm.

"Connie here has been tellin' me about those stolen gods you found last year. Says you made up a story out of just a couple of facts."

"It's not a very scientific method—hah—hah—hah."

"It is if it works," the sheriff said. "And it did then. We don't have much in the way of facts in this mess. So, you got a story?"

Mo found his bottle of Negra Modelo and took a sip. "Ahhh, thank you. A story. The problem is that there are so many little stories. The question is which ones add up to a big story. We have to reinvent a past, a past we don't know anything about really. It's like archaeology."

"Archaeology?" the sheriff said.

"Yep. See, those boys dig up old artifacts, try to figure out what they were and what they were used for. But the artifacts they dig up aren't the past. They're present objects. You got to infer from these present objects what they meant in the past."

Jack Knott sat back and sighed. He supposed he'd just have to be patient, let this boy spin it his own way.

"All we have," Mo continued, "are a few events that happened that we're sure of. Two deaths, one of which was surely a murder, and a couple of what you could call artifacts. Like that photograph."

A waitress appeared at the side of the table. "Would you like to order?"

"I'll try that stew you mentioned," Connie said. "The green chili stew?"

"That's two," Mo said.

"Three," said the sheriff.

"Well, you certainly are easy," said the waitress, beaming, and headed off across the room.

"Connie here," Mo resumed, "seems to have figured out when that photograph was taken. Why don't you tell him?"

Connie explained about the gray rocks in the background, the fire alarm, the flash of light, and how it seemed that only the director, Wheeler Fitzhugh, was in a position to have taken the photograph.

"Well, ain't that something," the sheriff said. "The director. So he's our man."

"More than likely. But it's difficult to say what he's guilty of. Smuggling? Probably. Murder? Possibly. But not necessarily."

"This ain't much of a story yet," Jack Knott said, scowling.

"It gets better. Let me explain. Connie and I talked about the reasons why he would take the picture. One is an ego trip, a memento. Another is, as you suggested, a marketing tool. Proof to some buyer that he had what he said he had. In either case, if he found out that Madero had found it, he would have reasons to kill her. A third possibility is that he took the photograph to use out of fear—cold feet. Things were heating up, the dead agent who had gotten awfully close, all that. So he plans to send an anonymous tip to, say, the FBI. Collins talked of some tip that made him think that the traffic was through this area and maybe even the center. But the cold-feet theory requires that Madero herself was in on the smuggling plot, found the picture, and was about to rat on Fitzhugh, so he had to kill her, make it look like an accident. This is plausible, but perhaps too complicated for our story. It's repugnant to Connie, who has a feeling for the kind of woman Madero was."

"Okay."

"There's a fourth possible story here. Maybe Connie saw the second of two flashes. He took one for marketing purposes, and one for his memory book. He sends one off to the customer and finds that Madero got the other one somehow. She confronts him and he kills her."

"Pushes her into the canyon."

"There's a fifth possibility," Mo said. He turned to Connie. "I just thought of this. Maybe Fitzhugh didn't take the picture. Maybe he was on the receiving end. Someone proving to him that they had what they said they had. Maybe he was, at this point, the buyer, not the seller."

"Sweet Jesus. Where are we going?" Sheriff Knott asked.

"But I saw a flash," Connie said.

"Actually you said you thought you saw a flash."

"Well, that's true. But there are those gray rocks—"

"Here you are. Green chili stew," said the waitress. She plunked the bowls down with a flourish and Mo asked for another beer.

"No," Mo resumed. "This artifact, this photograph, doesn't clear up exactly what happened, but it's very helpful. Because of it, we know that smuggling was going on, that Fitzhugh was probably involved. It doesn't make any difference whether he was a customer or a seller. In either case he could have had a motive to kill Madero, or have her killed. Even if she was in on it, he had a motive. Let's let that lie for now. Whew! This stew is potent." He swallowed and fanned his mouth with a big hand.

"An event we know occurred is that Madero's body wound up in Skeleton Canyon. As did the agent's, in a cave. But Madero wasn't pushed off the side of the canyon, because she wasn't there. At least not alive." Mo went on to explain the map coordinates.

"Our other artifact is the field notes. They tell us that she was on some high ground near Salt Canyon, a mile from Skeleton Canyon, that morning. Someone killed her there, we have to assume, and lugged her body over to Skeleton Canyon and dumped it unceremoniously over the edge. Now why do that? The agent's body was concealed, and was found through an utter accident. Madero's body was dumped into a canyon where it was almost certain to be found by your boys out on the manhunt. Oh, thank heavens, more beer. This stuff is volcanic." He took a long draft.

"You're the murderer," he said. "You trot up to the site where Madero is working and kill her. Why not just stuff her in some crevice, or throw her into Salt Canyon? There is only one answer. Hah—hah. That is because she was in the wrong place."

"I don't follow you."

"I called up the biology department at the University of Arizona. Back there in your offices, Jack. Madero was studying some shrub, mountain mahogany, and in particular how it is climbing higher and higher in elevation, possibly part of the greenhouse effect. Global warming, all that. And she happened to come across some specimen growing at an unusually high elevation in that particular place above Salt Canyon. The killer didn't want to take the chance of her body being found there, so he hauled it all the way over to Skeleton Canyon and dumped it there. Obvious to all who came through on the manhunt.

"It was a diversion. Given the manhunt, the body was likely to be found. If it was found near where she was killed, then a whole lot of attention would be drawn there. Why would that be bad?"

"Well—"

"Right. Because something else important was going on, or was going to go on, near where she was working. She had happened onto the place where the smuggling transactions take place. You don't want Sheriff Jack Knott and his boys, and the FBI and God knows who else mucking around *there*."

"I'll be damned."

Connie smiled. "Can I have a sip of your beer?"

"Too much capsaicin, huh?" Mo said. "Help yourself."

Mo took another bite of stew. "But I don't think Fitzhugh was alone in all this," he said.

"Why not?"

"Well, let me explain that to you. Hah—hah. See, you looked at the log at the center and you found that Fitzhugh was in El Paso on the eighteenth of June. That's the day the agent was killed. So someone else had to have done her."

"But the prints, the footprints, damn it, they match," Sheriff Knott said.

"There's a helluva lot of Nike running shoes sold in this country. They aren't like fingerprints, Jack. They're mass-produced."

"Well, yeah—"

"So I was thinking that if Fitzhugh's out of town, someone else killed the agent. Someone who's in on the scheme. Some-one who's out there, sees the agent snooping around the sen-sitive area, and does her in. Now who would that be? The other day I was eavesdropping on some good ol' boys in the Sidewinder Saloon and in comes some guy named Ned."

"He's a fire lookout for the Forest Service," the sheriff said. "Ned Fergusson."

"I thought that was what he is. Vern asked him why he wasn't up there looking out for *confragrations*. Anyway, he said something that struck me. Suggested that he saw every-thing going on up there. 'Eyes of a damn eagle' is what he said, and it got my attention. That lookout tower isn't more than a half mile from where Madero was working. Now what better place to have a colleague than old Eagle Eyes in his tower looking out over the site. Could even be a beacon at night."

"For what?"

"For the guy coming in to make a drop."

"Like an airplane?" the sheriff barked. "You can't land a plane up there in them hills. Jesus."

"I don't know," Mo said. "Maybe one of those ultralites. Built like bicycles. I don't know. It's not important."

The waitress appeared at the table. "Will there be any-thing else?"

"Just the check," Mo said. "I'll take it. You got the coffee the other day. Anyway, I'd bet that old Ned is in on it. Feel it in my bones. And there's another guy might be in on it."

"Jesus, this is gettin' awful elaborate. Who?"

"Jack, it's just a story. A harmless story." Mo yawned. "I can't believe that two beers've made me sleepy. Must be age."

"Okay, who?"

"The bug doctor. Armand."

"That's—"

"Listen. Connie, you remember the day we went in his lab and he was telling us how all that forensic work was done?"

"Sure."

"And he had all those killing bottles out for his fieldwork that day?"

Connie shuddered. "Yes."

"And do you remember that he had those bottles full of ethyl acetate? I could smell it."

Connie smiled. The sheriff said, "What the hell is ethyl acetate?"

"It's a chemical. Fumes kill bugs. Well, Armand told me the nearest forensic entomologist was a guy named Treadle at UCLA. So I called him just now, before lunch. And I asked him if he was running a forensic experiment, waiting for blowfly larvae to hatch, would he have ethyl acetate anywhere in the room and he said no sir, he wouldn't. Risk the whole experiment."

The sheriff's mouth popped open. He began to turn red. "You mean—"

"I mean the good doctor Armand didn't have the slightest intention of letting those critters gain their majority. He was gonna tell you that the agent died on the eighteenth whatever the bugs said, so he didn't give a damn if they lived or died. May have already killed 'em before we got there."

"Well, Jesus Christ, that's serious."

The waitress came with the check.

"Let's get out of here, figure out what the hell to do."

"Just a harmless story, Jack. Hah—hah—hah."

The deputy watched again as the man called Mo Bowdre walked into the sheriff's department, following Sheriff Knott and the Indian woman. It came to her that he was blind.

"Sheriff? You have a message here. From the FBI. In fact it's for both you and Mr. Bowdre."

She wondered why the FBI would be sending a message to a blind man about the agent who had died, Melissa Jenkins. And why was Sheriff Knott spending so much time with him? It didn't make a lot of sense. She handed the sheriff her written note.

" 'Larry Collins,' " the sheriff read out as he went through the door and down the hall, " 'said to tell Mo Bowdre that Melissa Jenkins was in Nueva Casa Grande on 18 June.' That's in Mexico. Says here he's still in the hospital."

"Hah. The scarecrow got his brains."

"Then—" Connie said.

"Confirmation. Always nice to have a wild conjecture confirmed."

"So the bug doctor cooked the report," Sheriff Knott said.

"Right," Mo said, sitting down in the sheriff's office. "Just made it fit what he wanted. That agent died on the nineteenth probably, not before dawn on the eighteenth. Both Armand and Fitzhugh were back from El Paso in plenty of time to kill her. And you know something, Jack? That's the only damn thing in my story that we can prove."

"Well, at least we can hang that little fucker—excuse me, ma'am—for falsifying an official report. That's a start."

"I am emboldened," Mo said, "to return to the lucrative world of conjecture."

Connie watched a strange smile creep across Sheriff Knott's

face. "You know," he said, "you talk pretty fancy for a Lincoln County boy."

"It's the altitude, Jack. Santa Fe's seven thousand feet. Goes to a man's head after a while."

"Well, I won't hold it against you." Sheriff Knott beamed and Connie watched the two men. Two good old boys, leaning on a rail, spitting . . . Mo made the strangest friends.

"See, Jack, I don't have to tell you that all we got here, besides that phony bug report, is a story. But there's a little bit more to it, the way I see it. Hah—hah—hah. If I'm right—if Fitzhugh made two photographs and sent one off to the customer, or even if he made another after he found out the first one was gone, and sent that off to the customer, then something's gonna happen soon. Say he did take the photograph on the twenty-seventh. Mailed it the twenty-eighth. Two days in the mail? It's possible. And today's the first of July. Get my drift?"

"I'm nodding my head," Sheriff Knott said.

"Well, I was telling Connie this morning that it might be fun to go camping up in those mountains. Hah—hah—hah."

"Now, you wait just a damn minute—"

Eight

Ned Fergusson punched out the numbers, stabbing violently at the buttons. He looked at his watch as the phone buzzed: four-ten.

"Yes," said Wheeler Fitzhugh.

"Get a load of this."

"What? What?"

"There's four people on horseback. Just came up out of Salt Canyon. They're headed right for—"

"Damn!"

"That old boy, Daniel Ascension? He's takin' a party out for a ride, it looks like."

"Who are the others?"

"How the hell would I know? Never saw 'em before. One of 'em is a big blond guy, beard, black hat. There's a woman with black hair."

"Christ. Bowdre. What the hell is *he* doing out there? What about the fourth?"

"I dunno, never saw him before either. Rides like a dude. What if they pitch camp?"

"Maybe they're just out for a late-afternoon ride."

"They're packin' a lot of gear."

"If they camp anywhere in the area, call me. Keep an eye on it."

"And?"

"We'll come out early and we'll get rid of them."

Ned Fergusson smiled and hung up the phone. He crossed his one-room eyrie, opened a metal locker, and fondly grasped the cold barrel of his old and reliable Winchester .30-.30.

He hadn't had a chance to use it lately, he thought. No more pussyfooting around. And in the mayhem he envisioned, he might emerge as the sole survivor.

"Daniel?" Mo said. "It's been a helluva long time since I was on a horse." The trail out of the canyon had been steep, involving a lot of switchbacks and heart-stopping heaves of energetic back legs and clattering rocks, and Mo had simply had to trust to the animal's surefootedness, knowing that much of the journey had to be along narrow ledges with stupefyingly precipitous drops awaiting any false placement of a hoof. Death at hand. A slip, a scratch of gravel, and he would plummet to his doom.

"You're doin' fine, Mr. Bowdre."

"Call me Mo, please, Daniel."

"It's the horse I'm in a fret about. Hasn't had anyone your size on her in her whole life."

"Hah—hah—hah."

"We only got another mile to go," Daniel said.

"Ruby here just sighed with relief."

"That ain't a sigh. It's a fart."

"Yeah, but relief anyway," Mo said, and began to regret that he had once referred to Daniel as a credulous rustic. He also began to worry again about the wisdom of this mission. Jack Knott had flat out said no when Mo had broached it. Mo had been able to persuade him that it had to look like an innocent camping trip—no recognizable fuzz—or otherwise the drop, if there was to be one, would be called off. Presumably old eagle eyes in the fire tower was pretty familiar with the local constabulary.

Jack had gotten even angrier when Connie said in a flat, firm voice, "If Mo goes, I go." Mo had figured that was her way of scotching the whole thing, but when Jack erupted, saying "For God's sake, the man is blind and you're a woman," Connie was silent for a moment. "Well?" Jack Knott said. And Connie said, "Sheriff, Mo is not blind when I am with him. I am his eyes."

"Well, goddamn it, this is absolutely bound to be dangerous and you're a damn woman," Jack Knott had said.

Mo recalled that there had been an agonizingly long silence. He imagined that Connie stared at Jack Knott the way a mountain looks down on the puny grasslands below.

Then Connie said, "Sheriff Knott, you may not know this, but Indian women . . . like the Apache women who used to live here? Those ladies used to have a lot of fun cutting off the ears, the fingers, and the balls of men who bothered their family. They were warriors, you know? You may have heard that the word *Hopi* means the peaceful people. That's not what it means. One way of translating is that we are right and you are wrong. So don't bother me. I'm going. It's real simple."

The room filled with silence again.

"Well, Jesus Christ—" is what Jack Knott had said, and like a prayer.

"Perhaps," Mo said, "we should see if the FBI should be in on this."

"You mean go up there as decoys?" the sheriff said.

"Yes."

"You ever see an FBI man that didn't look like an FBI man, even if he was buck naked?"

"Only one, I imagine," Connie said.

"Yeah, one. Hah—hah. Collins. And he's in bed."

So the sheriff had called in a young deputy named Jimmy Snyder and told him he had to shave off his handlebar mustache and try and look like a civilian and take his weapon and his radio, and he, Jack Knott, would be on the western edge of the Gray Ranch in a helicopter with four armed men waiting for a call, and goddamn it, he didn't like it one bit and he'd probably get his ass fired for going along with such a harebrained scheme . . . and so forth, but the four of them—Daniel Ascension, Mo, Connie, and Jimmy Snyder with a patch of white skin on his upper lip—had entered Salt Canyon at three-thirty that afternoon. After about a half hour of riding, his ass feeling like he had been forced to sit on a wooden church pew during a prolonged earthquake, Mo had said, "Connie? Did you Hopi women really do that kind of thing?"

"I made it all up, Mo. All we Hopi women do is make baskets and cook and grind corn. And sweep the dust out of the house, and tell the men what they're going to do. You know that."

They continued upward in single file with Connie behind him and Jimmy Snyder bringing up the rear. The late-afternoon sun struck the back of Mo's neck and he guessed they were out of the canyon altogether.

"Daniel, can you see that fire tower?" Mo asked.

"Yep. I can now."

"Then old eagle eyes can see *us*." Mo fretted again about the wisdom of this. The sun stopped burning Mo's neck.

"Storm's building up over the Chiricahuas," Daniel said.

"We'll have time to pitch the tents before it gets to us. Then it'll be clear. Starlight but not much of a moon. It's just a sliver."

"Good. A clear night is just what we need."

Tuck Eddy stirred and woke up in the gloom of the mine shaft. He stretched and walked slowly to the entrance and peered out. No one. Not a sound except a distant insect buzz. Then the trill of a rock wren. Tuck imagined it perched on some rock, bobbing up and down. He stuck his head out far enough to see the sky, gray with the coming rain and thunder. From his shirt pocket he pulled a piece of beef jerky and tore a piece off with his teeth. After the storm he could head out on his nocturnal prowls. He wondered how long it would be before he would see the sun, feel it burning into his body. Hadn't he read somewhere that without sunlight, you don't get vitamin D, so you get rickets or beriberi or some damn thing? It began to rain lightly outside the mine shaft. This is crazy, he thought to himself. I'm crazy. Went crazy, just like that. Maybe I always was crazy.

Crazy . . . And rich.

He squinched up his eyes and had the familiar, improbable, raging vision, like a shadowy, scarlet movie reeling through his mind.

From his tower Ned Fergusson watched the four riders dismount. Daniel Ascension and the thin guy started unloading the packs and bedrolls while the other two, the big guy and the woman, looked on, just standing there. They were in a small clearing among the oaks and pines. A couple of hundred yards beyond them to the east and ringing around to the north was a low escarpment, a wall of reddish rock with slabs and boulders at its base. He knew the place. He had watched the Mexican woman the other day from some of those boulders. The two men put up the tents, small backpacker tents, big enough for two friendly people each, and then fanned out collecting firewood. From his vantage point he could just make out the top of one of the tents. The big guy and the woman stood watching the west. Rain began spattering on the windows of Ned's eyrie and he reached for the phone. The drops descended the panes of glass in quirky squiggles, speeding up, then slowing down.

"They're pitched," he said when Fitzhugh answered.

"Damn."

"So?"

"We'll have to remove them."

"There's four of 'em. Old Daniel's pretty handy. You said you knew one of 'em?"

"Two besides Ascension. The woman's a Hopi Indian. The big blond guy is a sculptor. They were here at the center for a week. So there's only two of them to worry about. The sculptor is blind."

"A blind sculptor? That don't make sense."

"Never mind. We'll be at the bottom of the tower at nine-thirty."

"Nine-thirty it is."

The rain came harder and poured down the windows, obscuring Ned's view of the campers. Behind the loud rattle of rain on the tin roof, he heard the thunder—distant growls and then explosions and violent flashes of light. Through the open trapdoor, he could hear water splashing far below in the instant puddles. In the dim gray light he methodically oiled his Winchester and whistled tunelessly. Sitting ducks, he thought to himself.

When the rain had let up, a few drops pattering on the ground, Jimmy Snyder poked his head out of the little yellow tent and clapped an enormous, black, high-crowned Stetson on his head. He crawled out, turned, and began pulling old dead pine branches out after him.

"Daniel, you should get yourself some bigger tents. It ain't any fun spendin' time in one of these with a big man and a load of firewood."

Daniel crawled out and set his greasy hat on his head.

"Maybe tonight," Jimmy went on, "you can leave that hat outside."

Daniel looked at the deputy from his almost colorless blue eyes.

"I sure can't get used to you without that mustache. You look about twelve years old. Let's get a fire goin'."

"What d'you think I'm doin'?"

Connie emerged from the other tent, followed by Mo, who, on his hands and knees, looked like a huge bear with a hat. He sniffed. "Oh, a wonderful smell. Ozone and water. The world is new again." Connie took it in. The sandy ground was wet and quicksilver drops slid gently from the nearby pines. Overhead the sky was still solidly gray, but to the west, shafts of saffron sunlight streamed through the thinning clouds and lit up the tops of the distant Chiricahuas with a fine reddish-gold halo. It was exquisite and Connie thought how strange that such awful events could happen in such a beautiful place. She shivered.

"So you think it will clear up, Daniel?" Mo said, getting up on his feet.

"Oh yeah."

"You know this place pretty well, this part of the mountains?"

"Oh yeah," said Daniel, putting a match to the dry wood. Tiny flames tore through the dried grass and began to crackle against the pine branches. Out of his pack he took a grill and put it over the flames. "Nothin' fancy," he said. "Pork and beans. Campbell's finest. And coffee." He fished out a black skillet that might have derived from the Iron Age and put it on the grill.

"Yeah," he said, "I camped up here last year. Right over there." He gestured east toward the escarpment. "But this is a better place."

"Tell me, Daniel. Is there a place around here where you could land an airplane?"

"Up here?" Daniel's face wrinkled up in a rare grin. "Naw. You could *crash*-land one."

"How about an ultralite?"

"What's that?"

"It's a real small, light plane, made of mostly plastic tubes. Looks like a big tricycle with wings. On sandy ground like this stuff here, you wouldn't need more than a hundred feet to put her down. Big bump, but you could do it. You'd need more to take off. Maybe two hundred feet."

Daniel gestured eastward again with his head. "Up there. Above that cliff over east. About two hundred yards from here. It's pretty flat up there, pretty open, some scrubby stuff." He grinned again. "Funny idea."

"Does it slope up there?"

"It's a little higher to the north."

"Perfect. It could plop down on the upslope, come in from the south. And it could take off on the downslope."

"At night?" Daniel said.

"Best time. No updrafts. These babies are so light a little updraft'll throw 'em around like a pea in a whistle."

"How do you know about that?" Connie asked.

"Guy from Tucson was telling me about them once. Flies 'em. He's kind of a nut. Name of Doster."

Daniel squatted down and pushed one of the pine branches deeper into the fire. Sparks danced and died. He took three large cans of pork and beans from his bag, methodically opened them with a manual can opener on his Swiss army knife, and dumped the contents into the skillet. Then he fetched a large blue coffeepot, dumped some coffee in it, poured water in from a plastic jug, and set it on the grill beside the skillet. "Cowboy coffee. Nothin' fancy."

"From the smell, I'd bet this will be my best meal in three days," Mo said.

"A man does get hungry up here," said Daniel.

"Excuse me," Connie blurted out. "But don't you think we should be thinking . . . I mean, about what we're going to *do*? If you're right, a man's watching us right now. From that tower. Maybe the man who killed Vera Maria. Right here. We're like sitting ducks and we don't know what we're going to do."

"Not ducks. Decoys. We're doing just the right thing, sitting here around the campfire. Trekkers on a holiday, led by old Daniel here. Innocent as could be."

"But—"

"Anyway, they aren't gonna do anything until it gets dark. Wouldn't you agree?"

"Oh yeah."

"Well, what *then*?" Connie asked.

"Let me explain to you about that," Mo said. Jimmy Snyder, who had been tinkering with something in the entrance of his tent, walked over and squatted down on his heels next to the big man.

A pink telephone memo slip was taped to the door when Jeremy Armand returned from the field to his lab. *Please see me. Fitzhugh.* The entomologist opened the door, put away his equipment, and set eight glass bottles on the table. The nervous administrator, he thought, needing reassurance before every major performance. He sighed.

When he arrived at the director's office, Fitzhugh waved

him in with a grim expression on his face. When all around you are losing their heads, Armand thought . . .

"Close the door, Jeremy." Armand did so and sat down in front of the desk.

"Tonight," Armand said. "Then we're done for a while."

"Trouble, Jeremy. Bad trouble."

It sounds as though he really means it, Armand thought. Not the usual nervous frets and squeaks.

"There are four people camping out within two hundred yards of the landing site."

"Oh, no."

"Apparently one of that fellow Daniel Ascension's groups. Horseback. Two of them are the sculptor Bowdre and his Indian woman. I don't know who the other man is."

Armand remained silent.

"We have to get rid of them."

"Yes," Armand said. "We do." He wondered what Bowdre was doing up there. Just there, of all places. He had had the sense that the man was not completely what he said he was. He remembered him asking question after question in Armand's lab. Why would a sculptor, even if he had studied biology years ago, be so interested in such arcane—and to many, disgusting—matters? And why had he spent so much time with that little bitch Ingrid Freeman, touching and feeling the model of the Peloncillos? Twice he had done that. And why had he been in the Sidewinder Saloon with Sheriff Knott?

"Wheeler, Bowdre may not be a sculptor. He may be with the police."

"What?"

"Did you check on him?"

"Of course not. It never occurred—"

"What if he is? Police."

"A blind cop? Come here with his Indian girlfriend? It's

awfully farfetched. Maybe you're getting a bit paranoid, the way you accuse me of getting on these nights."

The little man folded his hands in front of his chest. "How do you know he's blind, Wheeler?"

The two men stared at each other.

"Whatever," Armand said. "We've got to get them out of there."

"I told Fergusson we'd meet him at nine-thirty."

Armand stood up. "We'll go in my car. Eight-thirty."

Whirrrr. Thump.

Connie jumped. "What was *that*!"

It came again. *Whirrrr thump.*

"That's a pair of nighthawks, ma'am," Daniel Ascension said. "They're over there behind you."

Connie turned and saw two dark shapes swooping up into the darkening, red-tinged sky to the east, veering, diving. *Whirrrr thump.*

"It's their wing feathers, make that big boom when they pull out of a dive."

The birds veered and flew up over the escarpment. Daniel put the last of the metal plates, washed clean with sand, into his pack, kicked the grill aside, and dismantled the fire, now only a few glowing sticks. He scooped up sand and covered the embers, and Connie shivered, not from cold, but from a sense of loss. The glowing embers had been alive, reassuring. Whenever, as a girl, she had spent the night camped out-doors, someone kept the fire going all night. Now she felt alone in the dead quiet, exposed. She dreaded the loss of the last light.

She looked over her shoulder. The reddish tinge in the east was gone. To the west, the angrier red still glowed weakly. She looked up, and saw a star, the first one of the night. A light breeze whispered almost inaudibly in the nearby pines.

"They're chasin' insects," Daniel said.

"Who?" Connie asked.

"Them nighthawks. Swoop down on 'em like that. Moths. Floating spiders."

"Floating spiders?"

"Little baby ones. Run out a bit of silk and let the wind carry 'em off. Air's full of 'em. That's what one of those scientists at the center told me once."

Connie shivered again. The air full of tiny spiders? The thought of it made her flesh crawl. Her neck and shoulders felt like a tightly twisted rope. Any minute now they were going to get in those tents and whatever was going to happen would happen. She was filled with dread. How had she let this happen? Why? She was Mo's eyes, but what could she do in the dark? She was his protection, but what good was she at protecting a man in the dark when people were going to try to kill him? She was sure that would happen. She expected to hear the sound of a gunshot any second. She could feel the place between her shoulder blades where the bullet would tear into her flesh. Any minute. The image of Mo, struck down, came into her mind, the big man, her man, toppling, falling.

She tried to conjure up the image of one of those powerful-looking, implacable Apache women warriors.

Next to her, Mo heaved himself to his feet and stretched expansively.

"Time to turn in, wouldn't you say, Daniel?"

"Oh yeah."

Connie moved to the tent, backed in, and as Mo backed in beside her the last glimmer of light vanished from the western sky.

"You know what?" she said.

"What?"

"I'm no warrior woman."

"Sure you are. Otherwise you wouldn't be here."

"I'm scared. Are you?"

"Well, sure. I'm not stupid."

At eight-thirty, Jeremy Armand was sitting in the driver's seat of his Trooper at the far end of the parking area. A leather satchel lay on the backseat and a snub-nosed .38 weighed heavily in his jacket pocket. What a mess, he thought. He had never directly caused the death of another human, and he didn't look forward to it. He took a deep breath. It would be worth it.

Gravel crunched and he looked out to see Wheeler Fitzhugh open the back door. He set a rifle on the floor, closed the door, and without a word, got in the front seat. The engine came to life and the Trooper eased down the driveway to the stone gate posts. It struck Armand that the center would not be getting a sculpture by T. Moore Bowdre after all.

Twenty minutes later they turned onto a long-neglected Forest Service road that led circuitously and ruggedly back up into the Peloncillos to the fire tower. Armand stopped the car, leaned down, and shoved the floor shift into four-wheel drive.

"Well?" he said.

"Well what?" Fitzhugh said, looking straight ahead.

"This may be the end of our little game."

"Why?"

"Wheeler, for God's sake, when this transaction is complete, there will be six people dead. In less than two weeks."

"Yes, I know."

They lapsed into silence and the beam of the Trooper's headlights bobbed and swerved as they bounced over the rocky dirt road running steeply up through black piñon and juniper trees. Before the road reached the ridge along which it ran for two miles to the tower, Armand turned off the headlights, lurching along in first gear, the light from the stars and a thin crescent moon barely serving to make the road distinguishable. Up on the ridge, tall ponderosa pines loomed like sentries in the night.

"How do you suppose this is going to work?" Fitzhugh said.

"Fergusson will have an idea. It's his métier. Calm down, Wheeler, it'll be all right."

Somewhere off to the north, a coyote yipped its high-pitched bark and another answered. The trickster, Connie thought, and listened, but the coyotes had nothing more to say to each other. She tried to think of the old coyote stories her grandfather had told her when she was a girl, but she couldn't concentrate enough to get through even one.

"Mo," she whispered. "How long are we going to have to wait?" She knew it was a stupid question.

"Maybe all night," Mo whispered. "But you Hopis are good at staying up all night. Whoops. Maybe not too much longer. I heard a car engine."

"You did?"

"Couple of miles away, probably beyond the fire tower. Now they turned it off so we won't hear it. Probably we'll get a visit in about an hour."

"Should we tell Daniel?"

"No, those boys aren't asleep over there."

Ned Fergusson was waiting under the tower when the two men appeared out of the shadows on the road, the little professor lugging a satchel. The old Winchester was in the crook of his arm and a cigarette glowed, dangling from his lips. He took a final drag and flipped it into a puddle where it went out with a *pfft*.

As the men approached Ned asked, "Nice night for it,

huh?" He noted Fitzhugh's rifle and asked, "What'd you bring, Professor?"

"A thirty-eight."

"What d'you think you can accomplish with a little pop-gun like that?"

"It's the only firearm I own. I'm very effective with it."

"This ain't target practice, here. Now here's how we can do this. Only needs two of us to take care of the campers. So I think the professor can go on up to the landing sight." He bent down and picked up a big eight-cell flashlight and handed it to Armand. "We're cuttin' things pretty close, so you better be up there, bring him in. Now, Fitz, you and me, we'll circle around west of 'em and get up against that cliff. I'll stay north of 'em up in the rocks, and you keep goin' till you're east of them in the rocks. I'll give you five minutes to get yourself in position and then I'll shoot down on the tents. They're those little backpacker tents, two people each, tight-packed like tomatoes in a can. Tents're yellow so you can see 'em good. Probably won't take more than fifteen, twenty seconds. Then we wait, see if anyone comes out. You see anyone come out, you shoot 'im. If no one does, I'll come up close and check. How's that sound?"

They went over it again. Fitzhugh seemed to be reassured by the feral composure of the older man, but Armand, never comfortable in the fire watcher's company, found his horizon streaked with doubts. As they made their way slowly and silently through the pine trees, he recalled the New Jersey art historian who had filled his apartment with a world-class collection of porcelain, all cleverly and boldly stolen from various East Coast museums. They finally caught up to him, and he got a few years in Allentown or one of those country-club federal prisons reserved for gentlemanly criminals—art thieves, corrupt politicians, and stock-market manipulators. The art historian was considered almost a folk hero by some

. . . but he hadn't sold the stuff for money. He simply had an addiction to porcelain and liberated pieces from the dust of old museum storerooms. More important, he hadn't left behind him a series of corpses.

It had all begun innocently enough. A whispered conversation one night with a colleague from the south, sitting around a campfire one night three years ago in the Guadalupe Mountains. The elaborate scheme, the small network, the timing—all worked out with the precision of a laboratory experiment. Two test runs, the methodology perfected. And it had become such a lucrative affair: Armand alone was now two million dollars richer. Two million dollars waiting for him in a Bahamian bank.

But then the hushed call—a woman prowling around in Mexico. She knew. At least she thought she knew. And when she appeared up here near the landing site, it was clear she did know. So Fergusson had killed her, put her in that cave he said practically no one knew about. The ill fortune of that vacant-eyed rube Ascension discovering her—the first thread to come loose. Then Vera Maria. Fitzhugh said that *she* knew, that she had seen the photograph, that he wouldn't leave it up to Fergusson. Another thread loose. But Fitzhugh had done well. The coroner had pronounced it an accident.

Now these four "campers." So certain had they been of the foolproof nature of their methodology, they never imagined it would come to what could only be taken as first-degree murder. Six of them. If they were caught.

This, clearly, was the last event. It was time to quit and become an expatriate. He had already picked the country, a place with plenty of room for a retired professor of biology and millionaire. There was plenty in the world besides biology to occupy his mind.

Up ahead, the shadowy figures of Fergusson and Fitzhugh halted. As he came up to them, carrying the satchel and the flashlight, Fergusson pointed east, pointed to himself and Fitzhugh, then north. Unnecessarily he cautioned silence by putting his forefinger to his lips.

Stepping carefully, Armand made his way through the trees, to the familiar path up the escarpment. He knew what he had to do and began working out the details in his mind. When he reached the top, about twenty feet above the boulders, he set down the satchel on the ground and waited, staring out to the south. Their colleague would arrive in fifteen minutes or less.

In a crouch, Ned Fergusson crept soundlessly through the trees toward the boulders under the cliff. He had spent a lot of time, he thought now, being stealthy, getting around unseen and unheard, day or night. In Southeast Asia, back before Vietnam had become a war, training "his" gooks to surprise the bad gooks. That had been the beginning. Then back home, hunting in the mountains over in Arizona. Then here in the Peloncillos. They had approached him three summers ago, the two scientists, and he hadn't been able to see a flaw in the scam. And his role was simple. That woman had made it a bit more complicated—nothing all that serious—but he hadn't expected that ol' boy Ascension would come along. Oh, well. You do what you need to.

He stopped behind a six-foot slab of rock and pointed east. He held up five fingers. Fitzhugh nodded his head and went on, disappearing into the shadows. Fergusson looked up at the sky, black velvet like you see in jewelry stores, filled with diamonds. From the dazzling array he picked out the familiar constellations—directly overhead in the Milky Way was the Summer Triangle, to the south the Scorpion. In the book, with a line connecting the stars of the Scorpion, showing a head and a long, curved tail, it looked more to Fergusson like a sperm than a scorpion. He looked south to the trees. The two yellow tents looked like white bubbles on the starlit ground.

Maybe he'd invest his $200,000 in diamonds. He looked at the green-glowing dial of his watch. Hell, $200,000 was nothing.

Four minutes to go.

A breeze whispered through the pines near the tents. Overhead, a bat fluttered past with frantic, silent wing beats, then another. Far off, a coyote yipped again, a lonely sound. The breeze died and the only sound was the nearly inaudible scratching of a pocket mouse, nervously prowling for insects in the dark. The first crack of Fergusson's rifle shattered the night and a thirty-caliber slug tore through Daniel Ascension's tent with a thump, followed by another before the first explosion could echo from the cliff walls. Then another. The mountains filled up with the awesome, awful racket as three slugs tore into Bowdre's tent, echoing for an eternity around the rocks.

Then silence but for the nervous whinny of a horse.

Wheeler Fitzhugh's rifle barrel lay on the top of a boulder. From behind the notch of the sight, his eyes were riveted on the tents two hundred feet away. He had watched as the fragile plastic leaped with each slug. Now silence. God, he thought. Four people. His hands shook.

Then he heard the voice whispering.

"Dr. Fitzhugh, I presume. Don't move. You move so much as a hair in your nose and you're a dead man."

The whisper, as quiet as a breeze, seemed to be coming from above him. "Who—"

"It's me, Tuck Eddy, Bigfoot of the Peloncillos. You out killin' more people, huh?"

"What the—"

"Don't move, Dr. Fitzhugh. Don't move. It was you killed Mel, wasn't it?"

"No." Fitzhugh was sweating. "What are you doing . . . ?"

"Ol' Mowgli the Snake Boy is out for vengeance. I got something here for you."

There was a rustle from above and something heavy landed on his left shoulder, like a piece of thick rope. Oh God, no! he shrieked inwardly and was hit, as though slammed by a train, when the two razor-sharp fangs sliced into his neck. He screamed, and the snake rolled off his shoulder. He was immobilized by the pain and the terror. His neck was exploding.

"That's a rattlesnake, you murdering son of a bitch. A Mojave rattlesnake. You'll never make it off this mountain. You're a fuckin' dead man, Fitzhugh."

Fitzhugh howled, a long, low sound that split the night as horribly as the rifle shots, ending with a high-pitched whine. From the rocks above, Tuck Eddy laughed maniacally. It flashed through Fitzhugh's spinning mind that he should not run, should not run, find Fergusson, walk, don't pump the venom through any faster, walk, and he ran toward the tents, screaming, "Fergusson! Fergusson! A snake! Christ! Help me!" The pain pounded and seared and spread into his chest, his jaw. He staggered and fell, pushed himself upon his knees, crawled a few yards, got up on his feet, staggered blindly toward the tents. He saw the black-haired woman standing there—what? Vera Maria? He saw her suddenly jerk her head, crumple and fall to the ground. Dead. She was dead. Pick her up. Pick her up.

No. She was already . . .

He reached the tent and his eyes filled up red, and he winked out, toppled, and fell across one of the tents, flattening it, unconscious, breaths like sandpaper.

•   •   •

Fergusson heard the scream, the howl, laughter—what the hell was that?—saw the figure staggering, reeling toward the tents, yelling his name. He leaped off the big slab like a mountain lion and ran, seeing the three dark holes torn in the first tent as he got near, Fitzhugh lying across the far tent. What the hell? This was wrong. Something wrong. He passed the first tent and stopped two yards from Fitzhugh. He stepped closer, put a hand down, and touched him. He was breathing. A snake, he had been yelling. He turned him over and stooped down to look closely at him. Something on his neck. He took a small flashlight from his shirt pocket and thumbed the button. In the thin beam he saw two fine holes. Fucking snakebite. Gotta get him out of here. Then he thought, no. One down. I can get the whole thing. Get up on that cliff, take out the professor, the pilot, the whole damn thing. He put the flashlight back in his pocket and a thought struck him like a bullet. Under Fitzhugh, the goddamn tent was flat on the ground. There was no one in it.

Shit! Every neuron in his brain fired with the same message: run.

He stood up, crouched, and turned.

"Ned, that's a bad thing you did," Daniel Ascension said. He was standing next to a pine tree, and the starlight glinted off the barrel of a rifle pointed at Fergusson's chest. "You'd best put that rifle on the ground, go over by that tent, and set on the ground with your hands on your head."

Desperate, Fergusson said, "What about him? Fitzhugh. He's snakebit."

"Go over there and sit," Daniel said. "I can't help him and watch you at the same time. I guess he's on his own."

Fergusson crossed to the other tent, sat down, and put his hands on his head in the posture of the prisoner of war.

"That's two of you," Daniel said, standing by the tree. "Where's the third one? The bug doctor?"

"Fuck you."

"Ned, you'd best tell me."

"I don't know where he is. Maybe he's behind you in them trees."

Perched ten feet up where the cliff curved to the east, Jimmy Snyder had the radio turned on before the third shot began to echo around him. "Mayday," he barked. "Mayday." He turned it off, listened to the final echoes die, and then he heard the scream, the howl, and the crazy laughter, some-where over to his left. He let himself down, and began creep-ing toward the sounds, and heard rather than saw a man running, falling, calling out: "Fergusson." Something about a snake. In the gloom he thought he saw the man crawling to-ward the tents, then standing, staggering forward. Someone fell. He waited a moment, then crept on, stopped again as he heard someone running, and crouched down. Presently a murmur of voices reached him. Slowly he made his way among the trees until he was a few yards from the tents and heard the voices again. He moved closer and made out Daniel and a guy sitting on the ground with his hands on his head.

"Daniel," he hissed. "It's Jimmy. You okay?"

"I got two of 'em here. One's out cold—Fitzhugh. Snake-bit. This here's Fergusson. Dunno where the bug doctor is."

"I'll go huntin'," Jimmy said. "You okay?"

"Oh yeah."

Deputy Snyder slipped off into the trees.

When the first shot rang out, Connie lurched and put her arms around Mo. They were down among the rocks and boulders near the far end of the cliff, east of the tents.

"Hold tight," Mo said, and clutched her. In a matter of seconds it was all over, but the echoes and, idiotically, the re-membered words to an old song went through his mind:

Hold tight, hold tight,
Boo-racka sackie
Want some seafood, mama.
Shrimpers and rice,
They're very nice.
Hold tight. . . .

Fats Waller. One of his father's favorites. Old 78 rpm record scratching away in the living room.

Jesus! What is my brain doing?

"We just wait," Mo whispered. "We're safe here."

"Eeeee." She shuddered, prayed, holding on to the big man, shielding him, protected by him. Maybe. They heard the scream, the howl, the laughter, the running, yelling.

"What's that?"

"Fitzhugh yelling for help. Running toward the tents, I think, yelling to Fergusson for help. Sounds like he got bit by a snake."

Connie shuddered yet again. Mo sat listening, thought he heard voices, but maybe it was just a breeze in the trees. He strained to hear. Then, after about two minutes, footsteps. The lightest touch of leather on rock.

"Bowdre." A thin whisper.

Mo remained silent.

"Snyder," hissed the voice.

"Yeah?"

"Daniel's got two of 'em. I'll look for the bug man. You stay here."

"Gotcha."

Hold tight, hold tight.
Boo-racka sackie . . .

Jesus.

Then another sound impinged on Mo's brain, sending Fats Waller off into the blackness. A distant whine.

On the edge of the cliff, standing next to the satchel, Jeremy Armand heard the shots—six in rapid succession—and then the silence. That was over with, he thought with satisfaction. He wished Lopez would come in the ultralite. The sooner the better. Then he heard the screams, and Fitzhugh's voice calling out. For what? Fergusson. A snake? What the hell was going on? More silence.

Come on, come on, Lopez. A breeze touched his face, coming from the southwest. He listened, urging the sound of the aircraft to come into being.

A snake? What the hell is going on down there?

He heard it, a distant whine, hardly louder than the breeze. He listened for a few more seconds, then pointed the flashlight toward the sky and turned it on. The whine grew louder, resolved itself into the low roar of an engine. He looked up, following the beam up to where it disappeared in the night sky. Closer, closer. The engine's roar softened, and wheels and a tiny fuselage hurtled through the beam of light and disappeared behind him. He turned off the flashlight and heard the ultralite bounce on the ground, bounce again, branches snap, the engine's low roar become a throaty murmur. He snatched up the satchel and ran toward the sound.

"That was it," Mo said. He stood up.

"What are you doing?"

"I gotta get up there."

"Mo, you can't—what can you do up there? No. No!"

"It's dark. I'm not at any disadvantage in the dark. They are."

"Mo, no."

"I got to. Those other guys are screwing around down here. Now you stay here, right here. Don't move. It'll be okay."

"I'll come."

"No!" Mo barked. "You stay here." He moved off toward the boulders, feeling his way, scrabbling up the rocks. Connie sat in the blackness, alone. She put her hand to her mouth and pressed her lips hard against her teeth.

As Jeremy Armand ran up he saw a silhouette climb out of the shadowy shape of the ultralite.

"Lopez," he said breathlessly.

"Where are the others?"

"Down below. Some campers showed up late this afternoon. They're down there, making sure—"

"Yet more to be remembered on the Day of the Dead?" Lopez said.

"Uh—"

"This is getting too bloody, too close. We need another way."

"Yes, we do. You've got it?"

"*Sí.*" He reached into the plane and placed a package on the ground. "Here. Shine your light on it. I will open it." He untied the cardboard box, lifted off the top, and unswaddled the cloth. The golden emperor gleamed up at them with a toothy smile, contented eyes. Armand gasped. It was unimaginably splendid. Lopez rewrapped the emperor and closed the box. "Now, the money," he said. Armand handed him the flashlight and Lopez knelt on the ground and opened the satchel. He riffled through the neatly tied wads of hundred-dollar bills. "I won't count it, my friend, because we trust each other, eh?" He looked up with a grin into the muzzle of Armand's .38, and before the grin vanished from his face, he saw the red flash and was dead.

Armand threw the satchel into the ultralite, then the box. He stepped over to his dead colleague and relieved him of the flashlight, which he put in the aircraft. With the strength of a man overdosed with adrenaline, he heaved the tiny, light craft around facing south and climbed in. His hands played over the controls and the engine burst into life. He shined the flashlight ahead to look at the course of his takeoff and gasped again. In the beam of the flashlight, a figure rose up onto the cliff edge—Bowdre!—and began to walk up the slope.

Knowing it was probably hopeless at that range, Armand pulled the .38 out of his jacket pocket. It caught on the cloth and he ripped it free, aiming as calmly as he could at the huge man a hundred feet away. He fired three times and, miraculously, the man lurched, spun around, clutching his stomach, and fell to the ground.

He heard the first two shots and the white-hot poker hit him in the side. Molten iron. He was on the ground. It had come, the other blow, the one he'd always expected since the explosion in the mine. He could see the orange flash, now the other shoe had dropped. He reached for the place that was burning, the source of the ache that spread like electricity throughout his frame, felt the blood, found the hole in his shirt, his flesh. On the side above his pelvis. Organs. Which organs?

Hold tight, hold tight.

The ground smelled fresh, new. The newness of water. Blessed rain. Seeping into the earth, endless cycle, birth, death, my blood seeping into the earth. Oh, Christ, this hurts. It hurts so bad it roars. Roaring sound. The plane. The fucking plane. Ow, shit! Getting up, getting up, yes. The roar louder. Over there. He lurched to his right. Timing, fucking timing. He crouched and the roar grew louder. Now, he guessed, and leaped, the pain in his side slamming him. Christ! He had it in his hand, jerking him backward an eternity, felt the pipe—the axle?—in his hand and pulled it down with him, let it go. Sank to the ground. Ow, Jesus. The engine roared, louder. He heard the crackling thunder as it plunged into the rocks below, *whap, whap, whap*, what the hell is that? *Whap, whap, whap.* A rush of wind, an explosion.

Oh God, not again.

The helicopter rose up above the rocks and the lights picked out Mo Bowdre two hundred feet away, down near the edge. He was kneeling on his hands and knees, head down, like a bear.

"That's Bowdre," shouted Sheriff Jack Knott. Then orange fire lit up the night, a sheet of flame from below the edge, behind Bowdre. The big man fell over on his side.

"Put it down, put it down!" Knott shouted, and the helicopter settled down on the sandy ground, a giant nocturnal dragonfly. In the lights, Sheriff Knott saw the Indian woman, Connie, pull herself up over the edge of the rocks and scramble over to Bowdre, her face a grimace of fear. He opened the door. "Let's go." A figure ran past the helicopter, and Knott, heaving himself out of the helicopter, recognized Jimmy Snyder in a black cowboy hat. The deputy skidded to a stop by Bowdre, bent over. The Indian woman was on her knees, holding Bowdre's face. Sheriff Knott and three men loped over to them. Bowdre was lying on his back. He looked naked without his dark glasses, glazy blue eyes staring unseeing up at the sky. The woman was crying, her face against his.

"Deppity, what's—"

"He's shot, Sheriff. In the side. It looks like it just went on right through, in the fat part."

Bowdre's big paw patted Connie's back.

"It's okay, it's okay," he said. His voice was weak, not much more than a hoarse whisper, a rasp. "Did someone here say fat?"

Sheriff Knott spun around. "Get the stretcher." He turned back to Bowdre, the deputy, the woman. "What's going on here?"

"Well, Sheriff," Mo said hoarsely. "Let me explain to you about that." And then he passed out.

Mo awoke, lying on his back on a comfortable bed. He sighed and felt Connie take his hand.

"Where am I?"

"In the hospital in Douglas."

"I thought so. Stinks in here."

"You're going to be okay. Flesh wound. Went right on through."

"How are you?"

"Okay. Shaky."

"Yes. You were brave."

"No, I wasn't brave."

"Who else is that here?"

"It's me," Larry Collins said.

"Your head back together, huh? What happened up there?"

"They flew you in here in the helicopter. And the director, Fitzhugh. He got bit by a rattler. Some kind that doesn't live up there in the mountains."

"Aha," Mo said, beaming. "The snake man."

"What?"

"I'll tell you about that later. Well, maybe I will."

"They brought in the other guy, Fergusson. Moved him to the Lordsburg jail this morning. Armand died in the plane crash. He had the emperor with him. It's ruined, the explosion and all. And it looks like a lot of money got burned up too. Evidently Armand shot the pilot. Guy named Lopez. Get this. Lopez was a scientist, a Mexican. Working over near El Paso. Armand was gonna run off with both the emperor and the money. You know, honor among thieves. It's all over. You did good."

Mo felt Connie's hand tighten on his.

"So now what?" Collins asked.

"Well," Mo said, feeling drowsy, "I guess I'll go home when they let me, grow another love handle, do a little art. That's what I do, you know. For a living?"

C o d a

The late-October air was crisp, cool, the sky overhead cloudless. Wind buffeted the red-brown leaves of the oaks inter-
spersed among the pines near the entrance of the Desert
Research Center. West, in the higher Chiricahua Mountains,
around nine thousand feet up, the aspens had turned to gold,
round leaves fluttering, quaking gaily, falling to the ground
like doubloons as they had each autumn since long before the
Apaches had arrived in these parts.

At the center, a handful of people had gathered: the director of the Denver Museum, the museum's general counsel,
the acting director of the center, a few board members, a
handful of scientists on sabbatical who had elected to spend
an entire year at the center, Larry Collins, Mo Bowdre, and
Connie Barnes. Mo had wanted simply to deliver the bronze,
get it set up, and leave—all without any fanfare. The center
was still suffering from the barrage of publicity. The papers,
even national TV, had had a field day: a smuggling ring; a
noted scientist dead in a crash, trying to run off with both

the money and the loot; the center's director along with some old reprobate Forest Service fire watcher in jail under indictment on multiple counts arising from the smuggling and the three murders, one of an FBI agent, the second of another noted scientist, a guest from Mexico, and the third a Mexican smuggler and scientist who had flown the ultralight. There had been murky stories, also, about a free-lance snake collector who had simply vanished.

But the director of the Denver Museum had insisted on a small unveiling ceremony—private, understated, but something to honor the event. After all, it was not every day that such a thing was donated free.

Unceremoniously Mo stood by the veiled figure, wearing a vast leather vest over a blue workshirt, with his slightly too small black cowboy hat pulled down on his forehead.

"Is it time?" he said.

"Yes, indeed," said the museum director. "We're all very excited."

"Well, folks, "Mo said. "Nobody but me and the boys at the foundry have seen this yet. Not even Connie here. Oh, I didn't make a mistake there. I seen it. Hah—hah. My way of seeing. Anyway, I hope it suits. Hey, Collins. You got me into this. Why don't you do the deed?"

"Sure. Be honored. What do I do?" He stepped over to the figure.

"Just pull that little rope hanging down there on the side."

"Okay."

Collins reached out and tugged the rope. The cloth fell away and a woman, about nine feet tall, stood before them, a bronze woman with long hair streaming behind her as if blown by the wind that was whipping the oak leaves. She was wrapped in a smooth blanket from neck to toe, nearly an abstraction, but her face had the unmistakable visage of an

Indian, high cheekbones, wide-set eyes that looked a bit Oriental. Her expression was grim, determined, yet somehow calm. From a fold in the blanket a strong arm protruded, the hand clasping a fierce-looking feathered lance.

The people gasped.

"Oh, Mo—" Connie said, and took his hand. "It's—"

"Well—hah—it's an Apache woman warrior. Indian women, they're strong of heart and will. Always were. And I thought all you folks might like a reminder about those people who used to live around here."

"It's splendid," said the museum director. "We are greatly honored, Mr. Bowdre." There was a buzz of excited conversation. Mo stepped away and motioned for Collins to follow.

"Hey, Collins," Mo whispered. "You on duty today?"

"No."

"Let's go get us a beer. I know where they keep it."

JAKE PAGE has been a ranch hand, a hard rock miner, an editor at *Natural History* and *Smithsonian* magazines, and a book publisher. His first Mo Bowdre mystery was *The Stolen Gods*. He has also written hundreds of magazine articles and columns and many other books, including *Hopi* (in collaboration with his wife Susanne, a photographer). Mr. Page lives in Corrales, New Mexico.